The Woman on the Beach

The Woman on the Beach

JULIA ROBERTS

bookouture

Published by Bookouture in 2021

An imprint of Storyfire Ltd.
Carmelite House
50 Victoria Embankment
London EC4Y 0DZ

www.bookouture.com

ISBN: 978-1-80019-532-5
eBook ISBN: 978-1-80019-531-8

This book is a work of fiction. Names, characters, businesses,
organizations, places and events other than those clearly in the
public domain, are either the product of the author's imagination
or are used fictitiously. Any resemblance to actual persons, living or
dead, events or locales is entirely coincidental.

PROLOGUE
September 2014

My hands are trembling as the border guard checks the passport I have just offered him. He glances down at the photograph and back up at me. I have my head slightly bowed, so my hair is falling forward over my face. He seems to be taking longer scrutinising me than some of the other travellers, which adds to my nervousness. Eventually, after what seems like several minutes but was probably only a few seconds, he hands the passport back to me and nods for me to pass through into the departure lounge.

I'm early for my flight to Guatemala City, but I'm cold and tired after the nightmare drive to Madrid from Denia in the torrential rain. In England, we're used to rain. That's not the case in Spain. The drainage channels at the sides of the motorways were overflowing, leaving excess water lying on the road surface. Despite driving slowly, I could still feel the car tyres losing contact with the tarmac from time to time. The irony of feeling out of control for a few seconds isn't lost on me. I've felt that way about my life for almost two years.

Once through passport control, I place my hand luggage on the conveyor belt. For one heart-stopping moment, the belt comes to a halt. Did the border guard radio ahead that there was something suspicious about me? There's nothing illegal in my bag, I tell myself, but it doesn't make me feel any better and it doesn't prevent me from looking as guilty as hell. Then the small case restarts its journey, trundling along without a care in the world, and I pass through the body scanner without setting the alarm off. It's a relief; I think my legs would finally have turned to jelly if I'd had to endure a pat-down.

I get myself a cappuccino and find a seat in a blissfully empty corner of the departure lounge. The cappuccino was a mistake. With the first sip, I'm transported back to Javea two nights earlier. Despite the rain, we sat outside under a canopy with the patio heaters on, reminiscing about our enduring friendship to the sound of the waves crashing against the rocks just a few metres away. And now she's gone and it's all my fault.

As the flight departure time edges closer, I reach into my bag for the laptop. The lounge is filling up now and I shrink further into my corner, anxious to avoid getting into conversation with anybody.

The television screens which have been blank up until now flicker into life. It's the news channel and the camera crews are live at the scene of the deadly train crash on the Denia to Benidorm line. I want to scream at them to turn it off. I don't need to see live coverage. All around me, people have stopped chattering and are staring in morbid fascination, some crossing themselves, grateful that they have not had their lives cut cruelly short. Across the bottom of the screen, a crawl is saying that there were only two survivors, but I know they are wrong.

I close my eyes, breathing in deeply through my nose and out through my mouth to try to calm myself.

'Are you okay?' a woman's voice asks.

'I'm just a bit of a nervous flyer,' I reply.

'You'll be fine. Flying is one of the safest forms of transport – much safer than the roads, or the railways for that matter,' she says, glancing at one of the TV screens. 'Those poor souls. I guess if your number's up, your number's up!'

I close my eyes again, trying to block the sound of screaming and metal grinding against metal from my mind. My heart is thumping so loudly, I'm almost certain the woman can hear it.

'Oh dear, you've gone even paler,' the woman says. 'I was only trying to help, but it seems like I've done the exact opposite. If it makes you feel any better, I'm feeling pretty confident my number's not up yet, so you'll be okay if you stick with me.'

At that moment, the announcement comes to start boarding.

'That's us,' the woman says. 'Do you need any help?'

'I'll be along in a moment. I just need to send a quick email.'

The woman gets to her feet and joins the queue forming to board the Airbus to Central America.

My hand is shaking as I hover the cursor over the icon that ironically resembles a paper airplane.

I hit send. This is it; there's no going back.

CHAPTER 1

Liv

Mexico, 2018

I love the solitude of the beach first thing in the morning, when the tide has washed away all trace of the people who enjoyed it the previous day. It feels like a new beginning; a chance to start over and see things through fresh eyes. That's exactly what I need, and one of the reasons I've come to Mexico.

As with every other day of my week-long stay, I was up before dawn to walk along the water's edge, leaving a trail of my footprints in the wet sand until the final ripple of each wave reached stealthily to erase them behind my back as though I was never there. I've loved watching the sky turn from inky blue through shades of orange until finally the sun broke the horizon to light the sky in a vibrant shade of azure blue.

There were a few feathery clouds when I walked today, which was disappointing, as it's my last day, but I can't really complain. The weather has been glorious for the most part. And anyway, by the time I return from breakfast to the sunbed where I spread out my towel at half past six this morning, the scattered clouds have evaporated. There is now a wide expanse of unbroken blue as far as the eye can see, and there's already heat in the sun.

My room has been a total joy. What a pleasant surprise it was to be upgraded to a beachfront suite on arrival as their more modest rooms were overbooked. They're not exaggerating when they say beachfront; my ground-floor room opens directly onto a small private deck area, just big enough to house a table and two chairs, which in turn leads straight onto the beach, with the sea a few metres away. The sound of the waves breaking on the beach has been my constant companion, the only one I've had since I got here. I've deliberately avoided eye contact with other hotel guests if they've greeted me. I didn't want to invite conversation, which is most unlike me.

It's the first time in my life that I've holidayed alone. For the past few years, I've always been with Jamie, and before that it was family holidays with my mum and dad and brother, Tom. Even when I went travelling during my gap year before university, it was with my friends Sophie and Grace. It's weird to think that all those years ago we three girls stood together a few hundred yards further down this very beach, our toes sinking into the soft sand as the waves washed over them, just as mine are now, and looking out to the same horizon. We had so many plans and hopes and dreams, but life had other ideas.

Grace and I were already drifting apart when she moved to Spain, but Sophie made an effort to stay in touch with her, never forgetting the promise we made when we met on our first day at senior school: *friends for life.*

I booked the trip to Mexico because I wanted to feel close to the best friend a person could ever have had. My life is in crisis and Sophie's ended far too soon. Two days ago, it would have been her thirtieth birthday, if she'd lived. The three of us had been celebrating Sophie's nineteenth birthday in a beach bar in Tulum when fate stepped in and changed the course of our lives. I miss my confident, beautiful friend. She was the closest thing to a sister I'd ever known.

It could be the dazzling sparkle of the sun reflecting off the sea that's making my eyes water, but I suspect not. Not wanting to draw attention to myself by dissolving into floods of tears, I turn away from the ocean and head for the sanctuary of my sun lounger. I reach into my beach bag for my book, mobile phone, and a tissue to wipe my eyes. Hating myself for doing it, I check my phone for messages. There are none, which is both unsurprising and disappointing.

When my husband Jamie had suggested a trial separation a couple of days after Christmas, saying, 'You're not the person I married,' I was not only shocked, but also more hurt than he will ever know. At least it made me stop and take a long hard look at myself. He's right; I'm not that girl anymore and never will be again after what happened, but I can't let tragedy come between us. I love my husband, and I won't give him up without a fight. The past four weeks of separation have given me time to think about what is truly important in my life, and top of that list is Jamie. Getting back what has gradually been eroded over the last three years won't be easy, but at least I'm now certain that it is what I want, and I'm prepared to do whatever it takes.

In case I doze off in the sun, I set my alarm for midday when I'll need to go inside and shower before starting my journey home. I lie on my front and undo the ties of my bikini top to avoid getting strap marks. Opening up the book I've borrowed from the hotel's beach library, I give myself a virtual pat on the back; I've paced myself beautifully, so the end of the book will coincide with the final few hours of my holiday. It must be the Virgo in me.

The sound of a dog barking wakes me. For a moment I panic, thinking that maybe I've slept through my alarm, but a glance at my phone reveals it's only just past 11 a.m. Lazily, I turn onto my side and prop myself up on my elbow while carefully holding my bikini top in place with my other hand to protect my modesty.

The dog barks again and I can now see it's a handsome golden retriever. He's sitting on the sand some fifty yards away, next to a pile of clothes, looking out to sea. I follow the line of his pointed nose and see two heads bobbing in the water, moving away from the beach. From this distance, it's impossible to tell if they are male or female, but both are strong swimmers.

As soon as they are in line with the end of the jetty, they turn left towards it, and as they do, the dog starts to trot along the beach as though tracking their movements. If he gets ahead of them, he sits for a few moments waiting for them, his tail flicking sand as it wags from side to side. As the swimmers approach the jetty, the dog races to the end of it, where he stands barking at them, his tail still wagging furiously. For a moment, I wonder if the dog is going to jump into the water, particularly as the two people have stopped swimming and are embracing, but then one of them points to the beach as they turn to retrace their path and the dog is off again, racing back in my direction.

I'm not the only one watching and, like me, no one seems concerned by the dog not being on a lead. He is obviously well trained and probably repeating actions he has carried out many times before. Once he is at the pile of clothes and his owners are on their way back towards the shore, the retriever alternates between impatient whining and excited barking. As his humans haul themselves to their feet, the dog can wait no longer and rushes into the water to greet them.

I can now see it's a man and a woman; she has waist-length blonde hair, while he is dark. Both are very slim and tanned, but what really strikes me is how happy they seem to be. I can't really see their faces among the tangle of hair and dog, but their body language speaks volumes.

A sharp pang of jealousy stabs at my chest. I close my eyes briefly; what I wouldn't give to be as happy and carefree as them.

It's not too late, I tell myself, it's only a trial separation. Jamie and I can still make it work.

When I open my eyes, the couple have their backs to me and are pulling on clothes over their wet swimming costumes, hindered by their dog, who seems to see it as a game. As the woman reaches her arms above her head to allow the bright red sundress to fall over her slender frame, I catch my breath. She has a large tattoo taking up the whole of her forearm from her wrist to her elbow. My throat tightens. Lots of people have tattoos, but unless I'm mistaken, I was there when the ink was applied one painful needle after another for hours on end.

'Sophie?' I call out. 'Sophie, is that you?'

The woman doesn't turn, but I'm fairly sure I see her shoulders tense.

I roll onto my front, fumbling behind my back to tie up the strings of my bikini top with fingers that feel as fat as sausages. Even so, it can't have taken me more than a minute to do, but when I'm finally able to get to my feet, the couple and their dog have gone.

Frantically, my eyes scan the beach, hoping for a flash of bright red fabric or the swish of a golden retriever's tail. My heart is pounding in my chest. They can't simply have disappeared into thin air.

'Excuse me,' I say to the woman on the sun lounger closest to mine. 'Did you see which way the couple with the dog went?'

She looks at me blankly before shaking her head and saying, 'Sorry, no English.'

I stumble over to where the couple were dressing moments earlier. There are footprints and pawprints visible, but the trail disappears into the soft powdery sand almost immediately.

Turning to face the ocean, I take some deep breaths to calm myself. I must be mistaken. I must have wanted to believe it was Sophie because I've been thinking about her so much this past week. Maybe coming back to Tulum wasn't such a good idea after all.

The sound of a mobile phone alarm going off breaks into my thoughts, getting louder with each repetition. Realising it's mine, I hurry back to my sun lounger to turn it off. My hands are shaking as I tap the screen.

I sit down and rest my hands on my thighs to steady them while continuing to take deep breaths. Whoever the woman in the red dress was, it couldn't have been Sophie. She died in the train crash more than three years ago.

CHAPTER 2

Sophie

Caterham, England, August 2006

The assembly hall of Birchdale School was already full of Year 13 students when Sophie, Grace and Olivia pushed open the doors to be met by a sea of faces and a wall of sound. Some of the expressions were anxious, worried that maybe they hadn't performed to their full potential in their A level exams, while others were happy and smiling, confident that they had.

Taking the lead as she usually did, Sophie pushed through the crowd to the table where Mr Reardon and Mrs Jessop were handing out envelopes containing the all-important exam results.

'Good morning, Sophie,' Mr Reardon said, dropping his gaze to leaf through the envelopes in search of hers. 'How do you think you've done?'

'Pretty sure I've aced it, sir,' she replied, smiling. 'If you pick the right subjects and put in the work, I can't see why anyone would be nervous.'

'Natural ability plays a part too, Sophie,' Mrs Jessop said, her voice gently reprimanding. 'Not everyone is blessed with the same brainpower and aptitude for learning. Which is not to take away from how hard you've worked. I hope you get the grades you need for your first-choice university. Cambridge, isn't it?'

'Yes, but I'm deferring for a year. Me, Grace and Liv are taking a gap year to go travelling.'

The three girls had been friends from their first day at Birchdale School after Liv had asked Sophie and Grace if they were sisters because they looked so alike.

'Don't you know about the birds and the bees?' Sophie had laughed. 'My birthday is at the end of January, so it's virtually impossible for us both to be born into the same school year. When is your birthday, Grace?'

'May the fifth.'

'And you, Olivia?'

'Please call me Liv. I only get called Olivia by teachers and my parents. I'm September the third, so it would just about be possible for me to have a brother or sister in the same school year.'

'Good point. You haven't, have you?' Sophie had asked, looking around as though expecting to see someone with the same mass of dark brown curls.

'No. I've got a brother, Tom, but he's about to start at university. How about you?'

'I'm an only child,' Sophie had replied. 'I guess my parents decided they couldn't improve on perfection. I am joking,' she added quickly, not wanting her new friends to think she was conceited. 'Mum had loads of miscarriages before me, so once they had a healthy baby, they decided not to push their luck.'

'I've got a younger brother,' Grace had said, her beautiful face momentarily clouded with a frown. 'Once Toby arrived, my parents lost interest in me.'

Liv and Sophie had exchanged a look before each linking an arm through hers.

'Well, you've got us now,' Sophie had said. 'We'll always make you feel wanted, won't we, Liv.' She crossed her arm over her chest and said, 'Friends for life, deal?'

'Deal,' the other two had agreed, each raising their arms to mimic Sophie's action.

*

'How exciting for you all,' Mrs Jessop said. 'I wish my parents had let me take a gap year, but things were a bit different in the 1970s. Here you go, Olivia,' she added, handing over her results.

'Thanks, Miss,' Liv said.

'Are you as confident as Sophie that you've got the results you need?'

'No one's as confident as Sophie,' Liv replied, digging her friend in the ribs, 'but fingers crossed I've done enough to secure the place I've been offered.'

She stepped aside while Grace got her results from Mr Reardon.

Envelopes in hand, the three friends battled their way back through the crowd and out through the double wooden doors.

'Come on,' Sophie said, 'let's get ourselves some privacy.'

Grace and Liv followed her up some concrete steps and over to a wooden bench that had been their favourite after-lunch spot for most of the last seven years. It overlooked the playing fields and had been a perfect vantage point from which to admire their latest crush or complain about girls who were outside their close-knit circle. Since February, it had more often than not only been Liv and Sophie chatting on the bench as Grace was preoccupied with her boyfriend, Gary.

'Ready to rip?' Sophie said, her finger wiggling into the envelope. 'One, two, three... go.'

There followed the sound of paper tearing, then rustling as three pairs of hands eagerly withdrew the results sheets.

'Yes! Straight As... Cambridge here I come,' Sophie said, punching the air.

'Phew!' Liv sighed, letting out the breath she'd been holding. 'Straight As for me as well. Looks like I'll be coming with you. How about you, Grace?'

The two of them turned to look at their friend, whose face was as white as the paper she was holding.

'My parents are going to kill me.'

'Stop messing about,' Sophie said. 'Have you got As too?'

Grace shook her head. 'I'm not messing, Sophie. Two Bs and a D. I don't know how I'm going to tell them.'

'There must be a mistake,' Liv said, taking the letter out of Grace's hand as though looking at it would magically change the grades. After checking, she raised her gaze to her friend's eyes. 'I don't understand. You were predicted As and Bs like me. What happened?'

A tear trickled out of the corner of Grace's eye. 'Gary happened,' she said, sniffing miserably. 'I've spent so much time with him, doing the things he wanted to do, that I guess I just let my schoolwork slip. Oh God! What am I going to do? My grades are nowhere near good enough to get into any decent university.'

'Listen,' Sophie said, 'it's not the end of the world. You'll just have to say you've not been feeling well lately and ask to do retakes in January. I'm sure Cambridge will hold your place if you explain it like that.'

'Do you really think so?' Grace asked, looking unconvinced.

'Yes,' Sophie replied confidently, although she had no way of knowing if her confidence was justified. 'You can't be the first person to not get the grades you need at the first attempt.' She linked her arm through Grace's and waited until Liv had done the same on the other side. 'Come on, let's go and talk to Mrs Jessop and see what your options are. It'll be fine; stop worrying.'

The girls were walking back towards the school buildings when Grace stopped abruptly.

'But if I have to do retakes, I won't be able to go travelling with you two.'

Liv and Sophie exchanged a quick glance.

'We'll work something out. If you still want to come, maybe you could join us after your exams.'

'Why wouldn't I want to come? We're friends for life, remember? We've got each other's backs.'

'Of course, but we weren't sure you'd want to be away from Gary for a whole year,' Sophie said.

'He's cool about it. He said we could have a non-exclusive relationship while I was away.'

Sophie wasn't sure how happy she would be with a boyfriend who'd suggested being non-exclusive, but she kept her thoughts to herself.

'Then that's sorted,' Liv said. 'There'll still be plenty of the world to see when you come and join us in February.'

'And we promise not to have too much fun without you,' Sophie added, laughing.

'Hmmmm, as if! Seriously, though, thanks for making me feel better about the mess I've got myself into. Now all I've got to do, apart from retaking my exams, is break the news to my parents. One more failure by their useless daughter, highlighted by Toby winning an effing scholarship to Whitgift School. Maybe if they'd showed me a bit more love, I wouldn't have had to look for it elsewhere.' Grace sighed.

Sophie couldn't help thinking she had a point. Throughout their schooldays, neither she nor Liv had ever been invited to a sleepover at Grace's, despite the numerous times she had stayed with each of them. Hard as it would be for them to accept, Grace's parents were partly responsible for her underachievement, although it wouldn't make telling them any easier.

'Well, *we* love you, don't we, Sophie?' Liv said, putting her arm around Grace.

'Absolutely,' Sophie replied, joining in with the group hug. 'We've got this.'

CHAPTER 3

Grace

Mexico, 2018

'Is everything all right, Grace? You don't seem your usual self.'

Luis is back early from his shift at the animal shelter where he helps out three afternoons a week. He's walked in on me taking a shower before I head off to the Pilates studio to teach my two evening classes. It's not the first time he's done this and won't be the last, but today I'm not in the mood. Normally I have no problem with him getting into the shower with me for a few minutes of passion, so I'm not surprised by the look of disappointment when I push him away. His expression is like one of the puppies at the shelter when they've been passed over for adoption.

'I'm fine,' I lie. 'I'm just running a bit late. I promised to show Josefina some of the new exercises I've been learning online before class tonight, but now I'm not sure I'll have time.' I reach for my towel and wrap it around my dripping body to make it clear to him that there will be no lovemaking before I leave for work.

I've been on edge all afternoon since I heard the woman on the beach call out. I didn't need to turn around; I instantly knew it was Liv. I'd recognise her voice anywhere, even though it sounded strained, filled as it was with a mix of doubt, disbelief and hope. After all, we were best friends for over fifteen years before I went to Spain.

Two things had shocked me though. What was Liv doing on a beach in Mexico after the three of us had vowed that it was the one place where we would never return? And why had she called out Sophie, when she knew Sophie was dead?

I glance down at my arm. Lots of people have tattoos and there's no way she could have seen it clearly from that distance, so why had her first thought been that I was Sophie? It had freaked me out.

The moment my dress was over my shoulders, I'd grabbed my sandals and raced up the beach without a backward glance, not stopping until I reached Luis's van. I'd had to fake laughter and pretend I'd been racing Luis and Vince, our gorgeous golden retriever, who we took from the animal shelter to prevent him from being put to sleep. He'd been too boisterous and badly behaved for most families to consider, but Luis had a way with animals, and judging by how Vince wagged his tail whenever I was around, he seemed to like me too. In fact, that was how he got his name. I'd laughingly remarked that his tail was like a windscreen wiper and Luis had misheard, asking me what a 'vincescreen' was. His English is very good, which had made it even funnier, but the abbreviation of 'vincescreen' stuck.

Luis has followed me through from the bathroom to our bedroom and is perched on the bed watching me dress.

'What time are you back tonight?' I ask, doing up my trainers.

'It depends what time the customers finish drinking. It's Friday; it could be very late if we get a crowd in.'

'I'll wait up for you,' I say, my voice filled with promise as I lean down to kiss him.

He responds with a passion that still makes me go weak at the knees, just as it did the first time our lips met.

Luis works in a bar in Tulum, which is where we met just over three years ago. I'd only been in Mexico for a few weeks and was living in a room above a hairdressing salon with a girl called Margarita. The salon employed us to braid hair on the beach and gave us a small percentage of our earnings as wages, as well as the roof over our heads for free. Neither of us had much money, so we mostly stayed in, but on Margarita's birthday, she persuaded me to go out to a bar with her, which is where I got talking to Luis.

During the evening, Margarita found herself an American tourist who was flashing his cash around and left with him at the end of the night. Rather than go back to our room and have to listen to the grunts and groans associated with sex, I decided to take a walk down to the beach and was slightly unnerved when I heard footsteps behind me. 'It's dangerous for a beautiful girl like you to be out on her own at this time of night,' was Luis's chat-up line. True or not, I fell for it and we walked along the beach together, chatting as though we'd known each other our whole lives, before finally sitting down on some rocks to watch the dawn break. He put his jacket around my shoulders when I shivered, probably assuming I was cold.

It wasn't the temperature that made me shiver; it was the memory of looking out on that same sunrise years earlier and sharing my hopes for the future with my friends. Things didn't go to plan, for any of us, and that thought, combined with Luis's kindness, made me cry. He held my hand while the tears coursed down my cheeks and then walked me home without asking any questions.

The next evening, he was waiting for me outside the hairdressing salon when I returned from hair-braiding on the beach. He remembered my love of Pilates and wanted to introduce me to his sister, who ran classes and was looking for an instructor. Josefina and I hit it off immediately and she offered me a job. I was about to decline because I would have nowhere to live if I gave up the salon job when Luis said I could sleep on his couch until I found somewhere. Within a week, I moved from his couch to his bed and I've been there ever since.

*

'I'm not sure I can wait that long,' Luis says now, voice low and husky, his hands caressing the rounded curve of my bottom. 'Are you sure you can't spare a few minutes?'

'Be patient. I promise I'll make it worth your wait,' I reply, pulling away from him and heading towards the door. 'We've got all the time in the world.'

Even as I say the words, I'm not sure I believe them. Yesterday, I felt safe in my adopted home with a man I adore and a life I love. With a handful of words, Liv has destroyed my inner peace. Most people would accept that it was a case of mistaken identity, but I know Liv. Once she gets the bit between her teeth, she doesn't let go. If she goes home and tells people that she thinks she saw Sophie, they just might believe her and come here looking; I can't allow that to happen. I found the courage once before to escape my desperately unhappy life, but I don't want to run now. Luis is the best thing that ever happened to me and I never want to be without him. I know what I must do.

My heart is thumping in my chest as I stride past the Pilates studio, where my first class is due to start in forty minutes. I'll just have time to drop a note in at the hotel asking Liv to meet me on the beach tomorrow afternoon. I've got a lot of explaining to do, but Liv and I go back a long way and I'm sure she'll understand.

I take the hotel front steps two at a time and smile my thanks to the doorman as he holds the door open for me. It's not the sort of establishment Luis and I would normally socialise in, it's a bit expensive for our limited means, but we have attended two parties in the function room. The first was Luis's grandmother's eightieth birthday, when I was introduced to the rest of his family, even though we'd been living together for over a year. There was no awkwardness surrounding my not being local, just happiness that Luis had found his soulmate.

Now that I'm actually standing at the reception desk, doubts start to creep into my mind. Am I doing the right thing? Maybe Liv has already dismissed what she thought she saw as an impossibility. By pre-empting what I think she might do, am I actually making things worse?

'Can I help you, miss?' the receptionist asks, a well-practised welcoming smile on his lips.

I have the opportunity to leave things alone, to hope that nothing further will come of the chance encounter on the beach. It would be a risk though, and it's not one I'm willing to take. I swallow down my nerves.

'I… I believe you have an Olivia Nelson staying with you. Would it be possible for me to leave a message for her?'

'Of course, miss. Let me find her room number and we can post a note under her door,' he says, checking the computer screen in front of him. It's only a matter of seconds before he continues. 'Oh, I'm sorry, but it appears you've missed her. She asked for a late checkout because of the time of her flight but was picked up by the hotel bus at 3 p.m.'

For a moment, I can't speak. Having reached the decision to approach Liv, I now don't know what to do.

'Is there anything else I can do for you?' the receptionist asks, his eyes flicking to the small queue that has formed behind me.

'Um, no, thank you,' I say, backing away from the counter.

I hurry out of the air-conditioned hotel into the heat of the early evening. I toy briefly with the idea of jumping in a taxi and trying to get to the airport before Liv's plane takes off, but it's now 5.45 and if she left at 3 p.m., chances are she'll already have gone through to departures.

Besides, there's the small matter of the Pilates class I'm due to start teaching in ten minutes. If I don't turn up, Josefina will be worried and will call Luis.

I break into a light jog. I don't want Luis to experience even a moment of panic because of me. I've already caused so much pain to people I love and who loved me. There's nothing I can do about the situation. For now, it's in the lap of the gods.

CHAPTER 4

Liv

Cancún Airport, 2018

Standing on the air bridge, waiting to finally board the plane after a two-hour delay, I'm feeling my usual sense of dread. To say I'm not looking forward to the flight home is an understatement. I can't think of anything worse than being stuck in a metal tube for hours on end, breathing in stale air and eating highly processed food. And the return always feels so much longer than the outward journey, which is filled with excitement and anticipation. Flying home, however lovely that home is, always has the feel of 'back to reality'.

I shuffle forward, show my boarding pass to the air steward and am directed to the right, along with the majority of other passengers. This time, I'm feeling the dread of the next few hours even more keenly, as I'm travelling alone and there's a huge question mark over what I'm flying home to.

To prevent my mood from deteriorating further, I cast my mind back to the words of a Virgin Atlantic ground staff member when Jamie and I were checking in for our flight home after our honeymoon in Barbados. She asked us if we'd enjoyed our stay and I said, 'It's been amazing; I don't want to go home.' To which she replied, 'But if you don't go home, you'll never experience the joy of returning to Barbados.' Put like that it made perfect sense and I often recalled those words to elevate my mood on return journeys.

And she was proved right about Barbados. I was over the moon when Jamie said he'd booked us a holiday there to celebrate our third wedding anniversary. It was made even more special when I discovered I was pregnant soon after our return.

I close my eyes briefly. Our happiness was short-lived. We lost our son to a miscarriage at eighteen weeks, too early to be viable, even with modern technology. There's no doubt it has tainted my memory of beautiful Barbados, so much so that I doubt I'll ever go back. It was devastating for both of us, of course, but I don't think Jamie really understood the guilt I felt that my body had cruelly let us down. He was so kind and supportive despite his own desolation. That's why I'm so certain we can fix things now; if we can survive losing our unborn child and come away from it stronger, we must be able to get through our current troubles.

After moving at a snail's pace, I finally arrive at my row and quickly lift my carry-on bag into the overhead locker before sitting down and sliding my handbag under the seat in front of me. Fortunately, I'm on the aisle, so I'll be able to get up and stretch my legs without having to disturb my fellow travellers. It could be a double-edged sword though, as if I do manage to drop off to sleep, I can almost guarantee that someone next to me will need to use the loo.

A smile plays at the corners of my mouth. *Listen to yourself. You're starting to sound as grumpy as your mum.* Penny, my mother, constantly moans about how inconsiderate people are these days and her criticism is usually directed at young people. I have to say that, in my experience, it's mostly people around her age who show a lack of awareness on airplanes. It's hard to believe that Mum turned seventy a couple of months ago and so sad that Dad couldn't hang on long enough to help her celebrate.

My smile from moments earlier disappears. It really has been a wretched three years: losing our baby, followed a few weeks later by the accident that claimed Sophie's life, and then my dad being diagnosed with bowel cancer. It's little wonder I'm not the happy-go-lucky girl that Jamie married. However, now I've had time to think things through, I realise that me moaning about my brother Tom may well have been the straw that broke the camel's back.

Jamie and Tom met at vet school and have been best friends ever since. Listening to me constantly criticising Tom for marrying someone so soon after we lost Sophie must have torn Jamie apart. I guess I was asking Jamie to make a choice between his best friend and his wife, but that was never my intention. As he put it in our most recent disagreement, 'Life goes on, Liv, you need to back off and let Tom be happy.'

At the time, I was really angry and upset. It escalated into a massive row, with me accusing him of taking Tom's side. 'If he's that perfect, maybe you should have married him rather than me,' I shrieked dramatically, flouncing out of the room and slamming the door behind me with such force that one of the baubles on the Christmas tree fell to the floor and smashed. Jamie came to find me an hour later, having allowed me time to calm down. By then, I'd realised he had a point and was about to tell him that I was going to make a real effort to be more friendly towards Tom's new wife, Polly, who I'd liked when our paths crossed at Jamie's work. But before I could say anything, my long-suffering husband suggested the trial separation. It was totally unexpected, and I didn't know what to say, so I just nodded mutely, despite it being the last thing I wanted.

I sigh. I don't know how Jamie's been coping because he hasn't been in touch since I texted to tell him I was going to Mexico for a week to try to sort my head out. I can only hope he's been missing me as much as I've been missing him.

*

Weirdly, I slept through the whole flight; a first for me. As soon as the dinner trays were cleared and the cabin lights dimmed, I settled back in my seat to choose a film to watch and the next thing I knew, the cabin steward was shoving a breakfast tray under my nose.

By the time the aisles are cleared of service trolleys, I barely manage to clean my teeth and have a pee before the captain turns on the 'fasten seatbelt' sign. Although I'm not in a window seat, I can see out when the plane banks to the left and it looks like there is a light dusting of snow covering the green fields around Gatwick. I'm not looking forward to standing around on the draughty platform at Clapham Junction when I change to my connecting train to Oxted, assuming they're still running. Leaves on the line, a light dusting of snow, heavy rain; all of these things seem to be dealt with quite adequately by other countries but render our transport system helpless.

Well, not all other countries, I think, closing my eyes.

An involuntary shudder runs through my body as I imagine what those final few terrifying moments of my best friend's life must have felt like as the train careered off the rails and plunged into a ravine. Sophie's face fills my mind, her eyes wide with fear and her mouth forming the words, *help me.* It's an image that has awoken me in a cold sweat many times. She was my best friend, and I wasn't able to help her because I was too wrapped up in my own grief after losing my baby. If only I'd been there for her, she wouldn't have gone to see Grace in Spain and she wouldn't have been on the train.

Grace sent me an email the day after the fatal crash, saying that she felt responsible for what had happened. She was leaving Spain to start afresh where she wouldn't constantly be reminded of the horror of the accident. 'Please don't try to find me, Liv,' the final line of her email said. 'I don't want to be found.' I was upset and shocked in equal measure. Grace was probably the last person to see Sophie alive and yet she was too damn selfish to share those final moments with the rest of us who cared so deeply about her. Our relationship was already strained after the thoughtless comment she'd made after my miscarriage. 'There'll be other babies, Liv,' were the words of someone who didn't have children and had no concept of what it was like to lose a baby when you've just allowed yourself to imagine cradling your little miracle in your arms. The email drove a further wedge between us. I had no intention of going in search of Grace to tell her I didn't blame her for Sophie's death because, if truth be told, I did.

For one fleeting moment, I wonder if the woman in the red dress on the beach could possibly have been Grace, but I dismiss the thought as soon as I've had it. Quite apart from the general improbability, Grace never did have a very high pain threshold, so I can't imagine her having even a tiny rosebud tattoo, let alone one covering her entire forearm.

I try to picture the woman on the beach more clearly. In truth, I didn't get a very good look at her because she was too far away. I instinctively cried out Sophie's name because I've spent a lot of the past week remembering the happy times we shared. Our minds can play very cruel tricks on us sometimes, I think, as the pilot makes a perfect landing.

Before long we are allowed to begin the long trek to passport control and baggage reclaim. Although there were mobile phones pinging all around me from the moment the jet's tyres made contact with the runway, I always wait until I'm through passport control before I turn my mobile on. I'm tapping my fingers impatiently on the handle of my carry-on bag when my phone chirrups that I have a message. It's from Jamie:

I'll be waiting for you at the barrier. I'll have a board with your name on it so you can recognise me. We need to talk xxxxxx

My heart leaps. Never in my wildest dreams did I imagine that Jamie would be here at Gatwick to pick me up. I don't allow myself to get carried away, but I'm hoping that the addition of a row of kisses is a positive sign.

CHAPTER 5

Sophie

Mexico, January 2007

'I can't believe you arrived in time to help me celebrate my birthday,' Sophie said, taking a strand of long blonde hair and smoothing it with her straighteners before bending the end into a soft curl.

'Did you really think I was going to let a little thing like retaking my A levels get in the way of partying with you two?' Grace replied, rummaging through her backpack and pulling out her make-up bag. 'I've been so jealous seeing the pictures of all the amazing places you've visited so far; I think photos of birthday celebrations at a beach bar in Mexico might just have pushed me over the edge.'

'We're not that mean,' Liv said, trying to talk while applying her mascara.

'Don't pretend you wouldn't have gone out.'

'Did I say that? I just meant we wouldn't have sent you any pictures,' she said, laughing, while ducking to avoid the cushion that Grace had launched in her direction. 'Oi, steady, you nearly had my eye out!'

'Ever the drama queen,' Sophie said. 'Seriously though, Grace, I'm so glad you got to see Mexico. I had all these preconceptions about wide-brimmed hats and gun-toting bandidos and it's been nothing like that.'

'I know,' Grace agreed. 'Powdery white sand beaches fringed with palm trees leading to impossibly turquoise water… It's the closest thing to paradise I've ever seen.'

The three friends had spent the day in Akumal, a short bus ride from the hostel in Tulum where they were staying.

Sophie was glad of the chance to relax after the previous day's trip to the archaeological ruins. There was no denying it had been magical, but it was pretty exhausting. Still, she had been particularly enamoured.

'I felt an amazing connection with the Mayan ruins,' she said. 'Imagine what it must have been like to live here centuries ago when it was first built.'

'Hot and sticky and riddled with mosquitos,' Liv replied, but her comment didn't dampen Sophie's enthusiasm.

'I love the idea that the Mayans worshipped nature, and the sun and the stars. Life was so much simpler back then. Although, their pace of life still seems pretty laid-back compared to ours.'

'The Mayans also sacrificed fellow human beings to appease their Gods,' Liv chipped in. 'It wouldn't have been quite such a great time to live here if you were chosen to be the sacrifice.'

'How do you know that?' Grace asked.

'I was paying attention to the guide while you and Sophie were climbing the ruins.'

'I wish you hadn't told me, Liv, I've kind of gone off them a bit now,' Grace said.

'It was just what happened all over the world,' Sophie said. 'The Spanish Inquisition wasn't very pleasant either and in England we used to dunk innocent women until they drowned to prove that they weren't witches. I hope history wasn't one of your retakes.'

'You know it wasn't,' Grace said, rolling her eyes. 'I've never been a fan.'

'How did your exams go?' Liv asked, seizing the opportunity to change the subject. 'We haven't had chance to talk about it since you got here.'

'I thought you might just have been avoiding asking since my dismal effort last summer.'

Liv and Sophie exchanged a glance, which didn't go unnoticed.

'Oh, so you were avoiding the subject. Well, you'll be pleased to hear it was a piece of piss. I'm quietly confident that I'll be taking my place alongside you girls at Cambridge in September.'

Sophie punched the air. 'Yesssss! A double celebration tonight.'

By the time the girls arrived at Las Iguanas, the bar where they planned to have a light late supper to soak up some alcohol before going on to Tulum's only nightclub, Sophie, Grace and Liv were already feeling pretty light-headed. The girls made a very attractive trio and once it became known that it was Sophie's birthday, they'd been bought drinks by fellow customers or offered free drinks by bar staff anxious to keep them for as long as possible. With men being drawn to them like moths to a flame, they were good for business.

'They do amazing grilled shrimp tacos here,' Sophie said, placing the menu card down on the table.

'Yes,' agreed Liv. 'I think I'll have those too and maybe some cheesy quesadillas.'

'I don't know what they are,' Grace said. 'In fact, I don't know what anything is.'

'They're a bit like toasted pitta bread pockets stuffed with cheese and chopped onion and peppers, oh, and they come with guacamole like you've never tasted back in England. You'll love them.'

'Sounds great. Do I need to order anything else or will that be enough for all of us?'

'It'll be plenty,' Sophie said. 'We don't want to get too full of food or we won't feel like dancing.'

'Nothing would stop you from dancing, it's in your blood,' Grace replied.

Of the three of them, Sophie was always the first on the dance floor. She'd been having dancing lessons from the age of three – ballet and tap at first, but when she got to an age when she considered them uncool, she started with modern jazz and street dance. She had a trophy cabinet in her bedroom at home to rival any of the top football clubs, although there had been no additions while she was studying hard for her A levels. She'd given up dancing in favour of yoga and Pilates and, after much persuasion, she managed to get Liv and Grace to go to classes with her. Grace had taken to it immediately, but Liv wasn't so keen.

'Is this your best birthday ever, Sophie?' Grace continued, taking a sip of yet another mezcal-based cocktail, courtesy of a group of men who'd followed the girls from the previous bar they had been in.

'It's up there with the best,' Sophie replied, 'but it would be difficult to top last year's birthday bash. Hard to believe that was only a year ago. We've done so much since then.'

'It was amazing; no one else's eighteenth came even close,' Liv said, her eyes shining.

'Especially mine,' Grace added, a frown darkening her perfect features for a moment. 'Dinner out with Mum, Dad and my precious brother at TGI Friday's because that was Toby's favourite restaurant. I was only allowed to invite one friend, even though my parents knew the three of us were inseparable and there was no way I would ever choose between the two of you.'

'Ah yes, I remember now,' Liv said. 'You took Gary as your plus-one and it was the first time your parents had met him. What are you smiling at?'

'I was just remembering the not so wonderful first impression Gary created, although, to be fair, by the end of the evening, Mum and Toby had warmed to him; he's such a charmer.'

'How have you left things with him?' Sophie asked.

Grace squirmed in her seat. 'Actually, we decided to finish things just before Christmas.'

'You finished with Gary and didn't tell us?' Liv and Sophie chorused.

Grace shrugged. 'I was going to be leaving him at the end of January anyway to meet up with you guys and I hadn't really been seeing much of him because of revising. I probably only stayed with him as long as I did because I knew my parents didn't approve. We called it a day after exchanging the Christmas gifts we'd already bought each other.'

'It all sounds very civilised,' Liv said.

'It was,' Grace agreed. 'And, to be honest, I never truly believed that he was my "special one".'

'We're all much too young for that,' Sophie said, pushing her chair back and getting unsteadily to her feet. 'We need to experience some frogs before we settle on our princes. Can you order the food while I pop to the loo? I need to eat something pronto.'

After splashing cold water on her cheeks in attempt to sober up, Sophie applied some pale pink gloss to her lips and headed back out into the crowded bar. As she started to make her way towards the veranda to rejoin her friends, she found her path suddenly blocked by a group of young men, clearly drunk, who had formed a circle and seemed to be shouting encouragement.

'Hey,' she said, squeezing her way closer to the centre of the group, 'what's going on?'

She stopped when she saw two young men squaring up to each other with their fists raised.

At the sound of her voice, one of the men turned his head towards her and, in that instant, there was the sound of breaking glass. Sophie could see the other man being handed a smashed bottle.

'Stop!' she shouted, rushing forward with her arms raised to try to protect the man she had distracted.

A shrill scream filled the air and then Sophie was sinking to the ground with blood pouring from her left arm. She heard Liv's voice shrieking her name before she saw her elbowing her way through the crowd who were making their way towards the exit in a small stampede.

'Oh my God, Sophie, what happened?' she cried, falling to her knees and placing both her hands over the gash on Sophie's forearm, from which blood was spurting in a gruesome fountain.

'He was going to slash his face,' Sophie mumbled, looking up into Liv's concerned eyes. 'I had to stop him. I can't feel my arm, Liv. I'm scared.'

Sophie glanced down and could see blood oozing through Liv's fingers despite the pressure she was applying.

'Grace,' Liv said, raising her voice to be heard over the commotion, 'tell the bar staff to call for an ambulance. Can you hear me, Sophie?' she asked, her voice becoming softer. 'It's going to be okay. You just have to try to stay awake until the ambulance gets here.'

'I'm sorry…' Sophie whispered, before drifting into oblivion.

CHAPTER 6

Liv

Oxted, 2018

It's a few years since we last visited the Pizza Express in Oxted, even though it's within walking distance of our home. It had been the ideal choice for spur-of-the-moment nights out, enabling us to share a bottle of wine without having to book a taxi to get us home, but it's usually full of families with children, and neither of us had wanted that after losing our son. Today though, it feels like the ideal location for our late lunch; not too intimate but quiet enough for us to talk on neutral ground.

Our conversation began in the car after Jamie picked me up at the airport, but as Oxted is only a twenty-minute drive from Gatwick, we still had a lot we wanted to say to each other. He dropped me at the house we haven't been sharing for the past month after agreeing to meet at the pizza restaurant at half past two. It gave me enough time to unpack, have a refreshing shower after my eleven-hour flight, and I'd even considered a short snooze. I skipped the snooze in favour of two strong black coffees. I wanted to have time to make a list so that I wouldn't forget anything I wanted to say. The vibes coming from Jamie have been promising, making me think that he wants a reconciliation as much as I do, but there's still a lot to be talked through.

The time on my own in Mexico has made me realise how incomplete I feel without Jamie by my side. I've now recognised that the triple helping of grief affected the way I behaved towards him. I think I was angry with myself for not showing my appreciation of his unfailing kindness, understanding and support even though I wanted to after we lost Alfie and Sophie in quick succession and throughout my dad's illness. By focusing my attention on Tom's decision to move on in the way he did, I gave myself an outlet for the anger I was feeling. Until Sophie's death, my big brother and I always had a close relationship, but it's been terribly strained since I tried to force my opinion on him. The further apart Tom and I have grown, the harder it has been for Jamie to cope with the rift between his wife and his best friend. I had no idea how much it was affecting him until he suggested the trial separation.

I've never come to terms with Sophie's death, and I don't suppose I ever will, but I need to show Jamie that I genuinely intend to be less judgemental and more understanding of my brother's desire to get on with the rest of his life. Tom and Sophie were married, but she had been my best friend for twice as long. From the age of eleven, we'd told each other everything, sharing our secrets and dreams; it was like losing my right arm when I heard the horrendous news.

It's one of those moments that you never forget. You know with absolute certainty where you were and what you were doing; a bit like the death of Princess Diana or watching the TV in utter disbelief as the planes crashed into the Twin Towers. It wasn't long after losing Alfie, but, as recommended by the hospital, we had begun trying for another baby after a couple of months to allow my body to recover. My period was late for the second month running, and just as with the previous month, I'd immediately bought a pregnancy tester kit. But those two words that no woman trying for a baby wants to see appeared in the little window of the stick. 'Not Pregnant.' It couldn't have taunted me more if it had been flashed up in neon lights in Piccadilly Circus.

Moments later, Jamie knocked on the bathroom door to tell me Tom was on the phone and needed to speak to me urgently. I'd brushed the tears away before opening the door to Jamie, feeling the need to hide my disappointment. I didn't want him to feel a failure that I hadn't managed to conceive, and I certainly didn't want to take the pleasure out of our lovemaking by placing the emphasis on me getting pregnant. I'd started to say, 'What's so urgent?' but when I saw Jamie's shocked expression, the words froze on my lips. He handed me my mobile phone, his skin as white as the sheets on our bed, saying, 'I'm so sorry.' There can't be an easy way to deliver such terrible news, but Tom made no attempt to soften the blow. 'Sophie's been involved in an accident. She's dead.'

I have less clarity over what happened next. I must have dropped my phone on the tiled bathroom floor, because the next time I went to use it, the screen was shattered. I do remember holding on to Jamie, gripping him so tightly that my fingers left small bruises all the way up his arms, howling the word 'no' repeatedly. I'm really not sure how I would have coped over the following few days if it hadn't been for Jamie. He's my rock and I have to do everything I can to get him back.

As I round the corner on my way to the restaurant, I see Jamie waiting outside, despite the freezing temperatures, and my heart starts to flutter in a way it hasn't since we lost Alfie. Maybe the trial separation wasn't such a bad idea after all, I think, quickening my pace. As I approach, he opens the glass door and stands back to let me pass. I half wonder if he's going to give me a quick hug or a peck on the cheek, but maybe I'm getting ahead of myself.

'Table for two?' asks the approaching waitress.

'Yes, please,' I reply.

'In a quiet corner, if possible,' Jamie adds.

We follow her over to a table against the back wall, although there are only a handful of other people eating, so the entire restaurant is pretty quiet.

'Can I get you anything to drink?' she asks, handing us our menus.

'I'll have a Nastro Azzuro, please. Jamie?'

'Same for me,' he says, unbuttoning his coat and shrugging it off. 'Do you want me to hang yours up too?' he asks as I unzip my quilted coat.

'Actually, I think I'll keep it on for now. After a week in the Mexican sun, the temperature is a bit of a shock to the system.'

'I'll bet. I'll nip to the loo while I'm on my feet. If the waitress comes back to take our food order, I'll have my usual.'

Jamie isn't gone for more than a few minutes, but in that time, our waitress returns with the beers and disappears again having taken the order for our two favourite pizzas, giardiniera and diavolo. In the past, we've always shared them half and half, and I really hope Jamie suggests doing that today.

In the car earlier, our conversation was quite stilted. Jamie talked a bit about his work and then asked whether I'd enjoyed my holiday. I didn't want to come across as needy by revealing that I'd been lonely on my own and had been checking my phone regularly, hoping for a text from him. Instead, I concentrated on telling him about my amazing room upgrade. 'It was dark when I checked in, so I had no idea that the room literally opened onto the beach, and it had a jacuzzi bath next to the full-length windows so you could sit in the tub and watch the waves crashing onto the shore. You'd have loved it.'

It killed the conversation until we both started to speak together.

'I'm sorry...' we both started.

'You go,' Jamie suggested.

I took a deep breath. 'I just wanted to say I'm sorry for putting you in such a difficult position. I wasn't trying to make you choose between me and Tom, really I wasn't. He has as much right to happiness as anyone and it was wrong of me to begrudge him it. Losing Sophie left a massive hole in all our hearts.'

'I'm sorry too,' he said, reaching to squeeze my hand briefly before returning it to the steering wheel. 'It's been a difficult time for all of us, but especially you. I should have realised that you were feeling engulfed by a tide of emotion that was preventing you from being your normal, caring self. You've always been able to see things from everyone's point of view; it's one of the things that attracted me to you in the first place.'

I looked up at him briefly from beneath my eyelashes, struggling to hold back the tears I could feel forming.

'That, and a great pair of boobs,' he added.

'Jamie Nelson, I can't believe you just said that!' I said, feigning outrage. 'That is such a sexist remark. And here was me thinking you liked me for my wit and intellect.'

'I like you for all of that, but I fancied you because you're bloody gorgeous. I've missed you like hell these past few weeks.'

'Really? When you didn't text or call, I thought it was because you didn't care about me.'

'I suggested a trial separation to give you some time. It wouldn't have been very fair if I'd been constantly messaging you; I wasn't sure if you still felt the same way about me.'

Even if I had been unsure, the sight of my husband hopping from foot to foot while waiting for me outside Pizza Express when he could have easily waited inside in the warmth would have swayed me. He's one of the kindest, most considerate people I've ever met, not to mention extremely handsome. What a fool I was to almost drive him away.

'Has she already taken the order?' Jamie asks as he returns from the loo, oblivious to the attention he is attracting from the female diners but clearly spotting the drinks on the table.

'Yes, and my guess is it won't take too long. It looks like we're the last lunch customers,' I note, holding my glass up to chink against his. 'Cheers.'

He takes a long drink before he says, 'Are we sharing?'

'The pizzas?' I ask, feeling warmth in my cheeks.

'And anything else you'd like to,' he says, putting his glass down and reaching for my free hand before raising it to his mouth and brushing his lips against it.

It may sound pathetic, considering we've been married for almost seven years, but it sets my skin tingling and my pulse racing in the same way as it did after our first kiss. I feel almost breathless with the anticipation of what may be to come, even though I've experienced it before.

The friendly voice of the waitress interrupts the moment.

'Who's having the diavolo?' she asks.

'We're sharing,' Jamie says.

'Great idea,' she says, placing the pizzas down in the middle of the table. 'The giardiniera will take the heat out of the diavolo – a perfect pairing. Enjoy.'

It's only later, when Jamie and I are snuggled together on our sofa enjoying a glass of the Prosecco that we had planned to open at New Year, that I tell him about seeing the woman with the tattoo on the beach.

'I don't know why,' I say, 'but I called out Sophie's name, even though I knew it couldn't be her.'

'It's pretty understandable. You were in a place that you haven't been back to since you visited it with her eleven years ago and she's been on your mind because of Tom and Polly. And wasn't her birthday around this time of year too?' he asks, gently twirling the curls of hair in the nape of my neck around his fingers in a way I always find very intimate.

I nod. 'It was three days ago. I got permission from the hotel to light one of those Chinese lanterns and let it float up into the sky after I explained that it would have been my best friend's birthday, but she'd died. I spent ages writing on it, telling her how much I missed her and how I would never let her memory die. Thank you for remembering.'

'I know how much she and Grace meant to you. It was a big blow for you not to have either of them for support when your dad fell ill.' He takes the glass from my hand and puts it on the coffee table so that he can pull me into a proper embrace. 'I tried to fill the chasm they left, but maybe I didn't try hard enough. I will from now on, I promise,' he adds, lowering his lips onto mine.

All further thoughts about the woman on the beach are swept from my mind as his kiss turns more passionate and his hands reach for me with an urgency that my body immediately responds to.

I know it won't all be smooth sailing ahead, but at least Jamie and I will be on the journey together.

CHAPTER 7

Sophie

England, 2007

Sophie's flight from Cancún arrived an hour later than scheduled. She had hoped she would be able to sleep for most of the flight once she'd taken her painkillers, but the throbbing in her arm woke her after a couple of hours and she couldn't get back to sleep even after a second dose. She wandered to the back of the plane and sat talking to the air stewardesses for a while, trying to take her mind off the pain, but by the time the jet touched down at Gatwick, she was feeling quite nauseous.

It had been difficult persuading her parents not to cut short their holiday in the Maldives in order to fly home and meet her when her plane touched down from Mexico. It was the first holiday they had ever been on without Sophie and she'd felt bad even ringing them to tell them what had happened, although she had played down the seriousness of the injury. In the end, Liv had come up with the idea of asking her big brother, Tom, to meet Sophie at the airport and her parents had agreed to it on condition that he would accompany her to their family doctor's surgery to make sure everything had been dealt with properly.

Despite being able to bypass the wait for hold luggage as her backpack fitted into the overhead lockers, Sophie's legs were feeling quite wobbly after the lengthy walk through the airport terminal building. She emerged from the customs hall and scanned the waiting crowd, looking for Liv's brother. Sophie had seen Tom occasionally over the years, but he'd paid very little attention to his younger sister and even less to her friends. Since he'd graduated and gone to a veterinary practice in Devon to get some hands-on experience, Sophie hadn't seen him at all.

Sophie could feel beads of sweat forming on her forehead and her eyes were starting to go blurry. Rather than risk fainting in the middle of the jostling crowd, she moved towards the nearest wall and leaned against it, taking deep breaths. She'd noticed a few spots of blood on the bandage around her arm when she'd reached up for her backpack, but glancing down at her arm now, she could see the spots had joined up to create a dark red patch that seemed to be expanding.

'Here, let me take that,' said a tall, dark-haired young man who looked vaguely familiar. Reaching for her backpack, he added, 'You look like shit.'

'Tom?' Sophie asked hopefully. 'I don't feel too good.'

'What the hell were you thinking, trying to stop a fight in a foreign country? No wonder backpackers get themselves killed. I'm just amazed that your parents, and mine for that matter, agreed to let you two go off travelling,' he said, barely able to disguise the irritation in his voice.

'I think I'm going to…'

Sophie collapsed into Tom's arms before she could finish her sentence.

When Sophie finally awoke several hours later, she found herself staring up into Tom's deep brown eyes.

'Where am I?' she asked, feeling dazed.

'East Surrey hospital,' Tom replied. 'I brought you here after you fainted all over me.'

Sophie could feel the heat rising in her cheeks.

'Oh my God, how embarrassing,' she said. 'I don't know what happened. I felt hot and a bit dizzy and then everything just went black. I bet you'll kill Liv next time you see her for dumping me on you.'

'It's a good job I'm a vet and recognised the smell of an infected wound. They rushed you straight into theatre for emergency surgery when I brought you in. Any delay and you might have lost your arm.'

Sophie looked down at her left arm, which was now heavily bandaged, and then back up at Tom.

'Have you been here the whole time?' she asked.

'It wouldn't have been very nice for you to wake up with no one here.'

'Thank you,' she said. 'That's really kind, but I'm fine now if you need to get off.'

'There's no rush. My partner Jamie has taken on my appointments that couldn't be cancelled. Can I get you anything?'

'Water would be great if I'm allowed. My mouth feels like the Sahara Desert.'

Tom poured some water into a glass and draped his arm across her shoulder for support while she drank it.

When she finished, Sophie lay back on the pillows and looked up at him.

'I don't know how I'll ever be able to thank you for your kindness.'

'We'll think of something,' he replied.

Sophie wasn't absolutely certain because she was still feeling pretty groggy after the general anaesthetic, but she thought she detected a flirtatious tone to his voice, which both surprised and excited her.

'I hate to ask you for another favour when you've already done so much, but would you mind not telling Liv what happened?'

'Why not? I thought you two told each other everything.'

'We do usually, it's just that she'll feel obliged to tell my parents and I've already put a dampener on their holiday. Nothing will be gained now by them rushing home.'

'All right, but you'll owe me big time,' he said, smiling.

'Don't worry,' Sophie said, looking coyly up at him from beneath her eyelashes. 'I always pay my debts.'

Tom visited Sophie at the hospital for the next few days and in the hours they spent together they discovered that, despite their age difference, they had a lot in common. Both were into fitness and adored animals. They even had similar taste in music.

A week after being discharged from hospital, Tom rang and asked Sophie if she'd like to meet up for a drink at The Harrow in Caterham on the Hill. It was around the corner from her parents' house and he said he thought she could probably do with a change of scenery.

She agreed, saying that she felt like a fourteen-year-old who'd been grounded for misbehaving.

Tom was already at the pub when she arrived. She raised her hand in acknowledgement and headed towards where he was sitting next to the open log fire.

He got to his feet, saying, 'You do know I got a ticket for breaking the speed limit in my rush to get you to the hospital.'

They stared at each other in silence for a second, then both started laughing. Sophie had wondered whether, outside the confines of the hospital, things might have felt awkward, but that was the ice-breaker they needed. She and Tom just seemed to click.

Over the following month, the two of them met up a couple of times a week until Sophie flew off to rejoin her friends. It was only then that she realised just how much she liked Tom.

The Bahamas was beautiful, Florida was fabulous and their road trip across America was amazing. The problem was, Sophie would rather have experienced it all with Tom at her side.

CHAPTER 8

Grace

Mexico, 2018

'Okay, girls, let's move into position for the one hundred,' I say, rolling onto my back and bringing my knees to my chest. 'Extend your legs at 45 degrees, raise your head and shoulders slightly and reach your fingers towards your toes. Breathe in for a count of five and beat those arms up and down in small movements. Good, now breathe out for five, making sure your core is engaged. And again, breathe in, remembering to bend your knees into the chair position if you are feeling any tension in your back.'

Teaching my Pilates classes has been my saviour for the past two weeks. Not only has it given me something to focus on instead of constantly worrying about any action Liv might take, it's also a relief to be in the air-conditioned Pilates studios now the outside temperatures are rocketing to an unseasonably high 35 degrees in the middle of the day. February in Tulum is usually mid to high twenties, gradually increasing as April approaches. The apartment Luis and I share has a barely functioning aircon unit in the living area and a rickety old ceiling fan in the bedroom that squeaks with every revolution. I've been claiming that as the reason for not sleeping well recently, but in my heart, I know that the actual cause is quite different.

Although we were only teenagers when we vowed to never set foot in Mexico again, both Liv and I have broken that promise. I know my reasons: I needed somewhere to escape where no one would ever think to look for me after the accident that claimed my friend's life. The guilt of knowing that we wouldn't have been on the train that plunged into the ravine if it wasn't for me has never left me. Inadvertently, I caused my friend's death, and although I have a new life now and am blissfully happy in a way I would never have thought possible, I'll never truly forgive myself.

I can only guess at Liv's reasons for revisiting the Yucatán Peninsula. The timing suggests that she wanted to mark her friend's thirtieth birthday.

I close my eyes in an effort to prevent a tear from escaping. I force myself to focus on my core, gently pumping my arms, breathing in for five and out for five, before eventually drawing my knees into my chest.

'And rest for a minute,' I say, relieved to take a moment to regain my composure.

This is the fourth birthday that's passed without celebration; I'm sad thinking about it. Maybe Liv felt the same way and had an overwhelming desire to come back to a place where it had been just the three of us, before our lives were complicated by relationships and marriage. Even the best of friends find it virtually impossible to maintain their closeness when there's someone else to consider, and that was certainly the case with us.

Initially, we tried to make time for each other, meeting up once a month for a meal or a trip to the cinema to see a 'girlie' movie, but the gaps between our meetings gradually lengthened until married life finally put paid to them completely. We stayed friends, just as we'd promised we would, but the special bond between the three of us was diluted. Until Liv called out on the beach, I hadn't realised just how much I miss my friend.

I change position, sitting on my heels in preparation for the 'mermaid' stretch. Reaching my left arm above my head, I glance up at the tattoo that might yet steal away my happiness. Why did I get that bloody tattoo? I think, bending my upper body over to the right and trying to concentrate on the feeling of release I usually experience.

My eyes scan the dozen girls through the mirror I'm facing to ensure they all have the correct posture. I smile. This is the intermediate class and my girls are all in the perfect position. Whatever else I am, I'm a bloody good Pilates teacher.

I raise my other arm, repeating the movement in the opposite direction and, in doing so, catch a glimpse of myself. If Liv had got a proper look at my face, there wouldn't have been any question in her voice; she would have known for sure.

I examine my face, searching for… I don't know what, the truth maybe. Suddenly, I know what I have to do. I've been agonising over whether or not to make contact with Liv, but now I know for sure that I can't spend the rest of my life looking nervously over my shoulder, fearful that she'll come back to Mexico and unintentionally spoil the new life I've created. I have to write to her and explain what I did and why, and trust that she'll understand my reasons for not wanting to go back to my old life.

My body is back in a central position and I reach forward to assume the Child's Pose, a move I've borrowed from yoga that I always end my classes with. I take a long deep breath in and then slowly exhale.

And once I've written to Liv, I need to come clean with Luis. Even though the thought of how he might react scares me, he deserves to know the truth.

CHAPTER 9

Sophie

Caterham, 2011

If I'd been able to order perfect weather for my wedding day, this would have been it, Sophie thought, gazing out of her open bedroom window in her parents' house and breathing in the warm air lightly scented with honeysuckle. There wasn't a single cloud in the sky, suggesting that the weather forecast was right and there would be no rain. It was a chance both she and Tom had been prepared to take when they'd chosen early May for their wedding.

She glanced over at the clock on her bedside table. It was almost half past nine. *The morning is running away with me,* she thought. *Liv and Grace will be here soon to help me get ready and I haven't even dried my hair yet.*

Although she'd set her alarm for 7 a.m., Sophie had actually woken with the dawn an hour earlier. It was as though her mind and body didn't want her to miss a moment of the most special day of her life.

She'd lain in bed thinking about the day ahead, her fingers subconsciously tracing the tattoo that had been meticulously applied to disguise the ugly scar that ran from the palm of her hand to the inside of her elbow. It was an intricate design based on the serenity prayer and had been carefully designed around the scar tissue: Give me the courage to change what I can, the serenity to accept what I cannot and the wisdom to know the difference.

Although Sophie had no way of knowing at the time, her dreadful experience in the bar in Tulum had changed not only the course of her life but also who she was as a person. She'd grown from being a happy-go-lucky teenager into a woman who realised there were consequences to her actions. Being with Tom, seven years her senior, had helped her to grow up much quicker than she might otherwise have done. The tattoo, though, was a visual reminder of the recklessness that had almost cost her her life.

She'd had it done over the course of a few weeks when the girls eventually returned from their travels. Tom wasn't particularly enthusiastic about her getting a tattoo, but Sophie was adamant, and once he'd seen the design, he had to agree that it was a work of art.

Despite the growing closeness between them, Tom had given Sophie space when she and Liv and Grace had headed off to Cambridge. They saw each other when Sophie was back for the holidays, but more as friends. It was only when she had returned home for the summer after her second year that the two of them became an item. A year later, the day after her graduation ceremony, Tom had proposed and Sophie had accepted.

As she gazed down at the stunning two-carat diamond solitaire ring on her finger, sparkling in the sunlight and casting a pastel rainbow of fairies which danced around the room in a dizzying way, Sophie could hardly believe her good fortune. She hugged her arms around her slender body, drunk on happiness. Tom was her soulmate; the person she wanted to spend the rest of her life with. The two of them had decided not to live together before getting married. He'd occasionally stayed over at the flat she had shared with Liv and Grace in their final year, and she sometimes stayed the night at his house, which would be her home after they were married, but both had agreed that they wanted their life as husband and wife to feel different and new.

She shivered, not with cold but with anticipation. It was exciting to think of the small feminine touches she would bring to his bachelor pad to make it more homely. Their wedding list had included cushions, bedding and fluffy cotton towels in shades of pink and grey, her favourite combination, not to mention the crystal mirror for above the fireplace and the matching lamps...

Her reverie was interrupted by a light tap on the door.

'Sophie, it's us. Can we come in?'

This is it, Sophie thought, padding across the soft cream carpet in her bare feet, *my last few hours as a single woman.*

Sophie made a truly beautiful bride. She had chosen a simple silk wedding dress that draped over her slight curves, becoming fuller below the knee, with an insert of fabric to create a short train. The neckline at the front was a soft cowl from between the shoestring shoulder straps and the back plunged to a deep V shape, showing off her perfectly toned body. She'd opted not to have a veil, choosing instead to have flowers in her hair, falling from the sparkly clip that held the front of her hair back off her face but allowed the rest to cascade over her shoulders in voluminous curls.

Her only jewellery was a scattering of pearls on an invisible thread necklace, giving them the appearance of floating against her chest, and matching stud earrings. She also wore the garnet friendship bracelet that Liv and Grace had bought for her while they were on their gap year travels. They each had one in their birthstone: Liv had sapphires for September and Grace had emeralds for May. They were only chips of the gemstone and not very good quality, but the girls never took them off, wearing them as a symbol of their lifelong friendship, and though it wasn't traditional, each was wearing a bridesmaid dress to match their bracelet.

There was one tradition Tom hadn't been prepared to break with though. Sophie had suggested the more modern wording of love, honour and cherish rather than love, honour and obey, for their wedding vows, but Tom had preferred the latter and eventually Sophie had agreed.

They left the evening celebrations before they were finished, a tradition both were happy to adhere to, and drove off in Tom's Mercedes, which had been suitably decorated with a 'Just Married' sign and a pair of boots dangling from the rear bumper.

Tom unlocked the front door and swept Sophie into his arms to carry her over the threshold. As her feet touched the ground, he tilted her face up to his and planted a kiss on her lips.

'Welcome to your new life, Mrs Sterling. You're mine now, until death do us part.'

CHAPTER 10

Liv

February 2018

I'm annoyed with myself for forgetting to ask Mum for my front door key back, after she borrowed it several years ago to allow the workman doing up her kitchen to have access to the house while she and Dad were out at work. Tom still has his, so can come and go as he pleases, but I'm standing on the doorstep of my childhood home in the freezing cold waiting for Mum to open it. My breath is forming clouds, and I can feel a drip on the end of my nose that I might have to wipe with the back of my woollen mitten if she doesn't hurry up. There's no way I'm taking them off; I can barely feel my fingers as it is, and my toes have long since lost sensation.

'Mum,' I say, pushing up the flap and calling through the letterbox. 'Are you in there? Can you let me in before I turn into an actual block of ice?'

I hear a shuffling noise and the bottom half of my mother comes into view. She's still in her pyjamas and dressing gown, despite it being almost midday, and she's wearing my dad's slippers, which are several sizes too big for her.

'Sorry, love, I was just on the phone to your brother,' she says as she unlocks the front door and stands aside to let me in. 'He's going to come over when he's finished his morning appointments.'

'Oh?' I say, unable to keep the surprise from my voice. 'Does he know I'm here?'

'Yes, that's why he's coming. There's something I want to talk over with the two of you,' she says, shuffling back along the parquet floor and into what was once the pristine dining room but which, as I can see over her shoulder, now resembles a jumble sale. There are clothes piled up on the chairs and the table is covered in books and loose papers. Hanging on the curtain rail are several suits that haven't seen the light of day for years. Everywhere is strewn with possessions and clothing belonging to my late dad.

Despite me assuring Mum that I would help her sort his things out when I'd settled back into my normal routine after the week away in Mexico, she's taken it upon herself to start without me and it has clearly taken its toll. She looks dreadful. She is hunched forward, her shoulders rounded and her chin dropping into her chest. Her hair is hanging limply and looks as though it hasn't been washed for days. It's an awful thing to say about your own mum, but I also noticed a slight waft of body odour as I followed her down the hallway.

My dad's death hit all of us hard, but, at first, Mum seemed to be coping surprisingly well. The downward slide started a week before Christmas, just after her seventieth birthday, when I popped in to help her put her Christmas decorations up. She told me she wasn't going to bother because she didn't feel like celebrating. I didn't argue because she had a point. All firsts without a deceased loved one, be it birthday, wedding anniversary or Christmas, are bound to be the hardest, as we'd already experienced when Sophie died.

Mum and Dad, as Sophie's in-laws, did their best to comfort her parents, but their efforts were largely ignored. I don't know if they somehow blamed my family for what happened to her, but I was already in a state after miscarrying Alfie so wasn't as much support as I might otherwise have been. Grace, of course, was unable to face them and simply disappeared from Spain with no forwarding address. Mind you, Sophie's parents did a pretty good job of disappearing too. They sold their house and went to live in the Shetland Islands off the north-east coast of Scotland, returning to their Scottish roots.

'Mum,' I say, trying to keep the exasperation out of my voice as I survey the mess before me that bears a close resemblance to the flotsam and jetsam washed up in the increasingly polluted oceans, 'I thought we were going to do this together.'

'It was getting on my nerves,' she says, her lips twitching. 'I feel like I need to get rid of everything that reminds me of your father so that I can move on with my life. Looking at all his stuff every day is like poking an open wound with a stick. It won't heal unless I stop torturing myself by looking through old photographs and holding his clothes against my face so that I can smell him.'

It's too soon. Mum and I have talked about this before. We only lost my dad in October; she hasn't given herself enough time to grieve.

'But, Mum,' I say, putting my arm around her, 'what if you get rid of something and later wish you hadn't? Once Dad's things are gone, they're gone. Other people will be wearing his clothes and reading his books. You can't just wipe away the past fifty years of your life.' My eyes alight on a pile of framed photographs, the top one of which is my parents' wedding day. 'When you're not feeling so emotional, you'll regret any hasty decisions, I know you will.'

'Tom doesn't agree. He came around to see me every day while you were on your holiday, so we had plenty of time for long talks.'

Whether or not Mum realises it, she has just made me feel terrible. I didn't want to go off and leave her, but, with things as bad as they were with Jamie, I had to have space to try to sort out my own life or I would be no good to her.

Tom and Dad always had the most amazing relationship, going to rugby matches together in the winter months and cricket in the summer, not to mention the hours they spent together on the golf course. But my brother was pretty noticeable in his absence throughout our dad's illness, particularly in the latter stages. It's not as though Tom's squeamish either – after all, he spends his working life looking after sick animals – but he just didn't seem able to accept that Dad was terminally ill. It was something else Jamie and I argued about. Jamie thought I was being harsh. 'It's hard to watch someone who has always been so fit and healthy just wither away,' he said, not seeming to realise it was equally hard for me. Someone had to be there to support Mum and that someone was me, right up to the moment Dad took his final breath.

'He says getting rid of everything that reminded him of Sophie helped him to get over the shock and move on with his life,' Mum continues.

'He's certainly done that,' I mutter, half under my breath. Clearly, he's influenced Mum based on his own feelings after losing his partner, but it's not the same for everyone and I'm not convinced it's the right course of action for her. 'Well, we don't have to make hasty decisions,' I say. 'I'm home now and I'm not starting back at work until Monday, so maybe we can choose a few things to keep that hold particularly happy memories for you. And there might be some things I'd like to have, if that's all right with you?'

She looks puzzled for a moment, as though wanting to keep mementos of my dad is an outlandish suggestion.

'What sort of things?' she asks.

'Oh, I don't really know. Maybe birthday cards I wrote to him when I was a little girl, or those drawings of animals he used to do for Tom and me. Tom always said he thought they influenced him to become a vet; he might like those if we can find them,' I say, my eyes once again scanning the mess.

'I doubt it, but you can ask him yourself. His car has just pulled up.'

Sure enough, I can see my tall, handsome brother getting out of his Range Rover and making his way down Mum's driveway.

I take a deep breath, trying to relax my shoulders which I can already feel tensing up at the sight of him. I stand slightly behind Mum in the hallway as he slips his key into the lock and the door swings open.

As a child, I adored my big brother and I was so proud of him when he graduated from university and later qualified as a fully fledged vet. I was a bit surprised when he and Sophie first started seeing each other, but that was mostly because of the age difference. It wasn't long before I realised that they were made for each other and I couldn't have been happier for them when they got engaged. Once Jamie and I started seeing one another, after meeting at Tom and Sophie's wedding, we often went out as a foursome, and sometimes as a six if Grace was dating. We had a lot of fun in the first couple of years of their marriage, and we turned the tables on them by having them as our best man and bridesmaid, along with Grace of course, when we tied the knot.

I'm not exactly sure when we started seeing less of them, but we went from being virtually inseparable to me rarely meeting up with Sophie even for a coffee. Maybe some of it was my fault. I was getting used to being a married woman and wanted to be with my husband as much as possible, particularly as we were both working full-time, so our leisure time was precious. In the two years leading up to my miscarriage, Sophie and I had seen very little of each other. I was dreadfully upset when Tom said he didn't think it was a good idea for Sophie to visit me after I lost Alfie as she'd been unwell herself. It was an excuse he used a lot and I had sometimes wondered whether it was to cover up problems within their marriage. Sadly, I never got the chance to ask her, but my suspicions seemed to carry more weight when Tom started dating Polly so soon after Sophie died, which put a lot of strain on mine and Tom's relationship. Before I went off to Mexico, we were barely on speaking terms, but perhaps I was being uncharitable.

'Tom,' I say, a touch too brightly, 'how are you doing?'

'Pretty good, all things considered.'

'And Polly?' I ask, anxious to follow through with my promise of being nicer to my brother's new wife.

'She's fine,' he replies. He turns to our mum and says, 'So what's with all the cloak-and-dagger stuff? I've only got half an hour before I need to get back. There's a cocker spaniel in a lot of pain with an abscess under her tooth that isn't going to get any better until I do the extraction.'

'The kettle has just boiled; shall I make us all a cup of tea?' Mum asks.

Tom shrugs.

'I'll do it, Mum,' I say. 'You go through to the lounge with Tom. Still having one sugar, Tom?'

'No thanks. Polly and I are trying to kick the sugar habit; it's no good for you.'

I don't know why he's telling me that. I haven't taken sugar in hot drinks since I was fourteen and went on my first diet, but maybe he's forgotten the way I take my tea. He hasn't made me one for a few years.

The kitchen is almost as messy as the dining room, only not strewn with Dad's possessions. Despite having a state-of-the-art dishwasher, there are cups and plates dotted around on the work surfaces and yet more soaking in the sink.

I flick the switch on the kettle and while I'm waiting for it to reach the boil again, I open the cupboard doors looking for clean mugs. Fortunately, Mum's amassed quite a collection over the years, although mine does have an advert for the local garden centre on it. I pour the boiling water onto the teabags and go in search of milk in the fridge while it brews, before carrying everything through on a tray.

'Is your dishwasher broken, Mum?' I ask. 'You should have said, I could have arranged to get someone out to look at it.'

'Well, you could have if you'd been here rather than swanning around in Mexico,' Tom says.

I bite my lip, refusing to rise to my brother's criticism.

Mum looks from one of us to the other, a nervous expression on her face. She must have noticed the growing tension on the occasions we have been together.

'Actually,' she says, 'it's not broken. I just don't see the point in putting that great big machine on and wasting all that water for only a few bits and pieces. I can do them in the sink.'

True, she could, but it doesn't look as though she has been. She's probably focused all her attention on clearing Dad's study and his wardrobes, and everything else has been left. I make a mental note to load everything into the dishwasher and put it through a cycle before I leave today.

'Decent cuppa as it happens, Liv,' Tom says, taking a sip from his mug. 'At least you haven't lost your touch in that department.'

It's amazing how my brother has somehow turned a compliment into a dig at me. I'm guessing that the department he thinks I have lost my touch in is being a good sister, which I'm intending to put right if he'll let me.

'So, what did you want to talk to us about, Mum? Tom's got to get back to work and we need to make a start on sorting through Dad's stuff.'

'You'll need to be quick,' Tom says. 'I've arranged for the charity shop's van to call around and collect everything this afternoon at three.'

I throw a glance in Mum's direction, but her face is impassive.

'Well, that will give us a couple of hours to choose what we want to keep,' I say, placing emphasis on the words 'us' and 'we'.

'That's your problem, Liv, you're far too sentimental,' Tom comments. 'Your inability to let go of the past almost destroyed your marriage. You're lucky you've got someone as understanding as Jamie, because most blokes wouldn't tolerate it. I know I wouldn't; you'd have been history with all your nagging and moaning.'

It's not my brother's words that hurt me, it's the thought that Jamie has been discussing things with him. Tom is Jamie's best friend, so I suppose I should have assumed that he might have talked about it, but I'm sure Jamie wouldn't have expected Tom to use it as ammunition.

'Well, thankfully, Jamie's not you and he'll completely understand that it's important to me to have some personal things to help me remember the wonderful, kind man Dad was,' I say, keeping my voice as calm as I can.

'Please don't argue, you two,' Mum says with a sigh.

'We're not; we just have a different point of view,' I reply, fixing Tom with a steady gaze.

I don't know if he was about to comment, but he's too late, because Mum says, 'Well, you're going to have to learn to agree on things, because I want you both to have equal power of attorney.'

'Is that really necessary, Mum? Isn't that something you put in place when there's something wrong?' I say, a bubble of anxiety in my chest. 'You haven't got any health issues, have you?' I add, unsure I would be able to deal with any more bad news at the moment.

'No, I'm fine. I just want to be prepared after what happened to your dad.'

'Well, I don't have a problem with it,' Tom says, knocking back the contents of his mug and getting to his feet. 'In fact, it's a good idea. You might want to make sure your Will is up to date too. What?' he adds, in response to my shocked expression. 'She's just being practical. We all know our final destination. The only variable is how long it takes to get there.' He glances at his watch. 'I'm going to have to go or Maisie the spaniel will be arriving at her final destination ahead of time. Give me a call later, Liv, and we can discuss how to go about setting it up. Or maybe ring Polly and arrange an evening for you and Jamie to come for supper, so we can sort it out then.' He kisses his fingertips and drops them on Mum's head, before striding out into the hallway and slamming the door behind him.

'You should do that, Olivia,' Mum says.

'What's that?'

'Arrange to have supper with Tom and Polly. It's not her fault that your brother fell for her so quickly after losing Sophie, and she clearly adores him. It breaks my heart to see the two of you being so confrontational, and it's not fair on Mia to have so little contact with her auntie.'

I know Mum's right. But Tom put me in a really difficult position. When he first introduced us to Polly, I thought she was a really sweet girl. She'd started working as a receptionist at Jamie and Tom's veterinary practice a couple of months before Sophie's accident and had offered him a shoulder to cry on. It was only when Tom announced their engagement three months later that I began to wonder if he'd actually been cheating on Sophie before the fatal train crash. Once I'd had the thought, I couldn't get it out of my mind. It felt as though by marrying Polly, he was removing all trace of Sophie from his life; I simply couldn't understand what his hurry was. After first telling me to mind my own business, he then used our dad's illness as his reason. 'I want Dad to go to his grave knowing that I've found someone else to share my life with. Surely you wouldn't want to begrudge him that peace of mind? Can't you at least pretend to be happy for me?'

So, I pretended; I managed to smile through most of his wedding day, except when Jamie, his best man for a second time, handed him the wedding bands. A tear slipped from the corner of my eye as I thought about my beautiful friend. I managed to escape from the evening reception early, citing a migraine, and had cried myself to sleep before Jamie arrived home. Since their wedding, I thought I'd been quite clever in hiding my disapproval from Mum, but her comment has made me realise that I haven't hidden it as well as I'd hoped. She's right, I can't continue distancing myself from my niece.

'You win, Mum. I'll call Polly when I get home and try to organise something for this weekend.'

Mum smiles her gratitude.

'Right,' I say, 'we'd better make a start if the collection van is going to be here at 3 p.m.'

'I've got these,' Mum says, looking down at her size 5 feet which are dwarfed by my dad's size 10 slippers. 'Do you think that's enough?'

'Well, let's have a proper look, shall we?' I suggest, wondering what made her choose something so random.

In the end, Mum kept hold of her wedding photo and a couple of albums after I explained to her that the charity shop would only keep the frames and books and shred the pictures. She also kept a white silky scarf that she said Dad used to wear in his teens and gave to her when they first started dating, but she was adamant she didn't need anything else. 'All my memories are stored in my head,' she insisted, as we watched the two men from the charity bundle Dad's clothes into bin liners and pile his treasured collection of records into boxes before carrying them out to their van.

I found the box of pencil drawings that he'd done for Tom and me over the years and I also rescued his golf clubs, even though Jamie doesn't play. Having looked through his things and shed a few more tears, I realised that actually Tom and Mum were right about letting most things go, particularly his clothes. At least they may provide comfort and warmth to other people. I did, however, keep the oversized sweater I had made for him when I'd first mastered the art of knitting. It ended up a couple of sizes too big for him because I was too impatient to start and hadn't done a sample tension square; it never stopped him wearing it around the house though. If Jamie and I ever get the puppy we've been promising ourselves, it will make a cosy bed lining for him to snuggle into and I know Dad would have approved of its new use.

I glance over my shoulder to the back seat, where it is neatly folded under the box of drawings, before I wave goodbye to Mum and pull away from the kerb. Her dishwasher is loaded and on, I've run her a bubble bath and the hairdresser is booked for a wash and trim first thing in the morning.

I'm just waiting for the traffic lights at the end of her road to change when my phone rings. It's Jamie.

'Hi,' I say.

'How was your mum?' he asks.

'Not too bad. She'd been having a sort-out of Dad's things so it was a bit of a mess when I arrived, but it's all gone off to the local charity shop now.'

'Are you okay with that?'

'Yes. Yes, I am actually.'

'Good. Are you on your way back?'

I glance at the clock on my dashboard. It's five past six.

'I'm sorry,' I say. 'I didn't mean to stay so long. I've just left, so I'll be about fifteen minutes.'

'Okay, I'll start dinner.'

I'm now feeling guilty about staying so long at Mum's. Jamie has been at work all day and it would have been nice for him to come home to me cooking. Tom's words about Jamie being so understanding flash into my head.

'Or we could get a takeaway?' I suggest.

'I've already got all the prep done and the oven's on, I just didn't want to start until I knew you were on your way back.'

'What are we having?'

'Toad in the hole, green beans and gravy.'

'My favourite. I knew there was a reason I married you,' I say, laughing as I end the call.

Much as I hate to admit it, Tom is right. I'm lucky to have Jamie. Seeing Mum so lost and bewildered, surrounded by my dad's things, has underlined the fact that objects don't make memories, people do, and I want to make my memories with Jamie.

CHAPTER 11

Sophie

Spain, 2014

The sun, noticeable by its absence since Sophie's arrival three days earlier, had finally put in an appearance and was reflecting off the ocean's surface, causing it to sparkle as brightly as a pile of faceted diamonds on a gem trader's desk. She took a sip of coffee from the mug she was cradling in her hands after breathing in the aroma of the roasted beans and tried to bank the feeling of calm that she hadn't experienced in almost two years. Coming to Spain to spend time with Grace had been the right decision; she just wished she had made it sooner, before things at home had got so bad.

Grace and Sophie hadn't seen each other in over two years, but if either was worried that it might have felt awkward, the ice was immediately broken when they realised they were both carrying the same Louis Vuitton cross-body bag when Sophie emerged into the arrivals hall at Alicante airport. The girls had air-kissed and commented on their remarkably good taste.

Sophie was happy to let her old school friend talk throughout the ninety-minute car journey to Denia. Grace had obliged by describing her arrival on Spain's Costa Blanca with a small amount of euros but a huge determination to make a new life for herself.

'There was nothing for me in England after that sleazebag Steve turned out to be married,' she'd said. 'You and Liv had settled down with your perfect partners and I still haven't spoken to my parents since they chose to go to Toby's trials with Surrey cricket team rather than our graduation ceremony.'

Grace had gone on to say that she'd chosen Alicante because it was the cheapest one-way ticket she could find and she'd got lucky in securing herself a job at an estate agent's in Denia within days.

'That's where I met Ricardo,' she'd added, 'and we hit it off straight away.'

'Is Ricardo your boyfriend?' Sophie had asked.

'Sadly not. He's drop-down-dead gorgeous but has no interest in girls, other than as friends. He lives in Alicante now, so we'll have to arrange to meet up while you're here.'

While Sophie unpacked, Grace had made a tasty dinner which was washed down with a bottle of Rioja while the girls reminisced about school and their gap year travels. They'd finally gone to bed around two in the morning, both slightly worse for wear after finishing a bottle of Soberano, Grace's favourite Spanish brandy.

Sophie hadn't emerged from her room the next morning until nearly midday, and when she did, her face was puffy and her eyes red-rimmed. She'd been woken just before dawn by the rain lashing against the patio doors and had been unable to get back to sleep. The mild-numbing effect of the alcohol had worn off and as the hopelessness of her situation at home overwhelmed her once again the tears had started.

'I'm making coffee; do you want one?' Grace had asked.

Sophie knew it must be obvious to Grace that she'd been crying.

'Can we talk?' she'd asked.

'I'm glad you feel you can,' Grace had replied.

She'd made them both a strong black coffee, which they'd carried through to the small round dining table, and as the rain streamed down the full-length glass doors, tears had streamed down Sophie's cheeks while she'd explained in stilted sentences that her perfect life wasn't quite all it seemed.

'What am I going to do, Grace?' Sophie had asked when the tears finally stopped. 'I can't live the rest of my life like this.'

'We'll work something out, I promise,' Grace had replied, pulling her friend into a hug. 'I'm so glad you came to me for help. It would have been tricky talking to Liv about this, with Tom being her brother. You know, I've been a bit jealous of you and Liv since the two of you got married, but I guess no one knows what goes on behind closed doors. Maybe there is no such thing as the perfect marriage.'

'Or maybe they just don't stay perfect for long.' Sophie had sniffed, remembering how ecstatically happy she'd been when she and Tom were first married.

'I'll give Ricardo a call and see if we can meet him for drinks and dinner, either tomorrow or the next day. His sister went through something similar, so he's probably better to talk to for advice than me.'

'I hope he can help. I'm desperate, Grace. I can't go on like this much longer.'

'I'm sure he will,' Grace had said in an attempt to reassure the fragile woman in front of her.

Of the trio of friends, Sophie had always been the most outgoing, self-assured and confident, but it was as though her spirit had been broken.

Sophie placed the coffee mug on the table at her side and wiggled her toes as she lay back on the sun lounger. The bright coral of her nail polish matched the sundress she had slipped on after her shower. She was looking forward to meeting Ricardo after all the good things Grace had told her about him.

'Hey, lazybones, are you ready to go? We need to leave for the station fairly soon.'

'Sorry, Grace,' Sophie said, blinking rapidly in an attempt to wake herself up. 'I only closed my eyes for a few minutes. I must have fallen asleep.'

'I hope you had sun protection on.'

'Of course, although I don't exactly need it now,' Sophie said, looking at the grey skies overhead. 'What have you done with the sun?'

'Not guilty,' Grace responded, raising both her hands with her palms facing outwards. 'Maybe you jinxed it by putting your sundress on. That was a bit optimistic, if you ask me. I think we'll be better off in jeans and trainers for our trip to Alicante; it looks like we've got even more rain on the way.'

Sophie swung her legs off the sunbed and picked up the cushion in one hand and her coffee mug in the other, before following Grace into the apartment.

'I'm all out of clean T shirts; I only brought two with me.'

'No problem. We're the same size, you can borrow one of mine,' Grace replied, heading into her room and opening a drawer stuffed with T-shirts in every colour of the rainbow. She pulled out several and handed them to Sophie. 'Here, take your pick, it's not as though I haven't got plenty to choose from.'

'Is there such a thing as a T-shirt hoarder?' Sophie teased.

'There is now,' Grace replied good-naturedly.

'Thanks, I'll be as quick as I can.'

Fifteen minutes later, the girls were huddled together under an umbrella, ready to make a dash for Grace's car.

'Is it always like this in September?' Sophie asked as the rain bounced up off the pavement and the water started to overspill from the gutters.

'Forget the fact that it's September, I've never known this much rainfall since I moved out here. All the riverbeds that are usually dried up apart from a trickle in the middle are gushing torrents, which should make our train ride even more picturesque than usual. I hope you haven't developed a fear of heights, because there are a few viaducts and sheer drops between here and Benidorm.'

'It was a good idea to get the train. At least I'll get to see a bit of the area despite the weather doing its worst. And it's so kind of Ricardo to offer to bring us back so that we can both enjoy a few drinks.'

'He's a good mate, and besides, his mum lives in Gata de Gorgos, so it gives him the chance to spend the day with her before driving you to the airport tomorrow evening. I'm just sorry we couldn't organise any sun for your few days here.'

'It wasn't the sun I came for,' Sophie said, squeezing Grace's arm. 'Thank you for listening.'

'That's what friends are for,' Grace said, returning the squeeze.

CHAPTER 12

Liv

Oxted, 2018

'How do you manage to get it so light and fluffy,' I say, savouring my last mouthful of toad in the hole. 'Whenever I attempt anything with batter, it's always as flat as a pancake.'

'Very funny, Liv,' Jamie replies, putting his knife and fork together on his plate and pushing it away.

'What? Oh, I see. Pancakes are made with batter. You thought I was cracking a joke.'

'You weren't?'

'No. This is me we're talking about. In the eight or so years you've known me, I don't think I've ever told a decent joke; that's more your department.'

'It's such a burden being so good at everything,' he says.

'And so modest with it too,' I say, laughing.

The thing is, he's right. Jamie is one of those people who seem to be able to turn their hand to anything. He's actually a much better cook than me. Although we do take turns in preparing the evening meal, there are more ready meals or takeaways on my nights than there are on his. Both he and Tom are excellent vets, but Jamie is always much more in demand because he's so gentle with both the animals and the owners. He plays football in a Sunday league team and has been voted Player of the Year for the past four seasons by his team-mates. Mum loves him, mostly because he lets her win at cards, and my brother definitely prefers him to me. He is just one of life's good guys, and to think I nearly let him slip through my fingers. What an idiot I am to almost have allowed my brother to come between us.

'Tom dropped into Mum's today,' I say, changing the subject. 'He suggested I call Polly and arrange to go round for supper.'

Jamie raises his eyebrows expectantly and says, 'And?'

'Have you got anything planned this weekend? I thought the sooner we arrange, it the sooner I can start to get to know Polly a bit better.'

He smiles. 'She's a nice girl, Liv. She was really popular when she was our receptionist at the surgery, both with other staff members and with the clients, and she's been sorely missed since she gave up work to look after Mia. I think you'll really like her if you give her a chance.'

I smile back at him. One evening meal isn't going to make me and Polly best friends, but I have to start somewhere and I really do want to build a better relationship with my niece. I often wonder whether Alfie would have inherited my curly dark mop of hair, as Mia has from Tom, or whether his hair would have been more sandy in colour like his dad.

Jamie's watching me, waiting for a response.

'Which day is better for you?' I ask.

'Either, although Saturday is preferable. I'd rather be slightly hung-over running up and down a muddy football pitch than with a scalpel in my unsteady hand trying to remove Mr Tiddles' testicles.'

'Gross,' I reply, shuddering. 'Just the thought of some of the things you have to do makes me want to retch.'

'Don't worry, I always wear gloves and then wash my hands thoroughly afterwards.' He winks.

'That's not what I meant, and you know it. I've never been great with blood and guts and stuff, even when I know it's fake in television dramas and films. I sometimes wonder how on earth I stayed so calm when Sophie was glassed in that bar in Mexico and the blood was oozing between my fingers. I'm surprised I didn't pass out along with her,' I say, feeling faint at the mere memory.

'Speaking of Mexico,' he says, stacking his plate on top of mine and pushing his chair back from the table, 'there was a letter for you with a Mexican postmark.'

'Really?' I reply, following him through to the kitchen, where he's loading the plates in the dishwasher. He's a really tidy cook, clearing up as he goes along, unlike me. The kitchen always looks as though a bomb has dropped if I've been making anything from scratch. Just something else my husband is good at. 'It's probably follow-up marketing from the hotel. I'm pretty sure I didn't leave anything there.'

'I put it on the desk in the office. I'll fetch it while you give Polly a call.'

He clearly has no intention of allowing me to wiggle out of making the phone call to arrange a supper date with Polly and Tom. My brother has offered an olive branch and I know it's in everyone's best interest to accept it.

I start the dishwasher before reaching for my mobile phone and selecting Polly's name. She answers on the second ring, almost as though she's been expecting my call. Maybe she has.

'Hi Polly, it's Liv,' I say.

'Yes, Tom said you might be calling,' she replies, a hint of hesitancy in her voice.

I plough on, anxious to get the call over and done with. 'He suggested that maybe we could meet up for supper at yours this weekend,' I say, nodding my head at Jamie, who is making the letter T with his fingers. What I could really do with is a glass of wine, but I'm trying to cut down on midweek drinking, so tea will have to do. He flicks the switch on the kettle, and I walk past him into the lounge to escape the noise of it boiling.

'We're free both evenings,' Polly is saying, 'so whichever is best for you. It'll be nice to have some company. We barely go out these days,' she adds.

It may be my imagination, but she sounds tense.

'Well, I suppose it's tricky with Mia to look after,' I reply, feeling immediately guilty that I haven't offered my services as a babysitter. 'Is she still having trouble sleeping?'

'She's a lot better than she was, but I'd hate for her to wake up and neither of us be here to comfort her.'

'Maybe I can help out with that,' I hear myself offer.

'Really?' Polly's voice sounds both hopeful and grateful. 'It would be lovely for the two of you to spend some time together.'

'We can talk about it when we come over,' I say. 'Jamie would prefer Saturday, so he doesn't have to worry about work the next day. It's probably the same for Tom.'

'Okay, great. Is six too early? It would be nice if you saw Mia before her bedtime.'

'That's perfect; we'll bring the wine,' I say, ending the call before she can object.

'All sorted?' Jamie asks, coming into the room carrying a tray with our mugs of tea and a packet of Jaffa Cakes. He places it on the coffee table before relaxing back in his chair, remote control in hand.

'Yes, Saturday at six,' I say, reaching for my mug and ignoring the Jaffa Cakes which I can't stand. As usual, Jamie is being thoughtful. He's still the same size he was when we got married, but I've struggled with my weight since the miscarriage. I try to avoid having anything after my dinner unless it's a special occasion. 'I told her we'd take the wine.'

'Good idea; your big bro can be a bit stingy in that department.'

He picks up the TV remote and immediately starts flicking through the channels. I've never understood why men do this. They don't stay on a channel long enough to make an informed decision on whether it's something they might enjoy watching. It's one of the few things that annoys me about my husband.

I give him a long hard glare, which he's oblivious to because he's already engrossed in his channel-hopping. The funny thing is, once he's been all the way through all the additional broadcasters, nine times out of ten we'll end up watching something on one of the main four channels.

He'll be a few minutes yet, so I pick up the letter from Mexico that fell face down on the tray when Jamie put it down. I turn it over to look at the address and let out a small yelp, almost dropping my mug of hot tea.

'I'm always telling you to let it cool down a bit first,' Jamie says, still distractedly flicking through the channels. 'You'll properly burn yourself one of these days.' When I don't speak, he turns to look at me. 'Christ, Liv, what's the matter? You look like you've seen a ghost.'

The writing on the envelope is small and neat; I'd recognise it anywhere. I occasionally used to try to forge it for her if she'd been at her dance classes until late and hadn't had time to finish her homework.

Jamie leapt out of his chair to remove the mug from my hand when it started to shake. He's standing over me now, a look of concern on his face. 'What's wrong?' he demands.

I look up at him, and then back down at the envelope.

'That looks like Sophie's writing,' I whisper.

'Liv,' he says, a hint of exasperation in his voice, 'why do you torture yourself like this? It can't be; she died over three years ago. The only way it could be her writing is if the letter has been lost in the post for eleven years. Here, let me see the postmark.'

I shake my head. 'She wouldn't have been sending a letter to this address,' I stammer. 'I didn't even know you back then.'

'Then it can't be from her; just open it and put yourself out of your misery.'

My hands are still shaking as I run my finger along the top edge of the envelope. The sound of tearing paper transports me back to exam results day. I can clearly picture Sophie's animated face and hear the delight in her voice.

I start to pull the sheets of paper out of the envelope, then change my mind. I can see Jamie's lips moving and hear his voice, but it seems to be coming from the end of a long tunnel and I can't focus on what he's saying.

'I'm going to read this upstairs if it's okay with you,' I say, getting to my feet.

'If that's what you want,' he replies.

I can't tell if he's hurt or annoyed that I want to read the letter in private when I reply, 'Yes, it is,' and close the lounge door behind me.

CHAPTER 13

Grace

Mexico, 2018

Wednesday is normally my favourite day of the week. I teach a lunchtime Pilates class and Luis is at the animal shelter all afternoon, but neither of us work in the evening. I'm not the best cook in the world, passable if I follow a clear recipe is probably the most accurate description, but I've made a special effort today. Instead of relying on the internet, I asked Josefina for her recipe for enchiladas, which I know Luis loves, and I've followed it to the letter. It smells amazing; tangy, tomatoey, spicy and garlicky without being overpowering. It's a good job we'll both be eating it though or there certainly wouldn't be any kissing later on.

Just the thought of kissing Luis sends a tingle down my spine. I wasn't even sure that I could truly love again after the trauma I went through, but Luis showed me the way. Not only is he the consummate lover, he's a kind-hearted and trusting human being, which is why I felt compelled to write the letter to Liv.

It's taken me almost a week since I posted it to prepare myself for what I'm going to tell him tonight. I hope that my revelation won't make any difference to us; what we have now is what I want forever, someone who loves me as much as I love them.

I can feel the palms of my hands becoming moist. It's a warm evening, but I'm pretty sure that's not why. I'm nervous, and unless

I'm very careful, Luis will sense it straightaway and the evening might not go as planned.

I've washed my hair and applied a touch of mascara and lip gloss, but otherwise I'm 'au naturel'. I've never felt so comfortable in my own skin as I have since Luis came into my life. If I want to wear make-up, he tells me I look pretty, and if I'm not wearing any, he says the same; he loves me for being me.

That's the problem. Luis loves the person he thinks I am; he doesn't know everything about my past.

The candles are lit, and I've got some soft music playing. I'm just wondering if it's all a bit too much when I hear Luis coming up the front steps.

'Something smells good,' he says as he opens the front door. He stops in his tracks, frowning. 'Did I forget something, Grace? Do we have friends coming for dinner?'

'No, it's just the two of us. I wanted to cook you something special to show you how much you mean to me.'

Shit; that's not what I wanted to say at all. Even to my ears, it sounded suspicious.

He's looking at me with a puzzled, slightly concerned expression, the sort of look a wife gives a cheating husband when he brings home a huge bunch of flowers for no apparent reason. I'm wondering if I can trust myself to open my mouth without putting my foot in it again when his expression changes.

'There are other ways that you can show me how much I mean to you without slaving over a hot stove,' he says, crossing the room and planting a kiss on my lips. He lingers a moment before pulling away. 'But that really does smell good, so I'm not complaining. Do I have time for a shower?' he adds suggestively. 'Or will I just wash my hands?'

It doesn't take a genius to work out his meaning, but I want that to come later in the evening when I know he still wants to be with me.

'Maybe just your hands… for now,' I reply, matching his mood.

'As you wish. I get the feeling you have our evening planned and I wouldn't want to spoil that.'

Luis disappears into our bedroom and I hear him use the loo before washing his hands. Some people like to keep these sorts of personal things very private, but Luis and I have always been very relaxed about them; it's only nature, there's nothing to hide. But I have been hiding something; something with the potential to blow my cosy world apart.

My heart starts pounding in my chest and my mind returns to the question that has occupied it on and off for the past three weeks. Does he really need to know?

Luis reappears in the doorway, his eyes as warm and trusting as the dogs he cares for at the sanctuary. There's my answer. I have no choice; he has to know the truth for better or worse.

Luis actually claimed that my enchiladas were tastier than Josefina's. I'm not sure about that, but they were really good.

When we've cleared the dishes away, we take our beers and go outside to sit on the sofa in our little courtyard garden. It was a square of hardened mud when I first moved in with Luis, but between us, we've created an oasis. I mean that almost literally, as there is a fountain and two palm trees – the most welcome of sights for a traveller in the desert.

I'm leaning against Luis's shoulder looking up at the bright stars in the inky sky and he's playing with my hair. I wish we could stay like this forever but now I've made my decision I can't put it off any longer.

'Luis,' I say, 'have you ever wondered what my life was like before I came to Mexico?'

'Sometimes. But I figured you would tell me about it when you wanted to. I'm a very patient man.'

'Yes, you are,' I agree, looking into his deep brown eyes. 'That's one of the things I love about you.'

He lifts my chin and kisses me. He tastes of beer and garlic, but then so do I.

I enjoy the moment, before pulling away.

'There's some stuff I think you should know.'

'Okay,' he says, taking another swig of beer, 'if that's what you want.'

I'm not sure 'want' is the right word; it's something I feel compelled to do. I take a deep breath before I speak.

'Do you remember on the night we first met, me telling you that I'd visited Mexico before with my friends from school.'

'I'll never forget a thing about the night we met,' he says, making no attempt to hide the love in his eyes. 'It was as though an angel had walked into my bar. I couldn't believe it when you left alone. I was worried that you would be afraid of me after I followed you to the beach. An English girl alone in a foreign country with a complete stranger.'

'It never crossed my mind to be afraid of you, but that might be because I'm not really afraid of much anymore. I was given a second chance at life, so every minute of every day is a bonus for me,' I admit.

'You're not really making much sense, Grace.'

This is it, the moment I've agonised over since seeing Liv on the beach. *Please, please let him understand why I did what I did,* I silently pray.

'Not long before I met you, I was involved in an accident when I was in Spain visiting my friend. It was a really bad train accident. People died, Luis, lots of people, including my friend, one of the girls I was in Mexico with.'

'Oh Grace, I'm so sorry,' he says, placing our beer bottles on the ground and extending his arms around me.

I can feel the solid, steady beat of his heart vibrating as I rest my face against his chest. I feel so safe in his embrace, but tears are pricking the back of my eyes.

'It's my fault she died,' I say, my voice unsteady. Despite my best intentions, the tears are now rolling down my cheeks. I've never said these words aloud to anyone, although the thought has tortured me since that September day.

'If it was an accident, how could it be your fault? You couldn't have prevented it from happening,' Luis says, his voice soothing.

'No, but we wouldn't have been on the damn train if it hadn't been for me.'

The floodgates have well and truly opened now. I want to tell Luis the rest of the story, but I can't speak I'm sobbing so hard. My breath is coming in short gasps and I'm starting to shake. Luis is holding me very tightly, trying to calm me I suspect.

'You can't blame yourself for that. Any one of us could be hit by a car when crossing the road just because we were in the wrong place at the wrong time,' he says, his words punctuated by the kisses he is dropping onto the top of my head. 'It was an accident, a tragic accident, but you didn't cause it, so it can't be your fault.'

'But she wouldn't have died if she hadn't been with me,' I manage through my tears.

'I wish you'd told me this before,' Luis says. 'This is a heavy burden to carry on your own, one I would have been happy to share with you.'

I have to find the strength to tell him the rest of the story. If I don't do it now, I never will and not only would it be on my conscience for ever, there's still the risk that Liv will come back to Mexico to seek me out. It would destroy Luis if he learned the truth from her rather than me.

I take several gulps of the warm evening air to try to steady my breathing. My careful plan for this evening did not take into consideration how emotional I would feel about reliving the horror of the crash. My voice is shaky when I start to speak.

'We'd been on the train for more than an hour. I got up to walk to the back of the train to take some photographs of the stunning views, when suddenly the brakes were applied. I was standing near the doors and as I reached out to save myself from falling, they opened, and I found myself in mid-air. I had no idea what was happening, but I could hear terrified screams and the sound of metal against metal as the brakes tried to bite. My body made contact with the springy scrub at the side of the tracks which broke my fall before I hit the ground. Despite feeling dazed, I was aware of a sudden silence; the squealing of the wheels on the track had stopped.'

I've started trembling violently, but although Luis holds me even tighter, he doesn't speak. Maybe he fears that interrupting me will stop me from finally releasing the horror of the memory; he's right, I need to finish what I've started.

'I… I thought the train had stopped on the tracks, but then… there was an explosion. The sound seemed to go on and on as it echoed against the steep sides of the ravine. The train was gone; she was gone. If I hadn't been at the back of the train, we would both have died.'

Finally, Luis speaks.

'But that wasn't your destiny. For whatever reason, you were spared and I'm so thankful you were. My poor love,' he says, releasing me from the tight embrace and placing his hands on my shoulders so that he is looking directly into my eyes. 'Poor, poor Grace.'

The truth in his words is excruciatingly painful, but I suddenly feel very calm.

'I took Grace's life,' I say, holding his gaze.

'No, you weren't to blame for…' Luis starts to say, then stops in confusion.

'What I'm trying to tell you, Luis,' I continue, taking a deep breath, 'is that I'm not Grace ... Grace was the one who died in the accident.'

I can see shock register in his eyes.

'But why would you do that? Why would you pretend to be someone you're not? I don't understand.'

'Because it allowed me to run away from my own life. I can't remember what I was running from, I just know I was desperately unhappy and afraid, and so I took the chance to escape. Please don't hate me, Luis,' I beg.

He still has his hands on my shoulders and is staring into my eyes, but his expression has changed from one of sympathy to one of utter confusion. I have no idea what he will do, but I had to be honest with him.

CHAPTER 14

Liv

Oxted

I close the bedroom door and cross our room to climb onto our bed. If it's possible to feel pale rather than look pale, then I do. I lean back on my pillows and take a few breaths to steady my nerves. My hands are shaking as I draw the pages from the envelope and start to read:

My dearest Liv,

I'm pretty sure you will have recognised the handwriting on the envelope, so it's a good sign that you're reading this. I had wondered whether to print a label, but I was worried you might think it was just a follow-up from the hotel and would bin the letter without opening it. I couldn't risk that, not after I've plucked up the courage to write to you.

My mind has been in absolute turmoil since you called out my name on the beach. I couldn't understand why you thought it might be me, when you knew that my life ended in the accident. I realise it must have been the tattoo that you thought you recognised, but lots of people have tattoos.

I ran, because I was hoping that you'd think it through and come to the conclusion that it was just a coincidence. But then I started worrying. I know you, Liv, and even if you'd decided it was probably a coincidence, you might have returned to Mexico for your own peace of mind.

I was so shocked to see you on the beach in Tulum after the three of us swore it was the one place in the world that we would never return to after what happened. And that, of course, was the whole point of me choosing Mexico. I wanted to disappear, to start a new life, and fate had handed me the opportunity.

I wasn't on the train when it plunged into the ravine. The doors had opened moments before, and I'd fallen from it. I was lucky there were bushes to break my fall, but I was so traumatised that, at first, I didn't know who I was. I couldn't remember my name or anything about my life. While I was trying to gauge if I'd broken any bones, I came across my bag. Inside it, I found a passport. It was Grace's.

I think I knew fairly quickly that I wasn't Grace and that's when a few things started to come back to me. I could see her laughing face behind the barrier at the airport because we both had the same designer handbag. I began to remember snippets of the conversations we'd had over the previous days, not everything, but enough to know that I was desperately unhappy.

Lying there in the pouring rain with the sirens from the emergency vehicles wailing in the background, I came to a decision. Grace couldn't have survived the crash; nobody who was at the front of the train when it left the rails could. She didn't need her life anymore, but I did. I wasn't a hundred per cent sure of what I was running away from, but I quickly recognised that I'd been given an opportunity to not have to return to it. Taking Grace's identity went some way to lessening the horror of what had happened to her. In my confused and desperate state, it almost felt as though she had sacrificed her life for me, and I couldn't let her death be in vain.

What I did might seem cowardly and cruel. I've had so many sleepless nights feeling terrible guilt for the grief I must have put you and my parents through, but I had to do it, I had to escape. Tom is your brother, and I know you love him. I've only been able to remember flashes of our life together, but it's enough to know that something was terribly wrong in our marriage and I can never go back. I think I would rather have died in the accident than continue living the life I was.

That's why I'm writing to tell you all this; I'm asking you to leave things as they are and not tell anyone that you've seen me. I came looking for you that afternoon because it would have been easier to explain all this in person, but you'd already left for the airport. I honestly didn't know whether or not I should write to you. I wondered whether you'd convince yourself that it was mistaken identity, or whether you'd come back looking for me? I had no way of knowing, but it did make me examine what I was doing. I was living a lie and it didn't seem fair on Luis, a man I love and have built a new life with. I'm going to tell him who I really am and hope that he loves me enough to forgive me for deceiving him.

Let me have this chance at happiness, Liv, I'm begging you. We live a simple life, Luis looking after animals and me teaching Pilates classes. We're not hurting anyone; please just let us be.

I'll always treasure our friendship. I think of you and Grace often, but that was another life, one that I cannot ever return to. I hope you can find it in your heart to forgive me.

Sophie x

I release the letter and watch as it falls first onto my legs and then continues its journey fluttering to the floor, almost in slow motion. My heart is thumping ponderously in my chest, but my mind is racing. I'm struggling to understand how any of what I have just read can be true. In two sheets of flimsy paper, everything I've believed about the fatal train crash in Spain has been thrown into doubt.

Sophie died, the police investigation said so, even though her body, like so many of the other victims, was never recovered after being washed out to sea by the raging torrent of water at the bottom of the ravine. Grace ran away because she felt responsible. If she hadn't invited Sophie to Spain for a visit, she would still be alive, that's what she'd said in her email. And yet, the letter, written in Sophie's handwriting, claims that was all a lie. And if it was untrue, and it was Grace who perished, will I ever be able to forgive myself for all the terrible thoughts I've had about her selfishness?

I wrap my arms around my knees and hug them into my chest. It can't be true; none of it. The Sophie I know would never willingly have left us all behind to start a new life, letting us believe that she had died, knowing how devastated we would all be.

The image of her grieving parents at her graveside, holding on to each other as if their lives depended on it, swims before my eyes. Both of them had been so calm throughout the funeral ceremony, which took place in the church where Sophie had been christened and, many years later, married.

I'd wanted to give the eulogy – after all I knew Sophie better than anyone – and when I'd written it, I was confident that I could deliver it. But as the moment approached, my legs had turned to jelly, and I knew I wouldn't be able to get through it without crying. Instead, I'd handed my speech to Jamie and my wonderful husband read out the words I had agonised over for days.

It was only as Sophie's coffin was being lowered into the ground, empty of her human remains but filled with some of the things that had been precious to her in life, including her childhood teddy bear, that the tears started slipping down her parents' cheeks. She had been so longed for, and such a treasured only child. My heart broke for them. Sophie wouldn't, couldn't, have treated them with such a lack of compassion. It's impossible... there has to be another explanation.

There's a light knock on the door and Jamie comes into the room. I lift my eyes to his and immediately he knows that something momentous must have been written in the letter.

'Can I read it, Liv?' he asks, stooping to pick the sheets of paper up off the floor.

I nod. I need Jamie to read it; cool, calm, sensible Jamie. He'll know what to make of it.

I watch his face as his eyes flick over the words, from time to time shaking his head in disbelief. When he is done, he sits on the end of our bed.

'Did you know?' he asks.

'Of course I didn't know,' I say. 'I'm as shocked as you obviously are – assuming any of this is actually true. You know how much I've struggled coming to terms with Sophie's death.'

'I meant, did you know that she and Tom were having problems? You were best friends. She told you everything.'

'Obviously not everything because I had no idea she was so desperately unhappy,' I reply, struggling to understand how Sophie could have kept something so huge from me. A thought occurs to me. 'You and Tom are best friends too. Did you know?'

'Of course not. I wouldn't have kept something like that from you.'

I reach my hand out to take the letter from Jamie and scan the final few lines again. 'Do you think it's true?'

Jamie's brow furrows. 'I can't think of a plausible explanation for someone else to copy Sophie's writing and then send a letter claiming to be her.'

He's right; what would be the point?

'This woman on the beach,' Jamie says, edging up the bed and taking hold of my hand, 'it couldn't have been Grace, could it?'

The image of the woman in the red sundress fills my mind. My first instinct was that it was Sophie, but I'm not sure I should say that to Jamie. She looked so happy, so carefree, so in love. Jamie idolises Tom almost as much as I did when I was a child and he was my grown-up brother. I don't want to believe that something was happening between Tom and Sophie which made her so unhappy that she'd rather be dead than return home to him, but there is a tiny bit of me that's wondering if it could be true.

There's no doubt that Sophie changed the longer they were married. She'd always been the one to instigate nights out, either with our partners or just the girls, but gradually that became less and less frequent. I was so involved in my own life with Jamie that I didn't pay it too much attention at the time, but thinking about it now, she definitely became quite distant, even on the phone, and if we did arrange anything, Tom would ring to cancel it, claiming that Sophie wasn't feeling well. What if they were having marital problems and Tom didn't want her talking to me about it? Or, worse still, what if he didn't want me seeing her because she was carrying visible signs of an argument? A shiver runs through me. As Jamie has just said, we always told each other everything, but something, or someone, stopped her from confiding in me.

Much as I love my husband, the last thing I want him to do is to speak to Tom about the letter before I've had a chance to confirm who it's from, even if it means being disingenuous. 'I suppose it could have been,' I say, choosing my words carefully so that it is not an outright lie. 'But why would Grace make up a story like this, unless she wants to punish me?'

'Punish you?' he says.

'Yes. When she sent the email after the accident, I never replied to her, not even to acknowledge I'd received it. With the benefit of hindsight, that was pretty unkind. She was obviously carrying a huge burden of guilt and I made no attempt to lighten the load. Maybe I should have made more of an effort, but I was too tied up in my own grief.' I raise my eyes to look directly into Jamie's; he doesn't look convinced. 'Perhaps the way I behaved has been eating away at Grace all this time and she's seizing the opportunity to get her own back.'

'Do you really think Grace would do that? You three were inseparable for years. And what about the handwriting? You seemed to be sure it was Sophie's when you first saw it.'

Again, choosing my words with care, I say, 'We used to fake each other's handwriting if one of us hadn't had time to do our homework.' It isn't a complete lie, but to the best of my memory, Grace was never involved in that particular scam at school, it was just me and Sophie.

'Hmmm. So, what are you going to do? Are you going to leave things alone, like she's asked you to?'

A whole range of emotions are having a battle inside my head. For years I've believed Grace to be selfish and heartless for not coming home to England for the funeral. Her explanation of feeling guilty because Sophie was visiting her when she died never really rang true with me, but she had no reason to lie. Poor Grace, she never got the love she deserved from anyone. Not from her parents, her boyfriends and, since the accident, not even from me. I feel wretched for all the wicked thoughts I've had about her, particularly if she perished in the accident. And my guilt is fuelling the anger that's building inside me towards Sophie. Even if she was having problems in her marriage how could she just cut us all out of her life and run away without a backwards glance?

Struggling to keep the fury from my voice, I say, 'You know I can't, Jamie. I have to know one way or the other who survived the crash.'

'But how do you propose to do that? There's no address on the letter, so you can't write back.'

'No, but I know roughly where she lives and there can't be that many Pilates studios in that part of Mexico. It should be quite easy to find a blonde European Pilates teacher.'

Jamie has a resigned expression on his face. He's known me long enough to know that once I've set my mind to something, it's virtually impossible to change it.

'Do you want me to come with you?' he asks.

I shake my head. 'This is something we need to sort out between us. If it is Grace, she needs to understand the extent of my grief, having still been so devastated after losing Alfie.'

Jamie squeezes my hand tighter. 'And if it's Sophie? What on earth will you do if it's Sophie?'

'I have no idea,' I admit, 'but until I find out, I'm asking you to keep this to yourself, and not say anything to Tom. Can you do that for me?'

'My lips are sealed,' he says. 'As long as you promise you'll tell me the truth when you find out who wrote the letter.'

Deep in my heart, I think I know. Maybe I knew from the moment I saw the woman on the beach but told myself that it was my mind playing games because I was feeling so emotional.

'Of course, I will,' I say, resting my head against his chest, inviting him to reach his arms around me, which he does.

'Tread carefully, Liv, you might be about to lift the top off a huge can of worms with pretty far-reaching consequences,' Jamie says, dropping a kiss on to the top of my head.

He's right, but there's something about the letter that feels like a cry for help, despite the plea to leave things as they are, otherwise why write it in the first place.

CHAPTER 15

Sophie

Spain, 2014

There were a few terrifying seconds while Sophie was in mid-air after being thrown from the train where she was certain she was going to plunge to her death, until branches started tearing at her clothes and skin and her body hit the ground with a sickening thud.

She lay stunned for a moment, the pouring rain drenching her from head to toe, listening to the sound of metal on metal as the train's brakes tried desperately to stop the stricken train. The eerie silence that followed the screeching sound was shattered by a massive explosion. Sophie began to tremble violently, her breath coming in shallow gasps as she tried but failed to cling on to consciousness.

Everything was hazy when she came to a few seconds later. She was in pain but had no idea why. Closing her eyes in an effort to focus, she tried to remember where she was and, more importantly, who she was. Her mind was blank.

Peering through the relentless rain, she became aware of an orange glow in the distance. The awful realisation began to dawn on her that the explosion she had heard before blacking out was the train she had been travelling on crashing into a ravine. As though in slow motion, the pieces of what had happened directly before the accident began to fit together.

She was sitting next to a woman she knew on a seat near the front of the train. She tried to remember the woman's name but it eluded her. The woman suggested going to the back of the train to get a better view of a stunning ravine they were approaching. She'd grabbed her bag which had her phone in it to take some photographs and walked to the back of the train. The next thing she remembered was the brakes being applied, the doors opening and her flying through the air. No one in the front half of the train stood a chance of surviving. *The person I was on the train with is dead.*

She started to sob, her body shaking uncontrollably as her miraculous escape from certain death truly sank in. The shaking was sending shockwaves of pain through her body. She had no idea if any bones were broken. Gingerly, she moved her limbs. They all seemed to be intact, so she moved her hands across her torso, gently pressing to see if anything felt tender and in doing so came across a narrow strap.

The bag, she thought, *I'm still wearing the bag, there might be something in there to identify me.* Following the strap with her fingers, she came across the body of the bag and unzipped the top. Moments later, she withdrew a passport and, edging herself up onto her elbows, opened it at the photo page. Staring back at her was someone she recognised, but immediately knew wasn't her.

An image flashed into her head of two woman greeting each other in an airport. One of them was the same woman who was staring up at her from the page which also revealed her name. *Grace,* Sophie thought, *the woman's name was Grace and she was my friend.* A wave of emotion momentarily engulfed her before she was able to feel around in the bag seeking out her own passport, but there was only the one. Her fingers did make contact with a mobile phone though and the screensaver picture was of three happy smiling young women. Two of them were blonde and very similar in appearance, but the third had dark curly hair. Sophie's fingers touched the screen as she whispered, 'Liv.'

For a few seconds, she couldn't understand why she had Grace's passport and phone in her bag and then she knew. *I must have picked up the wrong bag. Mine will be with Grace.*

The thought of her friend lying dead in the wreckage started the tears flowing uncontrollably again, and with the tears her reason for being in Spain came flooding back to her. She could feel her pulse quickening as a man's face filled her mind. Although he was handsome, he looked angry and Sophie instantly knew that she was afraid of him. Then the truth dawned. The man was her husband, and she'd come to Spain to seek Grace's advice because she was desperately unhappy in her marriage.

Grace was going to help me, Sophie thought. *And now she's dead and it's all my fault. Why couldn't I have died in the crash instead of her?*

Sophie's sobs began to subside as the thought flashed through her mind again only this time she thought, *What if I died in the crash.* Her hand was resting on Grace's bag which contained not only her passport and phone, but also her credit cards and the keys to her apartment and car.

Sophie closed her eyes for a moment. *Can I really steal Grace's life?*

Once her decision was made, Sophie knew she needed to take advantage of the huge amount of confusion over who had been travelling on the train when it had crashed. The rain would likely wash away evidence of her fall from the train and might also help in getting away from the immediate area.

Instead of climbing back up the hill to the railway track, where the rescue team would be looking for survivors, Sophie made her way down the rocky hillside and eventually found herself at the side of a main road. She checked to make sure that there was no blood visible from the minor cuts and scrapes on her arms, wincing in pain as she did so, before brushing bits of twigs and undergrowth off her clothes and out of her hair. There weren't many cars on the road, but less than ten minutes after sticking out her thumb to try and pick up a ride, a bread delivery van stopped to offer her a lift.

Sophie was in luck; the driver didn't speak much English and she only knew a few words in Spanish, so she didn't have to make conversation with him after he'd managed to explain that he was only going as far as Javea. From there, she picked up a cab to Denia which dropped her on the corner of the street where Grace had parked her car less than four hours earlier. Sophie paid for the journey in cash, and drove back to Grace's apartment.

Once safely inside, she turned on the television. Unsurprisingly, the train crash was all over the news. The footage from the scene was horrific and Sophie started to shake all over again as she imagined how terrifying the final few moments of Grace's life must have been. *She must have known she was going to die,* she thought, wrapping her arms around her body and rocking herself to and fro as tears coursed down her cheeks. *Poor Grace, but for me she would still be alive and yet here I am planning on stealing her life. I can't do it. Why couldn't it have been me who died?* she thought for the umpteenth time. Gradually her sobbing subsided as she fell into an exhausted sleep only to be woken by Grace's mobile phone ringing. Sophie reached into Grace's bag to retrieve it. She could feel her heartrate increasing as she glanced at the screen and saw Ricardo's name.

Of course he's calling, we were supposed to meet up with him an hour ago, she thought.

Sophie didn't know what to do. She couldn't answer the call because Ricardo would know it wasn't his friend's voice. But if she made no attempt to contact him, he might worry, put two and two together and report them as missing to the police.

She waited for a few minutes, then with shaking hands managed to send a text.

Sorry can't talk now – something has happened to my friend. I'll call you tomorrow x

The moment the message was sent, Sophie was galvanised into action despite wanting to do nothing more than curl up on the sofa and mourn her friend. Grace had made lots of friends since arriving in Spain. The moment they laid eyes on her, they would know she was not Grace so she needed to disappear quickly. The question was, where could she go where no one knew her or would go looking for her? The answer came to her in a flash: the one place where she and her two friends had vowed they would never revisit… Mexico.

Sophie opened up Grace's computer and was about to search for flights to Cancún before realising she would be leaving a trail that someone could follow if they wanted to. Instead, she checked for flights to the two countries that bordered Mexico to the south. No airlines operated a direct flight from Spain to Belize, her preferred option, because it would have been a shorter journey the other end, but one airline operated a direct flight from Madrid to Guatemala City. Using Grace's credit card, she booked herself onto a flight departing the next night and then went through to Grace's bedroom to start packing a suitcase of her clothes. As she handled the brightly coloured garments that Grace loved to wear, the tears started to flow again. *I feel so wicked stealing her things,* she thought, and once again found herself questioning whether she was doing the right thing before coming to the conclusion that she had no choice.

She decided it would be safe to stay in the apartment overnight which would give her time to think about what she was going to say in the other message she needed to write. People had to believe that it was Sophie who'd perished, and that Grace was so utterly devastated that she had run away from the situation. The best person to feed the lie to was Liv.

Sophie's hands were shaking as she sat down to compose the email, knowing that her words would end their friendship. In normal circumstances, she would have turned to Liv for help with her problems, but Sophie had remembered two things which had prevented that. Liv was barely functioning after a miscarriage three months previously. She blamed herself and had sunk into a terrible depression. There was no way Sophie could burden her with more problems. And secondly, she would have been talking about the brother Liv idolised. *Even if she'd believed me*, Sophie thought, *it might have pushed her over the edge and I would never have been able to live with that on my conscience.*

Details of why she was so desperately unhappy were still out of reach, but Sophie was certain it was to do with her marriage. She'd come to Spain to talk things over with Grace and now Grace was dead as a result of her willingness to help her friend. Sophie couldn't remember what she was so frightened of back home, but every time she wavered and contemplated returning, she felt a sense of fear so great that she was almost paralysed by it.

Big fat tears were dropping onto the backs of her hands poised over the computer keyboard. The words she was about to write might come more easily than she'd at first thought because Sophie was feeling enormous guilt about Grace's death.

She reached for a tissue to blow her nose and wipe her eyes. What she was about to do might free her from her past, but she was acutely aware of the agony she was about to inflict not only on her best friend, but also on other people who loved her.

She took several deep breaths in an attempt to keep herself calm before starting to write the email that meant the end of her life as she knew it. Maybe it would have been better for everyone if she'd died in the crash, but she didn't, so now she just needed them to believe it to be true.

*

Sophie read through the email several times before saving it to send the next day. The longer the delay in people finding out that she and Grace had been in the train crash, the better. Once the authorities knew they'd been on board, they would visit the apartment and Sophie didn't want to be there when they did. They would probably want to question her about the incident, as a witness, and then it would be revealed that Grace was the real victim.

Her flight from Madrid was due to take off in the early hours of the morning, so by sending the email just before boarding, Sophie had worked out that it probably wouldn't be read by Liv until the following day. Even if she and Jamie contacted the Spanish authorities as soon as they read the email, it would give her a few more precious hours to disappear in Central America. She was hoping to sell Grace's phone and computer in Guatemala, which would not only provide some local currency to get her started in her new life, but also show the GPS signal there rather than across the border in Mexico. Even as she was making her plans, she fervently wished things could be different. What she wouldn't give to be enjoying a boozy dinner with Ricardo and Grace in Alicante, but fate had intervened.

Sophie finally closed her eyes to try to get a couple of hours sleep at around 2.30 a.m. but was up again around six to make her early getaway having barely dozed. Every time she dropped off, she woke in a cold sweat, having dreamt she was falling.

She showered and dressed in Grace's clothes and put on some of her friend's jewellery. The thought that it might also need to be sold, along with her computer and phone, to give her some much-needed cash as she wouldn't be able to use Grace's credit card in Mexico, had feelings of guilt wash over her with a renewed vengeance.

Her hands were still shaking as she removed her wedding and engagement rings and zipped them safely into the coin section of her purse. As she returned the purse to her bag, the image of her wedding day and Tom placing the golden band on her finger flashed into her mind. Her heart contracted. *What could have happened to change things so dramatically between us?* she wondered.

A different image of her standing at the edge of a chalk quarry twisting her rings around on her finger replaced the one of her wedding day. Had she been about to take them off and throw them into the quarry? Or was her intention to throw herself off the edge in order to escape a life she could no longer bear?

Sophie grabbed the back of one of Grace's chairs to steady herself. However drastic the action she was about to take seemed, cutting all ties to her former life and family, it had to be better than them coming to terms with her taking her own life; families never really got over the grief that suicide caused. It was an immense decision, but one she felt forced to make.

Picking up Grace's keys, Sophie took a final look around at the life her friend had so cruelly been robbed of.

'Thank you, Grace,' she whispered under her breath. 'You'll never know how much this means to me,' she added, before pulling the door closed on Grace's apartment for the last time.

As she stood waiting for the lift to arrive, a middle-aged man came out of the neighbouring flat.

'Do you want me to give you a hand down the stairs with your bags, Grace? You'll be waiting ages for the that stupid lift.'

Turning slightly away from him and with her head down so that her voice was muffled, Sophie said, 'No worries, I'm in no rush.'

As the echo of his footsteps on the marble steps got fainter, Sophie exhaled the breath she had been holding. She had no way of knowing how well Grace knew her neighbour, but their similarity in looks had clearly fooled him. It might not be as easy under the closer scrutiny of the border officers at passport control.

*

Sixteen hours later, Sophie was sitting in the departure lounge at Madrid's Barajas airport amongst the other passengers waiting to board their flight to Guatemala City, Grace's laptop open on her knee, ready to send the email to Liv at the last possible moment. The conversation with the woman who had thought she was a nervous flyer had done nothing to steady her nerves. Having already survived a narrow shave with death, Sophie wasn't fearful that her number was up, but she was afraid that someone might realise she wasn't Grace and would stop her from boarding the plane.

The woman glanced over at her with a reassuring smile from her place at the back of the queue that was forming to board the Airbus to Central America. Sophie returned the smile with a slight nod of the head before focusing her attention on her laptop. Her hand was shaking as she pressed send.

This is it, she thought. *There's no going back.*

CHAPTER 16
Sophie
Mexico, 2018

Luis had been so understanding while I was pouring out my heart about the deadly train crash, but his demeanour changed when I revealed that I had taken Grace's identity to escape a life in which I was desperately unhappy. I'm not sure what he was more upset about. Was it the idea that I'd been lying to him for the past three and a half years and wasn't actually Grace, or was he hurt that I hadn't felt I could confide in him and share what had driven me to such drastic action? The truth is, even I don't know the full details of why I ran. All I know for sure is that I was so afraid of what was happening to me within my marriage that I would rather have died in the crash than go back to it.

He took me inside and put me to bed and then slept on the sofa, despite my pleas that I needed to feel his comforting arms around me. When I awoke the next morning, both he and Vince were gone. I honestly thought he had left me. I spent the morning in floods of tears, half of me wishing I hadn't told him the truth and the other half wishing that I'd been honest with him from the start.

I am still crying when he pushes open the front door just before midday. His hair is wet and both he and Vince leave a sandy trail as they cross the living room towards me. Vince reaches me first, his big pink tongue licking the salty tears from my face, and then Luis wraps his arms around me.

'You've been to the beach,' I say, stating what would have been blindingly obvious to a three-year-old.

'I needed some space to think, but it wasn't the same without you, was it, boy,' he says, addressing Vince. 'So we came home to get you.'

The relief that floods through me is indescribable, but it turns out to be short-lived.

We get back from a blissful afternoon at the beach, where neither of us mentioned the previous night, and Luis pours us both a glass of wine before coming to sit down next to me on our sofa in the garden.

'If we're going to be together,' he says, handing me my glass of wine, 'I want to know everything. I need to understand how you could walk away from your life, leaving your friends and family. I could never do that to my mother and father, and I'm struggling to understand what kind of person can.'

His words send shivers through me, despite the sweltering temperature. *If we're going to be together...* He made it sound like a very big if.

I start talking, faltering at first and probably not making much sense, but gradually I begin to tell him about my life as Sophie; how I was a much longed-for and much-loved only child who had never wanted for anything. I tell him about meeting Grace and Liv on the first day of senior school and how our friendship grew over the years until we became inseparable. I feel his body tense up when I talk about marrying the man I loved, but there's no point in me pretending that I didn't love Tom, because at the beginning, I did; I was completely besotted with him. I describe the early days of our marriage and our close friendship with Liv and Jamie, but when I get to the bit where we moved to a big house, my memories are less clear.

It's hard explaining to Luis that I was frightened of my husband when I can't really remember the reason why. I describe some of the flashbacks I've had: Tom's angry face, him squeezing my wrists until they were bruised, and the occasion where I remember being in the bath and Tom gripping me by my hair while I choked on the water. I stop at that point and Luis reaches for my hand to squeeze it reassuringly, but he doesn't speak. After a few moments, he releases it, as though signalling me to continue. I explain that I think maybe my husband wanted to kill me, but I seem to have blocked the worst things from my memory. What I do know is that my purpose for going to Spain was to escape from him for a few days and to talk to Grace.

When I stop talking, he says, 'Why did you turn to her rather than Liv or your parents? You say you were very close to them and that they loved you, so why didn't you tell them what was happening and ask them for help?' He's been avoiding looking at me while I've poured out my story, but he's turned to look at me now, his trusting deep brown eyes searching my face. 'I don't understand why you didn't just leave him, Grace?'

And therein lies my dilemma. I've asked myself the same question repeatedly since the flashbacks began. Why didn't I just pack my bags and walk away from him? What hold could he possibly have had over me that forced me to stay?

'I don't know, Luis, really, I don't. Maybe I was too scared of what he might do if I did. Perhaps he'd threatened me at some point, saying he'd track me down and do something awful to me.' I can feel my heart pounding in my chest and tears pricking the back of my eyes. I'm so frightened that my revelations might result in me losing Luis, and if that happens, I honestly don't know what I'll do. Meeting him had given me a new purpose in life. Without Luis, there would be no reason for me to carry on living.

'Try to remember,' he says gently. 'It's important.'

'I have tried,' I say, 'but there's some kind of fog surrounding that whole period of my life – the memories are sort of there, but it's as though I'm too frightened to retrieve them. I know I came back here because of what happened to me on my gap year. I felt safe in the belief that if anyone learned the truth that it was Grace who died and not me, this is the last place they would come looking.'

Luis is quiet for a few moments. He seems to be weighing things up, maybe wondering if he will ever truly be able to trust me again.

'I think you should have told your parents. I find it impossible to believe that my kind, caring Grace would sooner let them think their daughter was dead than reach out to them for help. It seems uncharacteristically cruel.'

It was the thing I had agonised over the most as I lay in shock on the hillside in Spain in the teeming rain. Liv had Jamie and would eventually get over my death, but my parents worshipped the ground I walked on and there would always be a huge hole in their lives that nothing could fill. Luis is judging my actions as cruel, but I think they must have been born of desperation. I've thought about them many times in the past three and a half years, wondering if they've managed to rebuild their lives. On the first birthday I spent in Tulum, I almost picked up the phone to tell them it was all a big mistake and that I was coming home like the prodigal son in the bible, but I still don't know exactly what made me run and I'm too afraid to find out. As time has gone on, it's felt better for my sanity to have them locked away in my past rather than fret about how they are coping.

I look up at him, wondering how on earth we will ever be able to get past this. He's looking at me as though I'm a stranger, which in a way, I am. Luis loves Grace; he doesn't know Sophie. It feels like I'm losing him. I can't let that happen.

'Sometimes, we have to be cruel to be kind,' I say in a barely audible voice. 'The last thing in the world I would ever have imagined myself doing is hurting my parents. My heart aches when I think of the distress I've caused them, but having them believe I died seemed preferable to me than the guilt and blame they would feel if I'd taken my own life.' I'm only just holding it together enough to speak.

'Did you seriously consider doing that?' Luis asks, unable to keep the incredulity from his voice.

Luis loves life; his life in particular. He appreciates every day as a gift and enjoys the simple things that make him happy. He probably finds it impossible to understand how someone could be desperate enough to contemplate suicide.

'I... I don't know for sure, but in one of my other flashbacks I'm sitting on my bed with a knife in my hand...'

Something seems to click with Luis. He sets our wine glasses down on the ground and envelopes me in his arms, cradling me like a child who has woken from a nightmare.

'I want to kill this man who made you so unhappy that he almost took you away from me before we had the chance to meet. And yet, maybe I should thank him. If he hadn't treated you as he did, you may never have walked into my life and that would have been the biggest tragedy of all. I love you, Grace, or Sophie, whichever you want to be called.'

The tears I've been holding back are starting to fall as I cling to the man who has made me whole again. He kisses my eyelids while stroking my hair back off my face and uttering soothing words in Spanish. We stay like that for several minutes as though nothing and nobody will ever come between us. He completes me and, judging by his words, he feels the same way about me.

Once I feel able to speak, I say, 'My name doesn't much matter. I've always been Grace to you and that's what my papers say, so I can carry on being Grace to make things easier. The life I've built with you is the only thing that is important to me and now we can live it with no secrets between us. I can truly leave the past behind and focus on our future, yours and mine, together. I love you, Luis.'

CHAPTER 17

Liv

Oxted

Jamie pulls the car into the driveway of Tom's house and turns off the engine. We're half an hour late, which I can't deny is down to me. Since reading Sophie's letter on Wednesday evening, I've been telling Jamie that there was no way I could sit down making small talk over dinner with Polly and Tom. The trouble is, having done such a good job of persuading Jamie that the letter has actually been written by Grace, he couldn't see any reason not to come. 'You need to give Tom the benefit of doubt,' Jamie kept saying. 'After all, he is your brother and my best mate and neither of us have ever known him to be anything but a great guy.' Jamie has a point; innocent until proven guilty. But I really can't fathom why Sophie would feel so desperate about her situation that she was prepared to fake her own death and leave everything she had ever known behind her unless there was some truth to her claims.

'Are you okay? Jamie asks.

'Sort of. I'm just going to try to blank out the letter and get through tonight,' I reply.

'It's for the best, trust me.' He smiles reassuringly. He reaches for the bag behind my seat containing the two bottles of wine we've brought with us. 'My gut feeling is that your brother's worst trait is being mean with the vino.'

I hope he's right.

As I'm getting out of the car, their front door opens to reveal Polly wearing a vibrant emerald-green silk shirt French-tucked into her jeans, which are most likely designer. She is effortlessly chic. Her blonde hair is caught back off her face but allowed to tumble freely over her shoulders, exactly as Sophie had worn hers on her wedding day.

A lump forms in my throat. Apart from my own wedding, that was one of the happiest days of my life; the three of us getting ready in Sophie's bedroom, the radiant smile on Sophie's face as she posed for the photographs on the church steps, and her mischievous wink before she turned her back and threw her wedding bouquet over her shoulder, aimed in my direction. If the letter does turn out to be from Sophie, what on earth happened behind closed doors in the following few years that turned her from my happy carefree school friend into someone desperate enough to abandon her family and friends and start over thousands of miles from home?

Polly is smiling warmly as we crunch across the gravel towards her. My brother certainly has a type; we have to get quite close before it becomes absolutely clear that it isn't Sophie standing on the doorstep waiting to welcome us into her home.

'I'm so sorry we're late,' I say, offering her the flowers we bought at the petrol station on the way over.

'You shouldn't have,' Polly says, burying her nose in the bouquet. 'And you remembered that freesias are my favourites!' She holds them to one side so that she can give me a quick hug and a peck on the cheek.

I now feel doubly bad. I chose the biggest, most expensive bunch of flowers to match the level of guilt I was feeling about not wanting to come. I didn't know there were freesias in it, and even if I'd known, I had no idea that they were Polly's favourite flower. I actually know very little about my new sister-in-law, although she's not really that new, since she and Tom have been married for almost three years.

'I'm glad you like them,' I manage to say, casting a warning glance at Jamie so that he doesn't correct Polly's assumption.

'I'm afraid you've missed Mia,' she says, standing to one side to allow Jamie and I to pass into their entrance hall. 'Tom's a stickler for bedtime, but she might still be awake if you want to pop up to her room.'

'Will that be okay?' I ask Tom, who has just appeared from the kitchen. Judging by the aroma, he is doing roast chicken and all the trimmings. He looks relaxed and happy, as he gives me a hug, always our greeting for each other before the accident in Spain. I hope he didn't notice how tense I am. Being hugged by a big brother who had made my best friend the happiest woman on the planet feels quite different now in light of Sophie's accusations about him in her letter.

'Sure,' he says, smiling. 'But don't wake her if she's already asleep.'

He takes my coat and the bag from Jamie with the wine in it.

I can hear the two of them laughing about vintages and grapes as I head up the carpeted stairs. Nothing much has changed since Tom and Sophie had the whole place decorated before moving in about a year after their wedding. It's a beautiful detached five-bedroom home on a private road in Warlingham with amazing views over Halliloo Valley, where Tom and our dad used to play golf together. All the years studying to be a vet have certainly paid off, although I have to say our house is nowhere near as grand as Tom's.

I cross to Mia's bedroom, smiling at the ceramic unicorn on the door which is ajar. I'm able to ease it slightly further open without making any noise. Even with the spill of light from the landing, it's quite dark within her room and I'm barely able to make out more than a lump under the covers and a tousled mass of dark curly hair against the pale-coloured pillow, just like mine and Tom's.

My heart contracts. Again, I can't help wondering if my little boy would have shared that same family characteristic if he had lived.

I have an overwhelming desire to go over to my niece, scoop her up in my arms and give her the biggest cuddle, but I resist. With the trouble she has sleeping, I'm pretty sure neither Polly nor Tom would thank me if I woke her. Instead, I make her a silent promise to be more present in her life from now on before pulling the door to and heading back downstairs to where I can already hear glasses chinking. I've volunteered to be the designated driver, so it will be just one glass of wine with my meal for me.

'Jamie was just telling us about the other night,' Tom says laughing, as I join them in the kitchen.

For a millisecond I panic that Jamie has betrayed my trust and told them about the letter, but Tom certainly wouldn't be laughing about that.

'The batter joke you cracked without realising,' Jamie says to enlighten me.

'Oh, right,' I reply. 'I'm glad you all find my lack of cooking ability so amusing. I think you got all the talent in that area, Tom.'

'Can I pour you a wine, Liv?' Polly asks.

'I'll wait and have one with my meal. Foolishly, I've offered to drive.'

'Well, it'll give your liver a chance to recover from all those cocktails on your holiday. Without Jamie there to keep tabs on your drinking, I bet you had a fair few boozy nights.'

I glance over at Jamie, but he avoids my gaze.

'You might as well pour it now, Polly, I'm about to dish up,' Tom adds.

'Red or white, Liv?'

Before I can answer, Tom says, 'Don't be stupid. We're having chicken, so of course it's white wine.'

There's a sharpness to his voice which seems completely unnecessary.

I'm tempted to reply that I'd rather have red, but I want the evening to go well, so I just say, 'White wine is fine; thanks, Polly.'

She smiles and pours the Sauvignon Blanc. Either she didn't notice the way Tom spoke to her or she's chosen to ignore it in front of guests.

The evening as a whole was actually quite pleasant, much better than I'd thought it would be. As always, Tom's roast chicken dinner, with roast potatoes, roast Chantenay carrots, steamed broccoli and Brussel sprouts lightly boiled and then tossed in butter, was delicious. It was something we'd enjoyed for Sunday lunch many times at his and Sophie's first house, along with Mum and Dad. After pudding, which was usually apple crumble and custard because Sophie, like me, was not the best cook in the world but found that easy to make, the 'boys' would go into the lounge and watch football, while we 'girls' would load the dishwasher and then take our coffees through to the sunny conservatory, where we could have a good old natter without the punctuation of a referee's whistle.

There was only one other slightly awkward moment, but it did cast a bit of a shadow over the evening.

When Polly walked into the room carrying a flaming Baked Alaska for dessert, I'd said without thinking, 'I half expected apple crumble and custard.'

Polly coloured up and Tom glared at me.

'I was only joking,' I said. 'That looks amazing, Polly.'

'It was nowhere near as funny as your "flat as a pancake" effort. Maybe you should leave the jokes to your husband in future.'

There was an edge to Tom's voice that Jamie must have noticed, because even in his slightly inebriated state, he raises it on the drive home.

'Tom wasn't too pleased with you for mentioning apple crumble. That was always Sophie's thing.'

'I know; it just kind of slipped out. I wasn't being deliberately insensitive; I thought he overreacted a bit.'

'He was just protecting his wife, Liv. I always stick up for you if I think someone has said something hurtful.'

'True,' I agree, 'but Polly didn't seem bothered, probably because she knew the Baked Alaska was going to be utterly divine. I couldn't believe it when she said she'd made the passion fruit ice cream in the middle too. I don't even know what a passion fruit looks like, do you?'

'No,' Jamie says, managing to slur a two-letter word.

Something tells me there won't be a whole lot of passion in our bedroom tonight. Jamie will probably fall asleep fully clothed while I'm in the bathroom taking my make-up off. It's a shame really because I'm right in the middle of my menstrual cycle and seeing the outline of my sleeping niece earlier in the evening has made me realise yet again how much I yearn for a child of my own.

CHAPTER 18

Sophie

Mexico

'See you later, boy,' I say, pulling the door to our apartment closed.

Vince is lying on his dog bed, his head resting on his paws and his huge brown eyes looking at me until the last possible moment. He hates it when Luis and I are both out working, but at least he seems resigned to it now. When we first had him as a six-month-old puppy, it was upsetting to leave him. As soon as I picked up my sports bag, he would circle my legs, leaning in against them so tightly that he almost tripped me up and whining pitifully. When I shut the door on him, he would start barking and for a while I worried that we would get complaints from the neighbours about the noise. At the time, I was only teaching one evening class a night, so I was never out for long. The moment I got home I would give him treats to reward him and eventually he became more accepting of me leaving because he knew to expect treats when I returned. He doesn't bark anymore when I leave, which is just as well as I'm now out for longer periods of time.

My Pilates classes have become increasingly popular, with the numbers swelling from four or five per class when I first started, to twelve more often than not, which is all we have room for. We've added extra evening classes to our timetable, which I take most of the time because Josefina has a young family to look after, except for Wednesday as it's Luis's night off. It feels good to have helped Josefina build her business over the past three years. Lately, she's been talking about the possibility of expanding even more, either by extending the existing building to add another studio or starting up a second studio elsewhere in Tulum. It's the reason I'm going in a bit earlier tonight, to discuss which might be the better option. Now that Luis knows my secret, but is still committed to being with me, I feel more comfortable planning for our future. More work means more money and will help Luis and I save up to buy a place of our own, rather than renting as we currently do.

Almost a month has passed since my confession that I hadn't been truthful with him about who I am, and our lives have returned more or less to normal. In fact, certain areas of our lives are better than ever. I allow myself a few minutes of reliving the passionate lovemaking from this morning and am still smiling when I push open the door to be met by the rush of cooled air.

Josefina is already settled on the wicker sofa in the reception area sipping a bottle of cola through a straw. I've tried to tell her that she would be better off with water, but it's the one suggestion of mine she always shrugs off.

'Right,' I say, 'we've got an hour before the girls start arriving for class. Where do you want to start?'

'*Hasta el lunes, si Dios quiere,*' I say to the women rolling up their Pilates mats at the end of my Friday night class. I still can't write a huge amount of Mexican, but my conversation is pretty good, mostly because I've had a patient teacher in Luis. He's helped me to say things in the most natural way rather than just translations from books or the internet. What I've just said to my Pilates students is, 'See you on Monday, God willing.' It's the *God willing* bit that makes the difference. It's helped me integrate with my students; they feel like I'm one of their own rather than an outsider.

Once all the girls have left, I roll up my mat and put it in one of the giant pigeonholes in the corner of the room, built by Josefina's husband to keep things tidy. He's got some great ideas for the extension Josefina showed me the plans for earlier. I'm glad she's decided to extend rather than open a new place in a different part of Tulum. I think it will be less pressure financially for her, and from my point of view it means I will still have a ten-minute walk to work rather than a trek across town.

I'm about to turn off the lights in the studio when I become aware of a figure on the other side of the frosted glass that divides the studio from the reception area.

'Did you leave something?' I call out, casting my eyes around the studio for a brightly coloured towel or a water bottle. 'I can't see anything in here.' I flick off the lights and take hold of the metal handle to pull the door open.

'That's the excuse I've had to make to come back to Mexico without arousing suspicion.'

The words stop me in my tracks. I would know her voice anywhere.

Slowly, I open the door to the reception area and come face to face with Liv for the first time in three and a half years. She hasn't changed much; maybe a little curvier than when I last saw her properly, and her hair is a longer, but otherwise she's the same old Liv, my best friend in the world for more than half my life.

'How did you find me?' I whisper.

'It wasn't difficult. You mentioned teaching Pilates in your letter, and since this is the only Pilates studio in Tulum, it was the obvious place to start my search.'

I nod, kicking myself for handing her the piece of information that has led her straight to my door.

'Just to be sure, I asked one of the women for the name of their teacher as they were on their way out. They all seem very fond of you…' She pauses before adding, 'Grace.'

I can feel the heat of colour rising in my cheeks. Although I told her in the letter that I'd assumed Grace's identity, it's still strange to hear Liv refer to me as Grace.

'Why are you here, Liv?' I ask, my voice low and breathless. 'I thought my letter explained that I've made a new life here because my old one was pretty awful, and that I wanted to be allowed to live it in peace.' My eyes are searching hers. 'I hoped you'd understand.'

'It's not as simple as that, Sophie,' she replies as though talking to a child who has been told they can't have a bar of chocolate thirty minutes before their lunch. 'I wasn't absolutely certain until you opened that door a few moments ago whether I was going to be confronted with Grace or Sophie.'

'But I told you in my letter that it was Grace who died in the accident. Why on earth would I lie about it?'

Liv laughs. It's mirthless. 'You've been lying to everyone about it for three and a half years, Sophie, surely you didn't expect me to take your letter at face value?'

She has a point. Although I explained about switching identities, I didn't go into much detail about my reasons for needing to escape my old life, just that I couldn't continue to live it. I still don't remember a lot, so it would have been pointless to drive a wedge between Liv and Tom and wouldn't have altered my decision never to return to England. It would merely have been one more thing to add to my already overburdened guilty conscience.

'I really wasn't sure who I was going to meet when I came here tonight. You see, I was having trouble accepting that the Sophie I knew could be so selfish as to run away from her friends and family with no consideration for their feelings, just because things had hit a rocky patch in her marriage,' she says, her voice increasing in volume and exuding a mix of anger and pain. 'We all have them, you know; it wasn't exclusive to you and Tom. In fact, that was why I was here in Mexico on holiday on my own. Jamie and I were on a trial separation and, ironically, it was mostly because of my fierce loyalty towards you.'

I want her to stop talking, but Liv is on a roll now. I've seen her like this before. She's like a racehorse with the bit between its teeth. Her eyes are blazing as she continues.

'What an idiot I was to risk my marriage for someone who couldn't give a toss about her own, let alone all the people who would be left devastated by her loss. Maybe you've always been selfish, Sophie, but I was so close to you I couldn't see it. I was blinded by your sparkling halo. Well, it's certainly slipped; you're no angel in my eyes anymore.'

Her use of the word angel reminds me of Luis. Although shocked, he managed to stay calm after I told him about stealing Grace's identity, in stark contrast to the anger Liv is oozing from every pore. I'll have to tell her everything I can remember, even though I'd hoped to keep it from her, and pray that she'll find it in her heart to forgive me. I need my friend to understand that I was faced with an impossible choice.

'Liv, I know it was a terrible thing to do to you and that you're angry with me…' I start to say, but she shuts me down.

'*Angry*? That's not even the half of it. Disappointed, disgusted, appalled; take your pick, Sophie, I'm all of those things. But what you did to me pales into insignificance when I think of the other people you hurt. I was standing by your graveside as your coffin was lowered into the ground. I witnessed your parents disintegrate before my eyes. You were their world, Sophie. How could you do that to them?'

I start to shake. Although I've always been aware of the heartache my death must have caused my parents, Liv's words have forced an image into my mind that I'd succeeded in supressing. Maybe I did make the wrong decision. Maybe I should have gone to them and asked for their help before things got as bad as they obviously did.

'I'm so sorry—' I start to say, but Liv cuts me off.

'I haven't finished yet,' she snaps. 'For the last three and a half years, I've been unable to forgive Grace for running away after the accident. I couldn't understand why she had made such a heartless choice when she could have brought a small amount of comfort to those of us grieving. But it wasn't Grace's choice, was it? She perished and because of your selfish decision no one has ever celebrated her life or mourned her passing. I doubt you've ever given that a thought.'

Liv is wrong. I had endless sleepless nights wracked with guilt. And when I did manage to sleep, I would wake up in a pool of sweat following nightmares in which Grace's face was gradually obscured by her long blonde hair swirling around her head as though in water. In front of my eyes it turned into seaweed, slimy and green and then parted to reveal a skull. I shudder at the memory.

'And then, there was my brother,' Liv adds, her icy voice breaking into my thoughts. 'You said in your letter that he made your life hell. Well, I can tell you now that he was beside himself with grief when he heard about the accident, after the initial shock had worn off. I'd never seen Tom cry before, even when his beloved cat was knocked down and killed just before he went off to university. He sobbed, Sophie.' She pauses, possibly to make sure that her next words will have the maximum impact on me. 'They were huge wracking sobs as though his heart had shattered into a million pieces. He just kept muttering over and over, "It's all my fault. I shouldn't have agreed to let her visit Grace. If I hadn't, this would never have happened." He was inconsolable; he loved you so much.'

I have to stop her talking. Tom was clearly upset at losing me, but I'm guessing that his reasons were very different from what Liv believes. I've felt trapped against the glass door while she's unleashed her anger on me, but I now move past her to sit on the sofa. I can understand why Liv is furious with me, but she doesn't know my side of the story. She and Tom were always so close; of course she feels protective towards him. I begged her not to come looking for me, but maybe a part of me hoped she would. After hearing her voice, I couldn't get her out of my mind and now here she is, my best friend in the whole world.

'There's stuff you need to know, Liv, and you're not going to like what you hear. You may want to sit down.'

I wait for a moment, but she ignores my suggestion. I have no idea if Liv will believe any of what I'm about to tell her, but I can't let her return to England believing me to be a spoilt and selfish wrecker of lives.

'You say Tom loved me, and you're right, he did, at first, but things seemed to change not long after we moved into Hailsham Crescent. I can't remember much detail, but I know he pressured me to give up work, saying that we didn't need the money, which, to be honest, we didn't.' Liv is staring at me, probably wondering why I'm making such a big deal about him wanting me to give up work.

I plough on. 'It wasn't just my wages I missed; it was people and feeling needed. One thing I do recall is feeling isolated and lonely. It was bad enough losing contact with people from work, but then he stopped me from seeing my friends, you included, Liv.'

She doesn't say anything, but a puzzled expression is forming on her face and she lowers herself down onto the other end of the sofa.

'Imagine what that felt like. Friends that I shared everything with since I was eleven years old. I wasn't able to see anyone and it began to feel very claustrophobic. We even started having supermarket deliveries. I'd always quite enjoyed pushing the trolley around the aisles, randomly choosing things for dinner. Gradually, he must have removed every tiny speck of pleasure from my life. In a weird way, I'm thankful that the trauma of the train crash wiped virtually that whole period from my mind. Just occasionally I remember odd details and Tom's face is always there, inches from mine, his eyes as black as coal. He seems furious with me, but I have no idea why,' I say, feeling the same sense of fear that this particular memory always evokes.

'Sophie,' Liv says, her voice gentle and calm, 'is there a possibility that your memory is playing tricks on you?'

I'm not sure what she is getting at. 'Such as?'

'Well, on the few occasions we did arrange to meet up, Tom almost always rang to cancel, saying that you were feeling unwell.'

'Unwell? In what way was I supposedly unwell?' I ask, feeling indignant that my husband had been telling lies about me behind my back.

'Oh, you know, headaches, tummy bugs, that sort of thing. And sometimes he just admitted that...'

'That what?'

Liv takes a breath, and says, 'That you were struggling to cope.'

'Cope with what?' I ask. 'Unless he was talking about the new house? Everything was fine until we moved, but then... it all started to go wrong. That house became my prison.'

'It happens. It was all so new for both of you. I wish Jamie and I had realised things were so bad. We would have made more of an effort to try to help. It hadn't really crossed my mind that you could still be suffering the baby blues after all that time.'

My skin starts to tingle. I have a sensation of pins and needles in my fingers which is travelling up my arms at pace. My heart rate is increasing, and I can feel the thumping against my chest.

'I... I had a baby?' I manage to say, my free hand moving involuntarily to my smooth flat stomach.

Liv's face registers shock as she nods.

'What happened to it? Did it die?' I whisper.

She doesn't speak.

'Please tell me, Liv. I need to know.' I'm beginning to wonder if the loss of my baby is the reason that I can't remember huge parts of Tom and my life together, after we moved into Hailsham

Crescent. 'I've watched television documentaries about it. Losing a child is so traumatic that people block its existence from their memory. Is that what happened to me, do you think?'

Liv's facial expression has changed from shock to pity. 'Oh my God!' she exclaims, 'You really don't know, do you?'

'Know what?' I say, raising my voice in exasperation. 'For God's sake, Liv, just tell me what happened.'

'That's what I couldn't understand when I got your letter,' she says, almost talking to herself. 'Even if you'd been able to walk away from the rest of us because you were unhappy, you would never have abandoned your little girl.'

I can feel blood rushing to my head as the impact of the words *your little girl* hits home. I'm a mother; I have a child and I abandoned her. The room is starting to sway and I'm struggling to breathe. I hear Liv's voice asking me if I'm all right, but it's as though it's coming from the end of a long tunnel.

A series of images force themselves into my mind in quick succession; bright lights and a woman in a nurse's uniform saying, 'Stop screaming and save your energy for pushing'; Tom standing at the end of my hospital bed cradling our new-born close to his chest, ignoring my arms reaching out to hold her; tears streaming down my cheeks as she suckles at my breast.

The images stop coming as I slip into darkness.

CHAPTER 19

Sophie

Oxted, 2014

After a very hot August, the weather had finally broken the first week of September. The previous couple of weeks had been humid, with clouds bubbling up most days and the threat of rain. Sophie couldn't help thinking that a downpour would have been a blessed relief and would have cleared the air but day after day nothing happened, making each day as oppressive as the previous one. The heavens had finally opened a couple of hours ago and the deluge had begun.

Watching through the window as the rain bounced up off the patio Sophie could draw a definite parallel with her own life. Every day, her anxiety built as six o'clock approached, the time Tom was due home from work. The slightest thing could cause their storm clouds to explode in a torrent not of rainfall, but angry words.

In an attempt to avoid Mia having to witness the scenes between them, Sophie had started bathing her early so that she would be in bed by the time Tom arrived home. Although Mia was not quite two, Sophie was pretty sure that certain things left a lasting impression, and she didn't want their daughter to suffer because of their inability to get along.

Mia's childish voice interrupted her thoughts.

'Mummy, come see what me and Mr Albert did.'

Turning away from the rain, Sophie walked over to the kitchen table where Mia had been colouring in her big book and looked down at the page. It was covered in squiggly lines.

'This is Daddy, and this is you Mummy, and this is me in the middle,' Mia said, pointing to a little pink blob with a black line above it, which was probably meant to represent her hair.

'That's very good, sweetie,' Sophie said, ruffling her daughter's dark curls. *How apt the drawing is*, she thought. *Mia is the glue that holds us all together and yet at the same time forces us apart. She is the cause of the nightmarish problems in our marriage and yet it's not her fault. Each morning I wake up hoping that the day will be different; that I won't feel so overwhelmed by the situation I find myself in. If things could just go back to the way they were before Mia was born and it was just Tom and me...* She immediately hated herself for having the thought. She loved Mia unconditionally, but things were not as she'd imagined they would be.

Mia had picked up the crayon again and was adding a small orange splodge next to the pink one that represented her at the centre of her masterpiece.

'Silly me,' she says. 'I forgetted Mr Albert.'

'Even better,' Sophie said, dropping a kiss onto her daughter's head. 'But it's time to put your book and crayons away now and get you in the bath before Daddy gets home.'

Mia did exactly what her mother asked her to, carefully placing all the waxy crayons back in their cardboard holder and then carrying them and her colouring book over to the cupboard where she kept all her toys. Sophie couldn't help marvelling at what a well-behaved child they had.

We are so lucky to have her, she thought, *especially after what happened to Alfie.* Tears welled up in Sophie's eyes. She hadn't seen Liv since her miscarriage and the feelings of guilt that she wasn't there for her best friend when she needed her most were almost overwhelming. But she was only just holding her own life together. The slightest thing could have snapped the fragile ropes that stopped her from falling.

Sophie was tucking Mia into bed for her nightly story when she heard the sound of car tyres on gravel. Immediately, her heart started thumping against her ribs.

'Is that Daddy?' Mia asked, a mix of hope and excitement in her voice. 'Can he read me my story?'

Instead of making the usual excuse that her daddy would be tired because he'd been out at work all day, Sophie hesitated. Tom would have to read to Mia for the three nights she would be away in Spain, unless he'd changed his mind about her trip to see Grace and refused to let her go.

'I'll go and ask him,' Sophie said, kissing her daughter's petal-soft cheek as the front door closed with a slam.

'I love you, Mummy,' Mia said, blowing a kiss with her teddy bear's paw, 'and so does Mr Albert.'

'I love you too, sweetheart,' Sophie replied, wondering how on earth she would be able to cope without seeing her little girl for three whole days.

She could see her husband sitting on the hall seat taking off his shoes as she padded down the stairs.

'Mia wants you to read to her.'

'You don't have a problem with that, do you?' Tom asked.

Sophie wanted to say yes. She wanted to tell him that it was her favourite bit of the day and he was stealing it away from her, but she knew he would see it as her being unreasonable.

Instead, she said, 'Of course not. I'll go and start dinner. Do you want a wine with yours?'

'No thanks, and you shouldn't either.'

Sophie clenched her fists. *Here we go again.*

CHAPTER 20

Sophie

Mexico, 2018

'What's her name?' is the first thing I say when I regain consciousness.

'Mia,' Liv replies.

'Mia,' I repeat, lingering over the two-syllable word. 'It's the Spanish word for mine.'

'Yes. You probably can't remember,' she says cautiously, 'but the plan was to keep with our family tradition and name her after her grandmother, our mum. Tom let you choose the name after you had such a tough time during labour.'

I furrow my brow, trying to remember, but nothing comes. 'I didn't know you were named after your grandma,' I say instead.

'Actually, I got lucky. My gran's real name was Marjorie, but everyone called her by her middle name, Olivia. Mum managed to persuade Dad that it would be an easier name for me to have throughout my schooldays, than Marjorie,' she says, wrinkling up her nose in distaste.

Despite the numbness I'm feeling on discovering that I have a daughter, who I currently don't remember at all, I feel a smile form on my lips. 'You're definitely not a Marjorie. Wasn't your mum called Penny?' I say, suddenly able to fish her name out of the recesses of my mind.

'Is. Penny's still very much alive, although we did lose our dad a few months ago.'

'Oh my God, that's awful,' I reply. 'What happened?'

'It started as colon cancer, but by the time he died it had spread to his bones. There's no way back from there.'

'I'm so sorry,' I say, experiencing a genuine pang of guilt that I wasn't around to help Liv through what must have been an incredibly difficult time. 'Your mum and dad were always really kind and welcoming. Your house was like a second home both to me and especially Grace.'

'Poor Grace,' Liv sighs. 'She never had the smooth ride that you and I had as teenagers, and even in her twenties she hadn't found anyone she wanted to share her life with.'

'But she was finally happy in Spain,' I say. 'Probably happier than she'd ever been in her life. And I had to go and ruin it all.'

'Don't say that, Sophie. Maybe it was her destiny to die young. None of us knows what life has in store for us. My dad is another example of that. Fit, healthy, never smoked and not overweight and yet his body let him down. It doesn't seem fair, but it's the way it is,' she says, her voice filled with sorrow.

'Your dad's death must have been dreadful for all of you,' I say. Despite my feelings about Tom, I can appreciate how heartbroken he must have been. They were very close, and his dad could only have been in his early seventies, which is no age these days.

'It was,' Liv replies, making no attempt to hide her obvious sadness. 'He was diagnosed a few weeks after you... after the accident in Spain, which we were all still reeling from, and I was still in a pretty bad way after losing Alfie.'

The moment she says the name, I have another flash of memory. Liv was over the moon when she'd discovered she was pregnant and had come around to our house after I said I wasn't free to meet up for a coffee. I remember she was wearing jeans and a pink vest top and was still sporting a gorgeous tan after their holiday in Barbados. I opened the front door, and the first thing she said was, 'Aren't you pleased for me, Sophie?' I can hear myself saying, 'Of course, I am. Why wouldn't I be?' She replied, 'Well, you didn't seem it when I rang to suggest meeting up. I was a bit hurt by your reaction, so I thought I'd pop around to give you a second chance to congratulate me.' I can picture myself standing there staring at her. 'Are you going to invite me in?' she persisted. I have a recollection of hesitating, looking over my shoulder as though someone was watching me. She came into the house, and we chatted happily for a couple of hours, losing track of time. The feeling of panic when I heard the tyres of Tom's car crunching on the gravel driveway was palpable. Tom was effusive with his congratulations, saying we should all go out for a meal to celebrate, but the moment Liv left the house, the smile left his face. I can't remember exactly what was said, but there were raised voices and I do remember running up the stairs to our room in floods of tears with Tom watching me from the bottom of them.

I'm trembling at the memory. Liv must assume it's a reaction to her mentioning baby Alfie because she says, 'It's okay, I think I've finally come to terms with losing him. It's taken me a long time to get to this point, probably much longer than it should have done with everything else that's been going on in my life, but seeing Mia when we were at Tom's for dinner made me realise the time is right to try for another baby.'

My palms are suddenly sweaty.

'Mia's living with Tom?' I whisper.

'Of course she is. He's her father.'

I need to tread carefully. Liv doesn't know the whole story yet.

'How was she? Did she seem all right?'

'Actually, she was sleeping,' Liv replies. 'We were late getting to Tom's, so she'd already gone to bed. All I could see of her was her dark curls spilling across her pillow, exactly like mine and Tom's when we were her age.'

'How old is she?' I ask, struggling to picture my daughter and I together, but coming up empty-handed.

I notice the wistful look in Liv's eyes when she says, 'She turned five last birthday. It's always tinged with sadness, of course.'

'Why?'

'Mia's birthday is the day after you were due home from Spain; the day after you... after we all thought you died...' Her voice tails off. 'Now that you know about Mia, I'm just wondering what you're going to do. You've built your new life here and say you don't want to return home, but I'm assuming Mia changes everything?'

It's as though Liv has looked inside my mind, which would best be described as being in turmoil. Even I'm struggling to understand how I thought it was okay to leave Mia in England with a man I was obviously scared of, rather than taking her with me to visit Grace in Spain... Unless he'd refused to let me take her. Maybe that was it; she was his insurance policy, his guarantee that I would return home. He must have known that I would never abandon my daughter, which explains why he believed it was me who died in the accident even though a body was never found.

It's as though a light bulb has gone on in my head. That was the hold he had over me, the reason I couldn't just leave him. If he loves Mia, he would never have let me take her from him.

I'm aware of Liv watching me. She's waiting for my answer, but I can't give it yet. I need time to think. Mia is my little girl. Just the knowledge that I have a daughter has triggered my maternal instinct. Even though I can't visualise us together at the moment, I want her to grow up with me as her mother. But, as things stand, that's impossible. I don't exist.

'I need to go home now,' I say. 'I need to tell Luis about Mia before I can even begin to think about what happens next. We made a vow to each other: no more secrets.'

'Do you want me to come with you?' Liv asks.

'No, thank you. This is something I have to do on my own. Are you staying at the same hotel?'

'Yes, The Helios.'

'Can we meet there tomorrow morning, around eleven, when I've had chance to talk things through with Luis?'

'I'll be in Reception,' Liv says, getting to her feet and heading towards the door to the street. 'Are you sure you'll be okay?'

I'm not sure of any such thing. My world has just been turned on its head for the second time in as many months and I have no way of knowing how Luis will react to this latest revelation.

I nod, and then with more conviction than I'm actually feeling, I say, 'I'm glad you came back to find me, Liv; I've missed you.'

'I've missed you too, Sophie,' she says as the door closes behind her.

I take another sip of camomile tea and lean back against the cushions that are propping me up in bed. It's not even ten o'clock, but after getting back from the studio, giving Vince his doggy treats and having a quick shower, all I wanted to do was climb into bed with a hot drink. It will be hours before Luis gets home, which gives me plenty of time to think about my conversation with Liv.

As she was leaving, I said I was glad she'd come back, but the truth is, I have mixed emotions about it. If Liv hadn't come back, I would never have known about Mia; she would probably have stayed buried in my memory forever and perhaps that would have been the best thing for everybody. But Liv did come back, and now I know I have a daughter I don't know what to do. Can I leave Mia to grow up in Tom's care? It might be the best thing for her, but will I be able to live knowing that on the other side of the globe my daughter is growing up without her mother? And I'm worried about Tom having sole control over her upbringing. I'm sure he loves our daughter, but no one knows for certain what goes on behind closed doors, as my relationship with Tom has proved.

I've been trying so hard to picture my little girl since Liv told me about her and, suddenly, I have a fleeting glimpse. Tom is holding her, but she reaches out her arms to me and in doing so drops the teddy bear she is holding. I bend to pick it up, but I hear Tom's voice say, 'Leave it.'

The image is gone as quickly as it appeared, but it makes me realise that I didn't ask Liv whether Tom told Mia what happened to her mummy. Has he kept my memory alive for our daughter's sake? What if I return home and she doesn't know who I am? She might be scared of me, not understanding why I disappeared from her life only to reappear several years later. What if she can't forgive me?

I must eventually fall into a restless sleep with those thoughts turning over and over in my mind because I'm woken by Vince's tail thwacking against the floor tiles. Luis is home and I have to tell him about Mia. We promised to be honest with each other from now on.

He'll know the moment he pushes open the bedroom door that something is wrong. I'm usually fast asleep by the time he gets home, barely stirring as he climbs into bed next to me. On the few occasions that I do wait up for him, I have soft music playing and fragrant candles lit. Tonight, the overhead light is on and I am bundled into an old T-shirt of his in an effort to warm the chill in my bones. I have no idea how I'm going to break the news to Luis that I have a daughter, but I'll have to find a way.

CHAPTER 21

Liv

Mexico

I haven't been so lucky with my hotel room this time around. Instead of a ground-floor suite opening directly onto the beach, I'm in a second-floor room with a small balcony overlooking the pool.

It's almost half past nine, which means the aqua aerobics class will be starting shortly. I always politely declined the invitation to join in when I was here in January, but I could hear the thumping bass beat of the music and could picture the enthusiastic instructor trying to encourage lethargic holidaymakers to 'get physical'.

There's no need to rely on my imagination this morning as my balcony is the perfect vantage point from which to view Pepe in his neon-coloured Lycra onesie moving between the sunbeds in his effort to justify his wages. I feel quite sorry for him really. Very few people seem up for the challenge this morning and that definitely includes me.

I pick up my coffee cup and head back inside my room, closing the glass sliding door behind me. I'm pretty sure it won't block out the music completely, but it should minimise it sufficiently for me to try and collect my thoughts before I ring Jamie.

I've been awake for hours already, trying to make sense of my meeting with Sophie. When I was with her at the Pilates studio last night, I believed every word she said. I could even see that some of the excuses Tom made on her behalf may have been him preventing her from seeing people which, according to the internet research I did in the early hours of the morning, were classic signs of controlling behaviour within a relationship. But what if Sophie was struggling to cope with her changed life as Tom had suggested on a couple of occasions? Was my brother just trying to protect his fragile wife?

On the other hand, why would Sophie lie about things? Something had made her run off to Spain and subsequently take on Grace's identity. Was it actually Tom's behaviour and how she was interpreting it or was she lying to cover her real reason for abandoning us all, whatever that may be? Rather than having a better understanding when I woke up this morning, I was more confused than ever about the truth. Maybe things will become clearer after I've talked things over with Jamie in response to his text messages from last night.

I'd got back to my hotel room a little after ten and considered ordering room service as I hadn't eaten but decided instead to raid the minibar and run myself a hot bath. While it was filling with water, I turned my phone on to check for messages and, sure enough, there were three from Jamie. The first one read:

Have you found her yet? xx

The second one, sent around an hour later, asked:

So, is it Grace or Sophie? xx

And the third one, sent around the time the Pilates class was finishing and I was confronting Sophie, said:

Sorry, Liv, I need to get some sleep, but ring me if you need to, regardless of the time difference. Love you, Jamie xx

He'd sent the message at midnight UK time, which was late for Jamie, so I decided to leave it and speak to him this morning, having slept on things.

Like me, Jamie has never had any reason to believe that Tom is anything other than a kind, considerate husband, and even the suggestion in Sophie's original letter that he might not have been had Jamie rushing to his best friend's defence. But there was something about the look in Sophie's eyes when she was relaying what she could remember about Tom's behaviour. I saw it in Polly's eyes too when he reprimanded her about the wine. Not fear exactly, more anxiety. Was it really possible that my big brother became someone else behind closed doors?

Thinking back to my childhood, Tom had always been the one to decide what card game we would play as a family, or which television show we would watch. I'd accepted it as normal because he was so much older than me. On the few occasions when my parents went out for the evening once Tom was old enough to babysit me, he'd always been very strict about bedtime, just as he had been with Mia when Jamie and I went around for dinner recently. There is little doubt in my mind that my brother likes to take control of situations, like organising the charity to take all of Dad's possessions before Mum had decided if she wanted to keep anything, but is that the same as controlling behaviour within a relationship? From what Sophie claims to remember, it seems as though he was deliberately isolating her from her friends and family so that she became more and more dependent on him. I really don't know what to think.

I've waited until now to call, early afternoon in the UK, as I couldn't remember if Jamie had said he was on call this weekend. He picks up on the second ring.

'Hey, how are you doing?' he says. 'I half wondered if you were going to video-call, so I've been tidying up just in case.'

'Trust me, you don't want to see me this morning,' I reply. 'I didn't get much sleep.'

There's a small pause. I can't decide if it's a delay due to us being thousands of miles apart or whether he's bracing himself for the news he's about to receive.

'So, I'm taking it you found her. Which one of your former friends, was it?'

'It's Sophie; and she's not a former friend, she *is* my friend,' I reply. Whatever Jamie thinks and despite the circumstances of our reunion, she will always be a very special person in my life.

'Jesus, Liv,' he says in a shocked tone. 'How can you still call her a friend when she deceived everyone into thinking she was dead, not to mention deserting you at a time when you really needed her? A true friend would never do that.'

I'm unsure how much detail I should share. Sophie has a lot of soul-searching to do about Mia. If she decides to stay in Mexico, living her life as Grace, then no one else from her past needs to know that she is still alive. People have already grieved for her; it would be unfair to put them through the emotional upheaval of discovering she survived but chose not to go home, whatever her reasons. I select my words with care.

'We know from her letter that Sophie was fragile even before the trauma of the accident. Maybe she just panicked and took flight because she didn't know what else to do.'

'Did she feed you that bullshit? Obviously, she had to come up with a story to cover the awful truth that she wanted out of her marriage. I'm just amazed that you're gullible enough to believe it. I think you should get on the next plane home and leave the selfish little bitch to her perfect life with her Mexican lover.'

Jamie, who is normally even-tempered and usually has the ability to see both sides of the story, sounds angry. He's angry for the hurt Sophie has caused not only to me but also to his best friend. In this mood, he's likely to get off the phone and ring

Tom immediately; I can't let that happen while I'm still not sure about the truth.

'I think you may be misjudging her,' I say, trying to stay as calm as I can. 'Although she has remembered what happened the day of the crash, there are huge gaps in her memory. I looked it up online in the early hours when I was struggling to sleep. It's called partial amnesia and is brought on by trauma.' I'm not lying to my husband; I did look it up because I wanted to be sure that it was possible for her to have complete memory loss in terms of Mia, while being able to remember other things with total clarity. 'It's not that common, but it can and does happen. Can you at least give her the benefit of the doubt?'

'All I'm saying is that she has lied to you before, so why would you trust her now?' he replies with obvious frustration in his voice. 'How did you leave things with her?'

'She's coming to meet me at the hotel this morning, after she's had chance to...' I was about to say, 'tell Luis about Mia,' but I think better of it... 'let the dust settle,' I finish lamely. 'Jamie, can we keep this between us for a while longer? Nothing will be gained by telling other people when we don't know what Sophie's intentions are. Even knowing what she now knows, she might think it's best for everyone concerned if she just stayed here.'

'And if she marries the Mexican boyfriend, that will make her a bigamist and you'll be an accessory to the fact,' he snaps. 'Holy crap! Does that mean Tom already is?'

It was something I hadn't even considered.

'I don't suppose so because he doesn't know Sophie's alive. Another reason why we should make this our secret. Surely you can see that's the best thing for now?'

Jamie makes a 'hurummmph' noise. 'I don't think we've got any choice. We're in the awkward position of knowing something illegal has taken place but not reporting it to the authorities. It's the sort of thing that could come back to bite us on the arse.'

I guess he's right. I haven't given much thought to the legal side of things, just the human side. I'm beginning to wish I'd never come to Mexico on my holiday in January. What we don't know can't hurt us, but both Jamie and I know about Sophie now; are we breaking the law by keeping it to ourselves?

'Are you still there, Liv?' Jamie says.

'Yes.'

'Here's what I think. Meet with Sophie today if you feel you have to, then check out and come home on the next available flight. I mean it; this whole situation is really complicated and the less tangled up in it we are, the better.'

'Okay. I'll check flight availability and call you after I've met up with Sophie. I'm sorry for getting you involved in this, Jamie.'

'It's not your fault, Liv. You just thought you saw someone from your past on a beach. If Sophie hadn't written to you, you would probably never have thought any more about it, and that's what's bothering me. Why did she send the letter? What possible reason could she have had? She must have known you would go looking for her, but why did she want to be found after all this time? You need to ask her that, because I, for one, really want to know.'

'I will, I promise,' I say ending the call. Jamie's right. Even knowing me as she does, Sophie can't have thought there was more than a fifty-fifty chance that I would actually come back to Mexico looking for her based on a glimpse lasting a few seconds. Something else must have prompted her to write. Maybe she was seeking some kind of forgiveness from me to soothe her guilty conscience.

Well, Sophie's not the only one who feels guilty. Two months ago, I came to Tulum to mourn the fourth consecutive birthday without my dear friend. I had no way of knowing that she was alive and well and living happily less than a kilometre away and that the person I should have been mourning was my other child-hood friend, Grace. I feel sick to the pit of my stomach for the countless uncharitable thoughts I've had about Grace since the accident in Spain. Cruel, heartless, selfish – you name it and I've thought it. And all the while she was lying at the bottom of the Mediterranean Sea along with the other victims of the disaster. My own unreasonable jealousy that Sophie had turned to her for help instead of me had prevented me from forgiving Grace. If I'd gone in search of her then and discovered that it was Sophie who had survived, I might have been able to persuade her to come home and face up to whatever was going wrong in her home life. I have a sinking feeling that it's all too late now.

And what of Grace's mum and dad? They might not have been the most loving and caring parents in the world, but they have a right to know that their daughter isn't staying away by choice. Grace deserves a proper burial, just like the one we held for Sophie, where we celebrate the person she was before tragedy struck.

It's all such a complicated mess and I can't help feeling that I'm responsible for it.

CHAPTER 22

Liv

Mexico

I've positioned myself opposite the main entrance in the opulent hotel reception area in order to see Sophie when she arrives. I usually love a bit of people watching, trying to guess what nationality they are by their clothes and whether or not they tip the hotel porter, but today my heart's not in it.

Although the hotel rooms are well-appointed, it's clear to see that this particular chain believes in first impressions. The driveway meanders through perfectly manicured gardens to a very grand entrance with pillars and half a dozen marble steps leading up to the revolving doors. Inside, there is black gold-flecked marble everywhere, from the floors to the countertop of the reception desk, and there are five huge chandeliers suspended from the ceiling two stories up. In one corner, a sweeping staircase, also in marble, leads to the VIP suites and a rooftop bar with daybeds and plunge pools. Back in January, I'd spent a couple of relaxing afternoons up there, but on this visit all I can think about is Sophie.

I glance down at my watch. It's nearly quarter past eleven. Maybe Sophie's changed her mind about meeting up with me.

'Sorry I'm a bit late,' Sophie says, catching me by surprise.

She looks stunning in a silk sundress in all the colours of the rainbow. Her hair is tied up in a high ponytail and she's wearing sunglasses that cover half her face.

'Sorry,' she repeats. 'I came up from the beach because I've got our dog with me and the hotel doesn't allow them inside. Are you okay to go for a walk while we talk?'

'Of course,' I say, reaching for my own sunglasses before following Sophie out into the bright sunshine.

As we go down the wooden steps onto the beach, I hear a dog barking and notice the golden retriever that had first caught my eye when I was here seven weeks ago. Just as he had been then, he is sitting patiently waiting for his owner, only this time he has a large stick across his front paws. As we get closer, he picks it up in his mouth and brings it to Sophie, then falls into step behind her as we head down to the shoreline and start walking away from the crowded part of the beach.

Once we're past the row of hotel sun loungers, and there are only a few people scattered randomly on their towels near the dunes, Sophie throws the stick into the water for the dog to retrieve. We stop to watch as he goes splashing into the water and proceeds to doggy paddle out towards the piece of wood. Neither of us has spoken since leaving the hotel reception area.

'Your dog's very well trained,' I say. He is, but my observation is more about breaking the silence that has fallen between us.

'His name's Vince,' Sophie says.

'That's an unusual name for a dog, 'but then you were never a fan of boring. Didn't you have a cat called Picasso when we were younger?'

'You've got a good memory,' she says, smiling. 'We called him Picasso because he trod in some gloss paint when he was a tiny kitten and left a trail of paw prints on our utility-room floor tiles that we never could get off.'

'Is there a story behind Vince's name?' I ask as we watch the retriever make a lunge for his stick, clamping his jaws around it before starting his swim back towards us with his prize.

'Only that he wags his tail like a windscreen wiper and Luis misheard my description.'

Sophie has mentioned her boyfriend's name and there doesn't seem much point in continuing with our small talk, so I just come straight out with my question.

'Did you tell him about Mia?'

'Yes,' she replies. 'Just warning you that you're about to get drenched. Vince will drop his stick and then shake himself vigorously.'

'It'll soon dry in this heat,' I say, glancing up at the sun, which is almost directly overhead.

'He'll do it every time he fetches the stick, but at least I've forewarned you.'

Unless I'm imagining it, there's a slight edge to Sophie's voice.

'By that, do you mean I should have forewarned you that I was going to come looking for you? The question is, if I had, would you still have been here? You've done a runner once before; how was I to know that you wouldn't disappear all over again?'

She shrugs and then bends to pick up the stick Vince has dropped at her feet. He shakes himself from head to toe, as Sophie predicted he would, before racing off after the stick again.

It feels as though she wants to say something, but the words won't come, so I fill the space.

'Am I right in thinking Luis didn't take it too well?' I ask.

She flops down onto the soft golden sand and gazes out to sea. Rather than towering over her, I follow suit.

'Talk to me, Sophie,' I say, gently. 'You obviously want to, or you wouldn't have come.'

'Luis has gone to stay at his mum's for a few days. He says we both need time to think about what we want our future to be,' she explains, fiddling with the hemline of her dress, twisting it back and forth in her fingers.

'I wouldn't read too much into that,' I suggest, putting my hand on her arm, my fingertips touching the outside edge of the tattoo that had betrayed her. 'It's a pretty big shock to find out that your girlfriend has a child, but even harder for him to accept that she had no recollection of it.'

'You know, the funny thing is, we've never discussed having children. I guess we were enjoying our lives, just the two of us. Three if you count Vince,' she says. 'I'd never given it much thought to be honest. We were happy and I assumed babies would come along when we both felt the time was right.'

She pauses, but this time, instead of speaking I allow the sound of the waves and the distant shrieks of children enjoying themselves to fill the space until she continues.

'It seems the time would never have been right for Luis. After I told him about Mia, he told me that he had a vasectomy when he was twenty-one because he didn't want to bring children into such an overcrowded and messed-up world.'

My heart starts thumping against my ribs. What must have seemed to Luis like a selfless decision at the time, giving up his right to father a child, becomes selfish when you don't tell the woman you love that she will never be the mother of your children.

'So, you see, Luis doesn't want Mia, but he said he completely understands if I do. Basically, Liv,' she says, turning to me and pushing her sunglasses up so I can see her eyes, swollen and red-rimmed from crying, 'he's given me a choice: him or Mia.'

I'm not often at a complete loss for words, but this has me speechless. I've spent my morning wondering about Sophie's reason for writing to me. Did she have some hidden agenda? Maybe a plan to return to England using me to back up her amnesia story. Perhaps she wasn't as idyllically happy as she was claiming. But looking at her now, I don't think that's the case at all. She looks utterly devastated. After pouring her heart out to Luis, admitting to switching identity with Grace, they'd agreed no more secrets. That's what she told me last night. To then discover that Luis has been keeping something this major from her has clearly shaken her world to its foundations.

Children are an integral part of family life for most people. I remember Jamie and I discussing it quite early on, after just a few dates. We talked about how many children we wanted, possible names for them and what they would be when they grew up. I'd been ecstatic when I'd found out I was pregnant with Alfie, which made losing him, and all the things we had begun planning for his future, all the harder to bear. I'm wondering if Sophie didn't talk about children because her mind had blocked out that she was already a mother. Maybe Luis took that to mean she had no interest in having babies either. But now that Mia's existence has come to light and she knows that she and Luis can't have children together, will her maternal instinct kick in? If she was leaning towards letting Mia grow up thinking that her mother died when she was a baby, will the thought of never having another child of her own have changed her mind?

'I'm so sorry. In a way, this is all my fault. If I hadn't called out to you, this would never have started, and you and Luis would still be blissfully happy.'

'It's not your fault. You only came back because I wrote you that letter.'

'Why did you write to me?' I ask. It's the million-dollar question and Jamie is not the only one wanting to know the answer.

Vince, having brought his stick back several moments earlier with no response from Sophie, has settled down on her feet and is looking up at her with his big trusting eyes. She reaches her hand out and fondles his ear.

'I don't really know. My life here is perfect. I love the beach, I love my job and most of all I love Luis,' she says, his name catching in her throat. 'But seeing you reminded me that it was all a lie. That one quirk of fate made me realise that I didn't want to live the rest of my life looking over my shoulder. I wanted to unburden myself and for you, at least, to know the truth.'

'Despite what you said in your letter about not wanting me to come looking for you, is that actually what you wanted?'

'I'm not sure. After carrying the guilt of Grace's death alone for over three years, I could have been reaching out to you for reassurance that it wasn't really my fault. Like you said last night, maybe Grace was destined to have a short life. She could have been on that train anyway going to see Ricardo in Alicante, or she could have been hit by a truck crossing the road. Perhaps I just needed to reconnect with someone from my past and to have them understand and forgive me for doing what I did.'

'Do you regret writing to me?'

She takes a deep breath, lifting her eyes to gaze out to the distant horizon as though trying to capture all that she stands to lose if she makes the wrong decision.

'No. It was the right thing to do, whatever the consequences. If I do lose Luis,' she says, her voice trembling, 'I'll be devastated, but I think it's unfair of him to ask me to choose between him and my daughter. Now that I know about her, I can't allow Mia to grow up with Tom. Goodness only knows what long-term psychological damage he might cause her.'

It upsets me to hear Sophie talk about my brother in this way, especially as I've only heard her side of things. According to Mum, Mia is a happy little girl, but that could in part be down to Polly. I haven't mentioned Tom's new wife to Sophie because there didn't seem much point in causing her pain, but if she's now planning on returning to England she needs to know what she'll be returning home to.

'There's something you should know before you make your final decision,' I say biting my bottom lip. I hope I'm doing the right thing in telling her. 'If your main concern is that Mia is growing up with Tom as a sole parent, you don't have to worry.'

She turns her head sharply to look at me, her eyes filled with both realisation and questions.

'Tom remarried three years ago.'

The shock registers first in Sophie's eyes, then the hurt, followed by the anger.

'You told me last night that he was broken-hearted by my death and wept at my graveside, but you didn't say that within six months he'd not only met someone else, he'd bloody married them! Poor grieving Tom could barely wait until my body was cold before he moved on to his next victim.'

Sophie's voice is raised and it's making Vince agitated. His tail is now curled beneath his body and he's making a whining sound.

'That's a low blow, Sophie,' I say in defence of my brother, despite having reacted to his marriage to Polly in a similar way. 'It really wasn't like that. He *was* broken-hearted. He didn't go out looking for someone to replace you, if that's what you're thinking. Polly started working at the practice as a receptionist a short time before the accident. According to Jamie, she was the only person Tom would speak to about what had happened, maybe because she'd never met you. Once Polly knew about Mia, she offered to help out with her care from time to time because she'd previously worked as a nanny. I guess things just snowballed.'

'How convenient for both of them. He gets a willing stepmum for his child and she gets to marry the boss; you couldn't write it.'

'Trust me, I was just as cross with him as you are. I kept telling him that it was too soon to get involved with anyone while he was still obviously grieving for you, but he told me to mind my own business.'

'Nice,' she says, her voiced dripping in sarcasm.

'When he announced that they were engaged and getting married a couple of months later, I didn't speak to him for weeks.

I had to go to the wedding because Jamie was his best man, but it was one of the worst days of my life. I just kept seeing you standing there by his side. Things have been slightly awkward ever since; I've barely seen him or Polly, which means I've not seen Mia much either. I've been a completely rubbish auntie. Even through Dad's illness, we rarely visited at the same time so that we could avoid seeing each other. Poor old Mum, stuck in the middle. Not to mention Jamie. Like I told you, it came between us to such an extent that we were on a trial separation when I was here in January.'

Sophie hasn't taken her eyes off me while I've been speaking. She reaches her arms around me and squeezes me tightly, as though her life depends on it. Eventually she relaxes her grip.

'I'm sorry you've had all this to deal with,' she says. 'No wonder you were so angry with me last night. I was wrong to take the coward's way out. I should have been braver.'

'It's not always easy to see things clearly when you're in the middle of something,' I say. 'If I'd been a better friend to you, I would have spotted that things weren't right. I was too tied up in playing happy families with Jamie to see how unhappy you were. When you didn't come to comfort me after we lost Alfie, I thought you were punishing me for being an absent friend. I can't even begin to describe how upset I was when you went off to see Grace without asking me if I wanted to go. I've never admitted this before, but when I heard about the accident, my first thought was, "It serves Sophie right for going without me." What kind of wicked person would have a thought like that about their best friend?' I risk a glance at Sophie, but she's not looking at me. 'That's why I never replied to Grace's email – the one you sent. I shifted the blame from you to her; I had to punish someone.'

Sophie is still gazing out to sea, but she reaches for my hand.

'I know he's your brother, but Tom is the cause of all of this and yet he's the one who has come out of it virtually unscathed. He has our beautiful family home, a new wife and our child. I don't care about the house and the new woman in his life, but I do care about Mia. Much as it will break my heart to leave Luis, I'm going home and I'm going to fight for custody of our child.'

It was never my intention to put Mia in the middle of a custody battle and yet, thanks to me, that now seems the most likely outcome of me returning to Mexico in search of the truth. Maybe I should have left things alone after all, but it's too late for that now.

CHAPTER 23

Sophie

Mexico

Tuesday

It's a long time since I've sat in the departure lounge at Cancún airport, eleven years to be precise, but, just like the last time, I'm on my own and unsure of what lies ahead when I get back to England. The only thing I do know is that this time I'll be met by Liv rather than Tom.

It's strange to think how events in Mexico have shaped my life. Back then, it was my forced return home after being attacked with a bottle on a night out. I may never have got to know Tom as anything more than Liv's big brother if I hadn't tried to break up a fight in a bar. I shudder. How different my life might have been had fate not taken my hand and led me off down a path that I thought was the right one at the time. I've since wondered if I should have spotted warning signs. Maybe I would have done had I not been so young and in love. I managed to put it all behind me and find new happiness in my borrowed life, but then fate stepped in again.

Until I knew about Mia, I'd lain awake at night questioning my decision to write to Liv after the encounter on the beach. The universe had decided to give me a choice. I could still live out my life as Grace with Luis at my side or I could face up to the decision I'd made to run away when things got so unbearable and try to rebuild my relationships with Liv and my parents. I've had time to think things through over the past four nights lying alone and sleepless in my bed.

I'm grateful that Liv came back to Mexico to find me. She's given me a chance, however slim, to be a mother to my child. If I'd started to unlock the memories that are now emerging about Mia in ten years' time, it might have been too late. It would have been like losing her for a second time. I don't know if I could have survived that.

Liv wanted me to travel back with her on Sunday after she'd managed to rearrange her flight, but there were a few things I'd needed to organise first, not least breaking the news to Josefina that I was going back to England for a while. Surprisingly, she didn't ask if Luis was going with me; maybe she just assumed he was.

I suppose I hoped that Luis would reconsider his decision to stay at his mum's house and come home so that we could discuss the situation we found ourselves in. When he was still a no-show by the time I got home from talking to Josefina at the Pilates studio on Monday afternoon, I knew I would have to take things into my own hands. I didn't want to talk or break down in tears in front of his mum, so I decided to write him a letter and deliver it, along with Vince, before my taxi to the airport arrived.

It took me several hours and half a box of tissues to compose and I still wasn't sure that I'd said all I wanted to say in the way that I wanted to say it, but it was the best I could do.

Dear Luis,

Never in my worst nightmares did I imagine I would have to write this letter to the person I love most in the world. You have been my rock and my soulmate since our paths first crossed. I love you, Luis, I think you know that, but finding out that I am a mother and that my daughter is growing up under the influence of the man who almost destroyed me has left me with no choice.

I know my little girl has survived without me for the past three and a half years, as I have without her, but that was because I'd blocked every memory of her existence, locking it away for safekeeping in a secure box in the depths of my mind. Now that I've been given the key, I'm starting to remember small things about her. I can almost feel the tug of her perfect rosebud lips as she suckled at my breast as a new-born baby and hear her cries when she was stung by a bee. These memories belong to me; they were moments that just the two of us shared and they are made even more precious because there may not ever be any more. I have no idea if I will be able to win Mia back, but I would never forgive myself if I didn't at least try.

It may seem foolish to you that I would even consider giving up our wonderful life together for the slim chance of being able to build a future with my child, but I think we both know that our lives will never be the same again, knowing what we now do about each other.

Don't get me wrong, my decision to return to England isn't about the choice you made years ago not to father a child of your own. Of course, I'm disappointed that you didn't think it was something I should know, and I would be lying if I said I hadn't imagined us with little Luises and Graces playing in the sand, but I can hardly talk about honesty after my own deception.

The thing is, once I knew I had a daughter, I don't think there was ever any doubt that I would want to try to win custody of her, despite the risks involved. For all I know, I could face a prison sentence for stealing Grace's identity, but it's a chance I'm prepared to take.

*I'm sorry that you felt it had to be a choice between you and
Mia. I think we could have made things work as a family, but
if that's not right for you, then I respect your wishes.*

*I will miss you and Vince more than you could ever imagine,
but I hope that you will be able to smile when you think of
our time together.*

*You'll always be in my heart
Grace xxx*

I signed the letter as Grace, because she was the woman Luis
had been sharing his life with. He doesn't know Sophie, and it
seems that he has no interest in getting to know her.

The letter stared up at me as I sat at the table this morning,
trying to swallow my breakfast granola. It wasn't the only thing
staring up at me. Vince was lying at my feet with his head resting
on his paws. Normally his tail would be wagging in anticipation
of his food, but he was completely still, as though he was aware
that something was wrong. Beyond his trusting gaze, I could see
my suitcase and carry-on bag waiting by the door. My life was
about to change, and in my heart, I knew there would be no going
back. Suddenly, everything felt very real.

After scraping the remains of breakfast into the bin and feeding
Vince, I'd put his collar and lead on him. Luis and I rarely bothered
with it, so he was a little reluctant at first. I was deliberately going
around to Luis's mum's house early because I knew she would be
out at the vegetable market and Luis would still be sleeping after
his late finish in the bar. My plan was to tie Vince's lead around a
post in the back yard and to slip my letter under the front door.
That way, I wouldn't have to see either Luis or his mum.

Vince and I both dragged our feet a little, turning the ten-
minute walk into a fifteen-minute one, but it was still only 9 a.m.
when we arrived at the small house on the outskirts of Tulum.

I lifted the latch on the side gate that led to the small courtyard garden and tied Vince up in an area which I knew would be in the shade for most of the morning. He whined when I squatted down to hug him; I wish I could have explained to him that I didn't want to leave him. With my arms around his furry neck and my heart at breaking point, the image I'd had before of me leaving someone I loved filled my head. Standing next to the front door of my home in Warlingham, my small travel case in my hand, I once again pictured Tom holding our daughter, while she reached her hands out towards me, waggling her chubby little fingers. I could clearly see his face and, as his lips moved, I could almost hear his words, 'It's all right, Mia, Mummy will come home to us soon.' But I couldn't picture Mia's face and it was both frustrating and upsetting.

Tom seemed sure that I would never desert Mia. It must have been why she didn't go to Spain with me. Despite the agony of leaving Luis and Vince, it reinforced that I was doing the right thing. I allowed Vince one final lick of my hand, then closed the gate on him, pushed the white envelope under the orange front door and quickly walked away before I could change my mind.

I returned to the apartment that Luis and I had called home and sat outside in the sunny courtyard, tears streaming down my cheeks, waiting for the knock at the door that would bring a very special part of my life to a close.

And now here I am, queueing up to board the plane that will carry me home to a life I was so desperate to escape from.

I hand over Grace's passport, aware that it is the last time that I will use it as my own. Once I've cleared customs at Gatwick, the process of establishing my true identity will begin, which will hope-fully eventually lead to me reclaiming my life and my daughter.

I slip into the seat next to the window and gaze out on to the tarmac, where steam is rising as the sun quickly dries the moisture from a brief shower of rain. It will be very different back in England. Days on end of cold rain falling from leaden skies. Just the thought of it makes me shiver, or is my reaction more to do with what and who I am leaving behind in Mexico? Liv has promised to lend me some of her winter clothes, but I doubt they will be able to warm the chill in my heart.

'Scared of flying, are you?' says the man who has just settled into the seat at my side.

I look at him questioningly and he directs his gaze to my hands, which are holding on so tightly to the armrests that my knuckles have turned white.

'Not so much the flying,' I reply, smiling weakly, 'more the possibility of crashing.'

I turn my head to look back out of the window in an effort to discourage further conversation.

How funny that a complete stranger has made me acknowledge that it's the fear of the unknown that is scaring me. If the authorities don't accept my story that I suffered total amnesia after the train crash in Spain and believed myself to be Grace because I was in possession of her documents, then there is little to no chance that they will listen to anything else I have to say regarding Tom and Mia. Liv has said she will vouch for my surprise when she called out to me on the beach, but she hasn't totally committed to supporting me in any other way. It's understandable, as she would be taking a stance against her brother while not really knowing if what I've told her is true.

I am embarking on a journey into the unknown without the person I hoped I would be spending the rest of my life with and the thought of that is simply terrifying.

CHAPTER 24

Sophie

England

Wednesday morning

I snuggle deeper into Liv's quilted coat while watching her in the wing mirror as she lifts my suitcase into the boot. Her expression is tense and I'm wondering if she's now regretting her offer to let me stay with her and Jamie. I don't want to be responsible for any further issues between them, particularly as her loyalty to me was behind the trial separation in January. Liv has told me that she's asked Jamie not to say anything to Tom for the time being, but that is going to be incredibly difficult for him if I'm living under their roof.

'Right,' Liv says, climbing into the car and switching the engine on. 'Let's crank the heating up, you must be freezing.'

'I'd forgotten how cold England in the winter can be,' I admit.

'Technically, we're now in spring,' she replies, 'although I can understand why you might find that hard to believe. We've had a really cold snap the past few weeks. In fact, before the plane could take off when I flew out to Mexico last week, they had to clear several inches of snow from the runway, so in a way you're lucky.'

It felt weird descending through the thick grey clouds and catching my first glimpse of England in over three years. During the flight, I wondered if it would feel like a homecoming, and make Mexico seem like an extended foreign holiday, but as the wheels touched down and the grip of the rubber against tarmac slowed the plane to a taxiing speed, I had the sensation that the brakes had been applied on my life. I'd thought Tulum was my forever home with Luis and Vince, but discovering I am a mother has changed all that.

The noise of the tyres squealing against the concrete surface of the car park make conversation almost impossible, so we remain silent until after Liv has inserted the ticket to raise the barrier and then negotiated airport buses and cars stopping at a moment's notice to drop people off.

'Does it feel familiar?' Liv asks a few moments later, glancing sideways at me before refocusing her attention on the road.

I'm not sure if it's a loaded question. Is she testing me to see how much I can remember of my former life? I wonder. The thing is, if Liv is doubtful about my selective amnesia, how much more difficult is it going to be to convince the authorities? The enormity of the task ahead feels overwhelming, and it will be even worse if I can't look to Liv for her support.

'It's pretty much the same as it's always been,' I reply, looking out at the green hilly landscape. The truth is, nothing seems to have changed at all since the last time I was at Gatwick, apart from some roadworks. 'I must have travelled this stretch of road hundreds of times with my parents after days out to the coast in Brighton or Littlehampton.'

At the mention of my parents, Liv says, 'Have you contacted them yet?'

She had given me their forwarding address before she left Mexico, but I couldn't see the point in writing to them from there as I would most likely arrive in the UK before my letter did.

'No; not yet. I just want to set all the legal stuff in motion first before I complicate things with the emotional side,' I reply.

'That's probably for the best, but you don't want to leave it too long, Sophie. It would be awful if they heard it from someone else.'

She's right, of course, but knowing what to say to them is beyond me at the moment. I'm not exactly planning on announcing my return with a fanfare, so hopefully I'll be able to get my head together sufficiently to speak to them before they hear it on the grapevine. For the next couple of days though, I'll be finding out what I need to do with the authorities. Liv rang the Citizen's Advice Bureau on my behalf, and they recommended doing everything through a lawyer. She then contacted a lawyer who I have a meeting with tomorrow morning, after which I have no idea what will happen.

'By someone else, do you mean Tom?' I ask, my mouth feeling suddenly dry. While I have thought about the possibility of having to face him at some vague time in the future, the reality that it might be sooner than I think is daunting. My fear of him is the reason I abandoned my home and my family; it isn't going to be easy coming face to face with him again. A thought occurs to me.

'Jamie hasn't told him that I'm not dead, has he?'

'Not as far as I'm aware. I told you I asked him not to, but you know Jamie. He's probably one of the most honest people on the planet and I'm worried that he might let something slip. If asked a direct question, he's totally incapable of lying, but I don't think he would deliberately say anything.'

'You will tell me if this puts too much of a strain on you two, won't you? I wouldn't be able to live with myself if I thought that by helping me it would drive a wedge between you two.'

'Actually, on that subject, there are a couple of things we need to discuss.'

Her tone is measured, suggesting that I might not like what I'm about to hear.

'Go on,' I say.

'Firstly, you should know that Jamie read your letter, so he knows that you only believed yourself to be Grace in the immediate aftermath of the accident. He doesn't want me to lie about you having total amnesia.'

My heart sinks. Without Liv backing up my story, it will be harder to convince anyone that I genuinely believed I was Grace until Liv called out to me on the beach.

'I'm sorry, but I think he's worried that because we didn't notify the authorities as soon as we received the letter, we could be accused of withholding information or something. You know how Jamie likes to play everything by the book.'

'That's okay, Liv,' I say, trying to keep the disappointment out of my voice. 'Maybe we could just avoid mentioning the letter altogether, then you wouldn't have to lie about what was in it. If you shred it, no one need ever know.'

'That's a good idea,' she agrees. 'I'll do it the minute we get home. It's bin day today and I'm pretty sure no one is going to go examining landfill looking for something that they don't know existed.'

She sounds relieved that one of her issues has been so easily sorted.

'I can tell them that I believed I was Grace until you called out to me and only from that moment, some of my memories started to come back. I genuinely had no clue about Mia until you told me, so it would help if you can back me up on that.'

'You know I will.' She seems about to say something else, but then stops herself.

'You said firstly; what else is on your mind?'

'We're nearly home,' she says. 'Let's talk about it over a coffee.'

*

The minute we're through the front door of my house in Oxted, I fetch Sophie's letter from my bedroom and bring it downstairs to our small home office where the shredder is located. We both watch as the flimsy sheets are drawn noisily into the machine, the metal blades whirring as they turn it into confetti. After removing the top from the shredder and mixing the contents thoroughly, I take it outside and tip everything into the bin. By making a point of destroying the only evidence that could prove I knew she was living under a false identity, I hope I've made Sophie realise how nervous I am about the whole situation. There is so much at stake for all of us, not least Tom. By supporting Sophie, I will in effect be betraying my brother, which doesn't feel very fair when I haven't heard his side of things. But if he was controlling her to the extent where she would rather be dead than continue with her life as it was, as she claims, then he has to recognise that his behaviour was unacceptable.

She follows me through to the kitchen, where I wash my hands before flicking the switch on the kettle and getting two mugs out of the cupboard.

'Tea or coffee?' I ask.

'I haven't had a decent cup of tea in years,' Sophie says, 'but I think I'll have a coffee. It might help me to combat the jet lag.'

A few minutes later, we carry our mugs through to the lounge, where the sun is streaming in through the bay window.

'You've decorated,' Sophie comments.

I'm taken aback for a moment. It serves as a reminder of how long it's been since my best friend was last in my home.

'Yes. We did it a few months after Alfie died. Jamie only wanted to repaint the nursery really, but I managed to persuade him to do everywhere so that it would feel like a fresh start.' We'd chosen a pale grey for the whole house. It had taken three coats of paint to cover the bright cheerful blue walls in Alfie's room. 'It didn't help; I still used to go and sit on the rocking chair in the nursery, where I'd pictured giving Alfie his middle-of-the-night feeds, torturing myself over what might have been.'

Sophie is kneeling at my feet in seconds, taking both of my hands in hers.

'I'm so sorry I wasn't there for you when you needed me, Liv,' she says, looking into my eyes. 'It will haunt me until the day I die. I wanted to come and see you, really I did, but Tom wouldn't let me.'

As awful as it sounds, I'm not sure whether I believe her. The Sophie I grew up with wouldn't have allowed her husband to dictate to her what she could or couldn't do, particularly comforting her best friend in her hour of need. And, not for the first time, I find it hard to believe that Tom would behave in that way. After all, by stopping her from visiting me when I really needed her support, he was hurting me as much as Sophie. I'm looking straight into her eyes but I can't decide if they are hiding something. What if Sophie has been lying to me all along and is simply using my loyalty to get what she has come back for: Mia. Am I a mere pawn in a very complicated game of chess?

I break eye contact with her to glance down at my watch.

'It's almost lunchtime,' I say, deliberately changing the subject. 'Why don't you take your coffee upstairs while you unpack, and I'll rustle us up something to eat.'

I can't quite read her expression as she lets go of my hands and gets to her feet.

'Good idea,' she says.

CHAPTER 25

Sophie

Wednesday afternoon

I'd been glad to escape to the privacy of Liv's spare room to unpack my case. The repetitive action of removing things and placing them neatly in the chest of drawers has had a calming effect on me.

For a split second as I was looking into her eyes, trying to decide whether or not she believed what I was saying, another memory fought its way to the surface. Tom was gripping my wrist very tightly and pushing his face close to mine, his eyes dark and threatening as he told me I couldn't visit Liv.

I close my eyes, and his face is there again. He's telling me that I would make Liv feel worse because I had a healthy baby and she'd been denied hers. Was Tom right? Would it have upset Liv to see me or would I have been able to comfort my best friend? Was he just afraid that I might let slip what was going on in our marriage?

Trawling through my mind, I'm trying to seek out happy memories of me with Mia. There must have been giggles at foamy bath times or when I tickled her while changing her nappy. I'm searching for the sound of her laughing; it must be there, but if it is, I can't reach it. All I find instead is Tom's face; angry or disappointed or threatening. Why was he so angry with me? What did I do to change the way he felt about me? He used to love me so much until we had Mia.

A thought suddenly occurs to me. I have wondered if maybe I was unable to connect with Mia, not love her as I should. But what if I loved her too much and Tom felt pushed out? A baby changes the dynamics of a relationship. Instead of couples doing everything together in a cosy little twosome, an intruder is demanding attention and, more importantly, love. Was it possible that Tom was the one who found it difficult to love Mia because she had stolen a piece of my heart away from him when he wanted it all? Was the whole situation born out of his jealousy and, if that was the case, does he love her now? I'd assumed he must do, being his flesh and blood, but now I'm not so sure.

I have a sudden and overwhelming urge to see my little girl. I know Liv told me she was happy, but I need to see Mia with my own eyes to feel certain that she is loved and, more importantly, that she's safe.

I finish emptying my case, putting shoes in the bottom of the wardrobe and taking my bag of toiletries through to the bathroom, and am heading downstairs as Liv appears in the hallway below.

'I was about to call you,' she says. 'Lunch is ready. Only beans on toast, I'm afraid. I hope that's okay?'

'Perfect,' I reply, following her into the dining room and sitting down opposite her. 'Something else I haven't had recently,' I add, scooping up a forkful of the pale beans and savouring the sweetness of the tomatoey sauce.

'Something else?' Liv asks.

'I mentioned the tea earlier,' I say, cutting the corner off the chunky toast and loading it up with beans.

'Oh yes, of course,' she replies, sounding slightly distracted.

We continue eating in silence for a few minutes before I ask, 'Which school does Mia go to?'

'Carlton House. It's a new private school in the next village.'

'I was wondering if we could go there?'

'When?' Liv asks warily.

'This afternoon. I'm desperate to see her,' I say, adding in my mind that I need to be sure Tom and his new wife are taking care of her.

'But I thought we agreed that you should keep your distance until we've met with the lawyer tomorrow,' Liv says, a note of anxiety creeping into her voice. 'It's only one more day. Will it really make that much difference when you haven't seen her in so long?'

'What if the lawyer instructs me not to go anywhere near her?' I can feel myself getting panicky at the thought. 'It could be weeks or even months before I'm allowed access to my own daughter. I can't wait that long, not now that I'm so close.'

'I'm really not sure, Sophie. Wouldn't it be better not to risk doing anything that might compromise your chances of being allowed back into her life?'

'Allowed back into her life?' I say, my voice rising in volume. 'What's that supposed to mean?' While I have contemplated the awful possibility that I might not get full custody of Mia, it's never crossed my mind that I might be denied access completely. Courts almost always find in favour of the mother, unless there's a real fear that the mother would endanger the child. 'She's my daughter and I would have been in her life the whole time if it hadn't been for your control freak of a brother. He doesn't deserve her, he never did.'

I immediately realise I may have overstepped the mark. Liv looks shaken by my outburst. I need to be mindful that Tom is still her brother; the brother she adored for twenty-seven years of her life.

'Please don't talk about Tom like that. H-he might not always have been the perfect husband from your point of view, but he absolutely worships the ground Mia walks on.'

Softening my tone, I say, ' How can you be so sure? You said yourself that you've barely been in her life.'

'Mum tells me stuff,' Liv says, fiddling with her hair. 'And Jamie. He says Mia has dancing lessons and goes riding on Sundays, and

I've seen photographs of them on holiday. She always has a smile on her face.'

Whether or not she realises it, Liv has just plunged a dagger into my heart. My throat feels too tight to swallow, so I push my unfinished plate of food away. Of course I want Mia to be happy, but if she is, why on earth have I come back? I persuaded myself that I was a knight in shining armour, or whatever the female equivalent is, coming back to rescue her, but maybe she doesn't need rescuing. Maybe I'm just being selfish because I want my daughter back.

I take a breath to calm myself.

'I won't approach her, I promise. We can sit in your car and you can point her out to me. I just want to see my little girl.'

Liv's elbows are on the table, her fingers interlocked. She rests her chin on them, her expression thoughtful. She appears to be wavering.

'Please, Liv.'

She raises her gaze and looks me straight in the eyes. It's as though she's searching my soul.

'All right,' she finally says. 'I'll take you this afternoon at school pick-up time, but I can't risk Polly recognising my car. I'll drop you on the next road and you'll have to watch from behind a tree or something.'

'How will I recognise her though? I haven't been able to picture her face at all and anyway she will have changed a lot since I last saw her.'

Liv gets up and goes into the hall, coming back moments later with her phone.

'They're from last summer, so not all that recent, but I doubt Mia will have changed much in just a few months. You know, I must confess I found it a bit strange that you didn't ask me if I had any photos of her when you first found out about her,' she says, swiping downwards on her screen as she scrolls through photographs.

Liv's right. I have no idea why I didn't ask her about pictures of Mia before. It would have been the obvious and natural thing to do. Maybe I was so desperate to remember what Mia looked like the last time I saw her that I didn't want the image to be tainted by what she looks like now.

'This is probably the clearest one,' she adds, handing her phone over.

My heart leaps and contracts in equal measure. In the centre of the photograph is a very pretty dark-haired girl who could easily have been Liv twenty-five years ago. She's holding her teddy bear in one hand and an ice cream in the other and she has a broad grin on her face. There could be no doubt that the man to one side of her is her father, the phrase 'two peas in a pod' springs to mind, but it's the woman on the other side who has caught my attention. If I didn't know it to be impossible, she could be me.

I raise my eyes to look at Liv.

'I don't think he ever got over you, Sophie. He replaced you with someone who looks just like you. Part of the reason I was so angry with him is because you were barely laid to rest before he proposed to Polly. But I was also worried that he was only marrying her because she looked so much like you. It didn't seem very fair to either of you, or to him for that matter.'

I glance back down at the photograph. Polly is smiling, but does the smile reach her eyes? It's hard to tell in a photograph and anyway, pictures don't always tell the full story. A small part of me wonders why Tom and I couldn't have been that happy. If I'd stayed instead of running away, might we have been able to work through our differences? An image of sitting in a crowded A & E department flashes into my head. I shiver at the thought.

'I hope he treats her better than he treated me,' I say my voice barely above a whisper. 'I know you don't want to believe it, but he was somebody different behind closed doors. I'm starting to remember more and more things about my life with him. Do you remember the night you looked after Mia because we had to go to A & E?'

'Yes,' Liv says. 'You'd had a fall and hurt your wrist, so Tom asked us to look after Mia because she was only a few months old and he didn't know how long you'd be at the hospital. She was such a little angel. She never so much as stirred when we brought her into the house,' she adds, smiling at the pleasure the memory evokes.

'It was broken; a clean break of both bones at the wrist, which was why I was able to have a brace rather than a plaster cast. But it wasn't the result of a fall,' I say. My pulse is racing along with my mind; things seem to be coming back to me at a terrifying rate of knots since I've been back in England. 'I can't completely remember what happened, but I do recall the agony as the fridge door slammed against my wrist.'

Liv's smile from moments earlier turns to a look of horror.

'He made me swear not to tell anyone what had really happened,' I continue, 'or Mia would suffer.'

Liv gasps, her hand flying up to her mouth.

'He didn't hurt her, did he?' she whispers.

I shake my head. 'Not as far as I can remember, but the threat was always there, just beneath the surface. What if he's using Mia to control Polly in the same way he controlled me? Mia is my flesh and blood; I would have done anything to protect her, but what if Polly just decides she's had enough of Tom and walks away? I can't bear to think what he might be capable of.'

Unsurprisingly, Liv appears to be having an internal battle. I'm sure she doesn't want to believe bad things about her brother, no loving sister would, but she is clearly thinking about what I've just said.

'Sophie, I need you to be honest with me. Is this your mind inventing reasons why you may have been afraid of Tom, or are you actually remembering things as they were?'

In truth, I'm not completely sure. The flashes of memory I'm experiencing seem pretty clear but it's all so fragmented. 'I think it's actual memories,' I say.

'Okay,' Liv says, her jaw set as it always is when she's reached a decision about something. 'I think you should stop trying to remember stuff until you've seen a specialist who can help you unlock your memories. In the meantime, I'll speak to Polly, and invite myself to theirs for coffee while Tom is at work so that I can try and suss out what her and Mia's homelife is like.'

'Thank you, Liv. It must be awful for you hearing bad things about your brother, but if there's any chance that he's treating Polly like he did me, Mia could be in danger,' I say, gazing down at the photograph of Mia one final time before handing Liv her phone back.

'There's no way I'll stand by and let anything bad happen to my niece, even if it means falling out with Tom,' she says squeezing my hand as she takes her phone. 'I'll do whatever it takes to protect Mia.'

'Thanks for having faith in me, Liv. Friends for life,' I say, crossing my right arm over my chest just as Grace, Liv and I had done on the day we first made our vow.

'Friends for life,' she replies, copying my gesture.

CHAPTER 26

Sophie

Wednesday afternoon

Carlton House Preparatory School is located on a quiet road with wide grassy verges traversed by narrow tarmac footpaths. It's a converted Edwardian house set quite a way back off the road, with bay windows either side of the double entrance doors. What must originally have been the driveway and the front garden has now been made into a playground, with markings for netball and goalposts at either end.

I took all of this in as I walked briskly past after Liv dropped me on the adjacent road. Having taken up my position behind an old oak tree whose huge trunk completely hides me from sight, I watch from the safety of my vantage point as the cars start to arrive. I imagine it must be annoying for local residents to have all the vehicles descend on the school twice a day at drop-off and pick-up time. Less than ten minutes after walking past the deserted school gates, cars line both sides of the road, their occupants gathered in various huddles along the path.

The sound of the school bell, signalling that lessons have finished for the day, carries me back to my own schooldays and the excitement I used to feel at the prospect of showing my mum my latest pasta painting or potato printing masterpiece. A lump of emotion starts in my throat as I recall the relief I felt every day once I found her in the crowd. I liked school, but Mum was my safe haven. Nothing bad could happen to me while she was around. Despite having a high-powered job in the city, she opted not to return to work after I was born in order to dedicate herself to raising me. She was always at the school entrance to meet me, come rain or shine, just like the groups who are collected around the gates now.

I can't imagine how she is going to react to the news that I'm alive. Shock initially, of that I'm certain, but then what? Will we be able to regain the closeness we had or will there always be the tiniest doubt at the back of her mind that I didn't lose my memory but chose to run away because I couldn't cope? Even though memories of feeling threatened by Tom are returning, I still don't understand why I didn't feel able to turn to the people I love, and who loved me. If only I'd reached out then, I wouldn't be in the bizarre position I am now, hiding behind a tree in the hope of catching a glimpse of my own daughter. I should be in one of the huddles of mums waiting for Mia to come out of school and share stories of her school day. I feel cheated.

The first few children are starting to spill out into the playground. They seem to be a slightly older age group, but it's difficult to tell from this distance. I don't want to miss Mia, so I cross to the other side of the road from the entrance and start to walk fairly slowly back along it.

I can't help wondering if I know any of the other mums, which is not beyond the realm of possibility as I grew up and went to school in this area. Not that they would recognise me. Once again, I'm wearing Liv's navy-blue quilted coat, with the fur-trimmed hood pulled down over my head. The only visible parts of my face are my eyes and nose as I have a scarf pulled up to cover my mouth. This is partly to help with my disguise but mainly to keep out the cold. I did ask Liv if she thought I should wear my sunglasses, but she said that might draw attention to me. She's right; the bright winter sunshine from this morning has disappeared, so no one in their right mind would be wearing them. Even without them, I feel adequately disguised; I'm not sure I would recognise myself in a mirror.

I've put on a pair of Liv's lace-up brogues. My plan is to drop down to tie up my laces once I'm close enough to the gates to have a clear view of Mia when she comes out. I'm fairly sure no one will pay me any attention, but I need to be careful as a woman on her own loitering outside a school could arouse suspicion. Mothers seem to have a built-in protection mechanism when it comes to their children which I'm only just experiencing now that I know I have a daughter who could be at risk.

As I get closer to the scattered groups, I try to spot Polly. If I can locate her, then it will be less likely that I'll miss Mia among the hustle and bustle of home time. The problem is, they're all as well wrapped up as me under hats and hoods.

The playground is filling with children now. I follow my plan and peer from beneath my hood, scanning each face for the familiar features while I fiddle with my shoelaces. After several minutes, my hands are numb from the cold and I decide to get to my feet in case someone thinks I've fallen and comes to my aid.

In the space of those few minutes, most of the children have located their parents and are heading towards parked cars for the journey home. Some stragglers are crossing the tarmac of the playground, but they seem older. I'm pretty sure I haven't seen Mia come out, but in case she is one of the ones yet to appear, I cross the road to mingle with the few remaining adults who are stamping their feet and rubbing gloved hands together in an effort to keep warm. It doesn't take me long to realise that Polly is not among them.

I'm not sure which emotion hits first: disappointment or panic. It took a lot to mentally prepare myself to see my daughter, but I hadn't considered she wouldn't be at school today. Of course, it's entirely likely that she has a minor ailment that has kept her away, but what if it's something else?

As the wooden doors are closed, indicating that the last of the pupils have left for the day, I start walking briskly down the road in the direction of Liv's car, panic rising in my chest. I'm perspiring heavily by the time I wrench her passenger door open a few minutes later.

Before Liv can speak, I say, 'She wasn't there. Something's wrong; I know it.'

'Calm down, Sophie,' Liv says. 'You probably just missed seeing her with everyone so wrapped up.'

'No. I was watching every child that came out and she definitely wasn't among them.'

'Well, perhaps she's ill, so Polly and Tom decided to keep her away from school,' Liv suggests.

'What if that's not the reason she's not at school? What if Tom hit her and she's got a black eye or something, so they had to keep her off to hide it?' My words seem irrational even to me, but what if I'm right?

'You're overreacting. I'll bet there are loads of children off with coughs and runny noses at this time of year. Come on, let's go home,' she says, turning the key in the ignition. 'We can come again tomorrow afternoon after you've met with the lawyer. Even if they advise against you seeing her, they're not exactly going to know if we do the same as today, are they?'

I place my hand over hers to prevent her putting the car into gear and pulling away. 'Can you ring Polly to be on the safe side?'

'And say what? *Hi Polly, I'm just calling to ask if my brother has been hitting my niece?* Even if he had, which is highly unlikely, she's hardly going to say yes, is she?'

I know Liv is right, but now I've got the idea in my head that Mia might be in danger, I can't shake it.

'Earlier, you said you were going to ring her and suggest going around for a coffee. That could be your reason for calling. If you suggest tomorrow, she might say no because Mia's not well.'

'And if she doesn't say that? What if she just says no? You'll panic even more. It's a bad idea, Sophie.'

There's a hint of irritation in her voice. I need to keep Liv onside, so I have to try and be calm.

'But what if the panic is justified? You promised me you wouldn't let anything bad happen to Mia and yet you have no idea if she's lying in her bed bruised and broken. Please just make the call,' I urge, clinging on to her arm as though my life depends on it.

I'm not sure what I see in her eyes. It could be pity or it could be worry. Either way, she turns off the ignition and reaches into her handbag for her phone. She puts it on speaker and raises her finger to her lips. Moments later, a woman's voice fills the car.

'Hello? Is that you, Liv?'

'Hi, Polly; yes, it's me. I didn't know whether you would have stored my number in your phone.'

'That is okay, isn't it?' she asks.

She sounds very young and anxious.

'Yes, of course. I said to Tom that I'd like to get to know you better. I think maybe we got off on the wrong foot, but I want to put that right if you'll let me.'

'I'd like that,' she replies. 'It feels as though I made things awkward between you and your brother and that was never my intention.'

'I'm sure it wasn't,' Liv says. 'You just came into our family at a very difficult time, which wasn't your fault at all. Anyway, I was wondering if you fancy meeting up for coffee tomorrow?'

'Oh, that would have been lovely, but I can't do tomorrow.' There's a slight pause before she adds, 'Mia's off school with a bit of a cold. Maybe next week?'

I shake my head at Liv. We only have her word that Mia has a cold. What if that's not the reason she's off school?

'Or I could come around to yours? I could bring something for Mia to take her mind off her sniffles. It would be nice to see her since she was sleeping when we came for dinner.'

There's another short pause while Polly appears to be weighing things up.

'Actually, that might be quite nice. I think she's getting a bit fed up only having me for company. What time were you thinking?'

'Any time after lunch is good for me,' Liv says.

'How about half past two?'

'Perfect,' Liv replies, giving me a look as though to say, *you see, everything's fine.*

I'm just thinking how ridiculous I was to panic so much when Polly continues.

'Oh, and Liv, don't say anything to Tom about coming around. I'm not sure he'd approve of Mia being well enough to have a visitor if she's not well enough to go to school, if you see what I mean.'

There is anxiety in her voice, which immediately sets alarm bells ringing in my head.

'No problem,' Liv replies without skipping a beat. 'It can be our little secret. See you tomorrow.'

Liv ends the call and returns her phone to her handbag.

'Don't go reading too much into that, Sophie,' she says. 'Our parents were exactly the same when we were younger. If we weren't well enough to go to school, we weren't allowed to see friends.'

Liv seems convinced that Polly's reasons for not mentioning anything to Tom are legitimate, but I'm not so sure.

'Mia's five,' I say. 'And you're not a friend, you're her auntie. More to the point, did you not get the sense that Polly was afraid of Tom?'

Liv doesn't answer as she turns the engine back on and puts the car in gear.

'Well, I did,' I continue. 'But maybe that's because I know what he's like to live with. I never thought I'd say this, but I actually feel quite sorry for her.'

Liv still doesn't say anything. She pulls away from the kerb while I reach for my seat belt. As I'm fiddling around trying to slot the end of the belt into the buckle buried under the quilted excess of Liv's coat, Tom's face looms large in my mind. He's shaking his head, standing in our front doorway, with his arms folded as though preventing me from leaving. I can hear my voice begging him to allow me to go and see Liv: 'She's my friend; she needs me.' His reply is cutting: 'You can't help her; you can't even help yourself.' Again, I can almost feel the tightness of his grip as he turns me away from the door and propels me up the stairs to our room. Why wouldn't he let me see his sister in her hour of need? How could he be so cruel?

I steal a quick glance at Liv. Her eyes are fixed on the road ahead, her jaw set in a way that suggests further discussion about her brother is off limits, for the time being at least. I turn away, wondering if maybe Liv is finally starting to believe me that her brother isn't necessarily who she thinks he is.

CHAPTER 27

Sophie

Thursday morning

Meeting with Natasha Swann, the lawyer Liv contacted on my behalf, gives me a feeling of relief that the wheels are in motion for me to regain my former identity. She was very direct and to the point in the brief phone conversation we had yesterday after getting home from Carlton House School, and has a similar approach in person this morning. I think I've made the right decision to attend on my own. Understandably, Liv doesn't want to lie about the letter in which it was quite clear that I was aware I wasn't Grace long before the chance encounter in Mexico. Since she's not with me, I don't have to worry that she might inadvertently say the wrong thing.

After telling Natasha about the accident in Spain, she appears convinced that I'm telling the truth about having total amnesia until I heard Liv call out to me on the beach. She voices her opinion that hearing my real name could well have unlocked my memory, frozen by the trauma of the crash, but adds she's not an expert in such things. While I'm talking, she emails a psychoanalyst friend of hers and sets up an appointment for tomorrow morning, explaining the urgency of the situation. I'm hoping that she too will be convinced that my memory of my life before the crash is recent, thus corroborating my story in terms of the authorities, but also that she will help me retrieve the memories that are still tantalisingly out of reach.

Natasha has already been in touch with the authorities after our brief conversation yesterday, about me arriving in the country while travelling on someone else's passport. She said it was important to do that as soon as possible or it could seem that I was trying to hide something. And she's started the process of applying for a new passport for me, which will, of course, require proof of identity, in the form of fingerprints and possibly blood tests and dental records.

Now that all the practical stuff is in hand, we move on to talk about Tom and what I can remember of his behaviour towards me. She is taking notes, throwing in an occasional question for clarification, but mostly just listening. It's only when I mention my fears for Mia's safety that she engages with me more actively.

'Do you believe your daughter to be in immediate danger?' she demands.

'I'm not sure,' I answer truthfully.

'Then why did you say you fear for her safety?'

'I have a feeling that he used Mia as a way to stop me from leaving him. Almost like a pawn in a game of chess.'

'Can you remember him hurting her or doing anything to make you believe that he might?'

I close my eyes in an effort to concentrate my thoughts on our home life, but as usual I find it impossible to visualise the three of us together.

'I don't remember him ever laying a finger on her,' I say. 'Although I have huge gaps in my memory regarding Mia. It's possible that I just blocked them out because I felt guilty for not being able to protect my little girl better.'

'This is really important, Sophie,' she says, staring intently into my eyes. 'If there is even the smallest possibility that Mia is at risk of physical abuse while she's in her father's care, we can apply to have her removed and placed in social care for her safety.'

I'm not sure what social care entails, but the thought of my daughter being forcibly removed from her home seems a little extreme. I wish I'd been able to see Mia yesterday to reassure myself that she's being well cared for; at least Liv will see her this afternoon and be able to report back. I'd rather nothing was done to upset Mia prior to that though.

'I'm fairly sure Polly wouldn't let her come to any harm. My sister-in-law, Liv, the one who arranged for us to meet,' I explain, 'says she's a really nice girl.'

'And Polly is who?' Natasha asks, her pen poised over her big blue book to note it down. 'A live-in nanny?'

'No. I was getting around to telling you about Polly. She's Tom's new wife. Apparently, he remarried six months after my funeral.'

To say that Natasha raises her eyebrows would be an understatement. They positively shoot up as she scribbles down this latest piece of information. 'He didn't waste much time in finding a replacement for you.'

'No,' I agree.

'It's not against the law – at least it wouldn't have been if you'd actually been dead, but, of course, he didn't know that you weren't. However, it could be construed that he wasn't really grieving your passing, which may work in our favour as we try to build a case of abuse against him,' she says, tapping her pen against her notebook as though deep in thought.

'What will happen to their marriage?'

'Good question and not one that comes up very often. He can't be married to two people at once and, as you're not actually dead, he is in theory still married to you, making his current marriage null and void. But if the Spanish police gave him reason to believe that you'd died, I doubt criminal charges would be brought against him. Do you know what proof they gave him?'

'Liv told me that my bag washed up on the beach a week after the accident. It had my passport in it, so although a body was never recovered, it was enough to presume my death and proceed with funeral arrangements.'

'In that case, he didn't do anything wrong. It just seems a bit soon to have met and married someone else. The most likely course of action is for him to divorce you and then remarry his new wife, assuming she'll still want to marry him.'

'What do you mean?'

'In my experience, the type of behaviour you describe Tom as subjecting you to would probably be repeated in subsequent relationships. Once Tom has won the object he desires, his behaviour changes and he becomes possessive to the point of obsession. I think that's what happened with you and Tom and I wouldn't be surprised to learn that his new wife has found herself in a similar position. It might be worth trying to find out,' she says, fixing me with a pointed look and raising her perfectly groomed brows again, but more in an unspoken question this time.

This takes me by surprise. I was worried that Natasha would suggest that I keep my distance from Tom and his family for the time being, which is why I was so anxious to see Mia the previous afternoon. Yet here she is, if my understanding is correct, suggesting that I make contact with Polly.

'Liv has arranged to have coffee with Polly this afternoon,' I say, which is met with more eyebrow action. 'Do you think I should tag along?'

'I can't advise you to do that,' she says. She surreptitiously glances down at her watch, as our appointment has overrun by several minutes already. 'But if you wanted to tag along, as you put it, I don't see that as a problem.' She gets to her feet, signalling that our meeting is over, and I follow her over to the door. 'I'll be in touch once I've got something to share and I'd appreciate if you'd do the same.'

Walking down the front steps of the imposing Georgian building, I can't help thinking that I've struck it lucky with Natasha

Swann. Not only did I really warm to her, and have total trust that she is doing all the right things legally, she also seems to be pretty au fait with personality disorders such as Tom's. Part of me is wondering whether that's in a professional capacity or a personal one; either way, it definitely feels as though she is on my side.

Liv has done a great job in finding Natasha, which I'm sure she'll be pleased to hear. But as I approach the car park where Liv has been parked up waiting for me, I'm not quite so sure she'll be happy with the idea of me going with her to talk to Polly. I'll have to broach the subject carefully.

'So how did it go?' she asks the moment I open the car door.

'Natasha was brilliant. To be honest, I thought she was a bit abrupt on the phone yesterday, but having met her, I think it's just her eagerness to get things done,' I say. 'She'd already informed the authorities about me arriving in the country on Grace's passport and has started an application for a new one after our phone conversation yesterday. And she's arranged an appointment with a psychoanalyst friend of hers for tomorrow morning.'

'Wow. It sounds as though she's really on the case,' Liv says.

'She seems super-efficient. How did you find her? Was it a personal recommendation or just good fortune?'

'I remembered her name being mentioned by one of the women I work with when her husband was threatened with deportation. It turned out to be a computer error in the end, but Natasha managed to get them some compensation for all the stress caused. I thought she might be the best person to help. Do you want to nip into Fuego for a bite to eat or shall we just head back to mine?'

Much as I want to revisit one of our favourite haunts, I'm nervous about being recognised, particularly as I'm with Liv. I can't risk anyone seeing us, putting two and two together and mentioning it to Tom. When he does eventually find out that I'm alive, I want to be in control of the situation.

I glance down at my hands; they're shaking. It makes me angry that even from a distance Tom has the ability to frighten me. Hopefully my session tomorrow with the psychoanalyst will explain why and also start to build a case against him so I can get Mia back.

'Actually, Liv, I think I'd prefer to be out in public as little as possible. And if my memory serves me right, Fuego is rammed at lunchtime. We don't want to be late getting to Polly's.'

'We? You can't come with me, Sophie. The purpose of calling around for coffee is for me to make sure that Mia is okay, isn't it?'

Damn! That's not the way I intended suggesting that I accompany her.

'Yes, of course. But Natasha seemed to think that Polly might be enduring similar psychological abuse to what I went through with Tom. She suggested I should contact her and try to find out. She said it might help build the case against him.'

I can see Liv's knuckles turning white as her grip tightens on the steering wheel. Until now, I'm not sure Liv has really considered how damaging my accusations might be. It wouldn't only have an effect on his private life, it would impact on his veterinary business too, which could in turn affect Jamie.

'I'm not sure I can go through with this,' she whispers. 'I don't want to be forced to choose sides between you and my brother.'

'You're not choosing sides; this isn't the school playground. I loved Tom as much as you do, if not more, but he almost succeeded in destroying me. If I hadn't taken hold of the lifeline I was thrown when that train careered off the rails, I wouldn't be here now talking to you. I'm pretty sure I was at the end of my tether and would have done almost anything to stop the nightmare. You remember I told you about the flashback I have where I'm holding a knife?' Liv doesn't answer, so I carry on. 'I'm not sure whether I was planning to use that on Tom or myself. Either way, I wouldn't be sitting in this car with you now. I'd either be buried in my grave for real or I'd be serving life for killing my husband.'

Liv leans forward to rest her head on her hands on the top of the steering wheel. I can't imagine what she must be thinking. My words sounded dramatic, even to my ears, but they were the truth. I don't know all the details yet, but I do know I suffered terribly. If Natasha is right and Polly is now locked into that same nightmare, it's my duty to try to save her before it's too late.

'Liv? Talk to me.'

Slowly she turns her head.

'What if you're wrong?' she asks. 'What if you'd fallen out of love with Tom and your mind made up these stories, these... these half memories to excuse your actions in stealing Grace's life and abandoning your child? I've taken everything you've told me at face value, believing that my own brother could treat you badly, but what if that's not how it was at all?'

'I promise you I'm telling the truth as I remember it.'

'I only have your word for that,' she says, her voice raised, her eyes glinting in anger. 'You keep claiming that you suddenly remember things, but what if you're using me, playing me for a fool and pitting me against my own brother just so that you can steal Mia away from him after he's been caring for her these past three years. How do I know you're telling me the truth?' she shrieks, pushing her face towards mine in an action that is scarily reminiscent of Tom. 'For all I know, Polly and Tom are blissfully happy, and you're so jealous at the thought of it that you want to march in there and smash their happiness to smithereens because you couldn't find that same happiness after Mia was born. I can't let you do it, Sophie. I don't want to hear you make any more accusations about Tom until after your psychoanalyst session and we have a better idea if what you are remembering is the truth. It's your turn to choose now. Either I visit Polly alone, as planned, or I cancel this afternoon all together.'

I feel crushed. I suppose I should have expected some kind of reaction from Liv at some point, but this outburst has sent me reeling. I have no one else I can turn to. Jamie doesn't really want me staying with them but is tolerating me because Liv has faith in my story. If she stops believing in me, I have nowhere else to go. The really awful thing is, I'm half wondering if she's right and my crazy head has invented all the bad memories. Seeing the analyst may or may not help me regain my memory, but that could take weeks or even months. By then Tom will know that I didn't die in Spain because he will have had legal notice about his marriage being invalid. If I am right and he is slightly unhinged, there is no knowing what he might do to our daughter as punishment for me daring to leave him.

I'm taking deep breaths and trying to think clearly. I simply don't know what to do for the best.

'Well,' Liv says, holding her mobile phone up, 'what's it to be? Do I cancel or do I go and make sure Mia is safe and while I'm there try to find out if things are okay between Polly and Tom?' Her voice is calm now, in fact totally devoid of emotion.

'Let's leave the plan as it was,' I manage to say. 'I-I didn't realise how much this whole situation was upsetting you. I'm sorry.'

Without speaking, she drops her phone back in her bag, turns the key in the ignition and backs out of the parking space.

'You will tell me if you suspect that Mia is not being treated well, won't you?' I ask, my voice quivering.

'Of course; what kind of a monster do you take me for?'

I say nothing. One monster in the family is more than enough. Liv is not like her brother.

CHAPTER 28

Liv

Thursday afternoon

While Sophie was at her appointment with Natasha Swann this morning, I popped into The Bee's Knees on Oxted High Street. It's one of those shops that sells a delightful mix of greetings cards, candles, decorative mugs and other quirky gift ideas. They also have some beautiful traditional games and toys for children. I love browsing in there just for the sake of it, so it was nice to have an actual purpose for a change.

I selected a fifty-piece wooden jigsaw puzzle, apparently suitable for up to eight-year-olds, depicting a unicorn trotting along a sparkling path through a magical kingdom, with a little girl at its side. The child had long red hair, woven through with flowers, but I didn't think Mia would mind too much that the colour of the girl's hair wasn't the same as her own. Astrid, who owns the shop and greeted me as a regular, offered to gift-wrap it for me, but I declined, not wanting to confuse Mia into thinking it might be her birthday.

After pulling into Tom and Polly's driveway, I reach for the gold and black striped bag and climb out of the car. Astrid insisted on the fancy bag, which she wouldn't let me pay for, and also put tissue paper around the puzzle. 'Part of the fun of receiving a gift, whatever the occasion, is the anticipation of what might be inside,' she said. I'm not sure if the experience is quite the same for a five-year-old, but there seemed to be little point arguing with her.

I've calmed down after my outburst earlier. In fact, I'm feeling a bit guilty about rounding on Sophie the way I did. However confused I am about the situation, it must be twice as bad for her and until she contacts her mum and dad she has no one to talk to apart from me and Jamie, and we don't mention Tom in front of him. I've suggested she call her parents tonight. Fingers crossed, they are still on the same number.

Just as before, when Jamie and I came here for dinner, Polly already has the front door open in a welcoming gesture. The difference this time is that Mia is standing by her side, holding on to the folds of fabric in Polly's midi-length skirt, and peering at me shyly from behind it.

My heart lurches. Was it really too much to ask for Sophie to come with me this afternoon? She must be desperate to see Mia and I've denied her that pleasure.

I push my guilty feelings away and plaster a smile on my face as I stride across the gravel driveway towards them.

'Hello, Polly,' I say, kissing the air next to her cheeks. 'What a lovely skirt. You have such fabulous fashion sense.'

I'm not lying just to pay her a compliment. I've always considered myself to be reasonably stylish, but next to Polly I feel positively dowdy.

'Thanks, Liv. I can't take the credit though. It was a birthday present from Tom.'

My mind starts to race. Have I forgotten Polly's birthday?

As if she's read my thoughts, she adds, 'I couldn't get into it back in October, but I've slimmed down a bit since then.'

With her sentence, she has quashed the fear that I forgot her birthday but also alerted me to the fact that she is indeed very slim; almost too thin. I can't help wondering if the weight loss is deliberate or the result of something else.

'You remember Auntie Liv, don't you, Mia?' Polly asks, directing the attention away from herself.

'This can't be Mia,' I say, feigning surprise. 'This young lady is far too tall to be my niece.' I look her up and down in examination. It allows me to check for any signs of physical abuse and I'm relieved to see there aren't any, at least not visible ones.

Mia releases the skirt from her grasp and announces proudly, 'I'm five and a half. I'm a big girl now.'

Although she is no longer holding on to Polly, Mia is still firmly gripping a teddy bear in her other hand. Albert bear was a first-birthday present from Jamie and me and for a moment I wonder if she's chosen to hold him because she knew I was coming around. On closer inspection, I can see Mr Albert is a bit on the bald side, where he has obviously been hugged a lot over the years. It makes my heart sing to think she has gained comfort from cuddling him, but is a reminder that I would have known how fond of him Mia was if I'd been around her more.

'Come on, Albie, let's show Auntie Liv the tea party we're having in her honour,' Mia says.

Although her voice is high-pitched and childlike, her words sound very grown-up.

I follow her into the hallway and then through the kitchen and into the conservatory, where a wicker table is set with four places. For one awful moment I think that maybe Tom is home until Mia settles her teddy into one of the chairs and ties a bib around his neck before climbing up onto the chair next to him.

I'm grateful that because of the disagreement with Sophie I wasn't able to eat much at lunch; the table is crowded with plates of sandwiches cut into fingers, biscuits and cakes.

'This all looks lovely,' I say. 'You shouldn't have gone to so much trouble.'

'It was all Mia's idea,' Polly replies, sliding into the chair on the other side of Albert bear. 'She got very excited this morning when I said you were coming to visit because you'd heard she wasn't feeling well.'

'Are you feeling a bit better today, Mia?' I ask, taking the final seat at the table. She does look quite pale, which is understandable if she hasn't been well, but that apart, there are no outward signs to indicate that she isn't well looked after.

'Yes, but Albie's still got a cough,' she says, making a small coughing sound and patting him on his back. 'Polly thinks we need to stay off school tomorrow as well, just to be on the safe side.'

Again, her words sound very adult for a five-year-old, making me wonder if she mixes much with other children of her age outside school.

'Would you like tea or coffee?' Polly asks, opening the lid on a box of tea and coffee sachets and offering it in my direction. There is one of those vacuum flask jugs that you get at business conferences on the table between us, which I'm assuming is filled with hot water.

'Me and Albie are having tea,' Mia says, picking up her plastic teapot and pouring what looks suspiciously like orange squash into the cups in front of her and her bear.

'Then I shall have tea too,' I say, selecting a sachet that has the words English Breakfast Tea printed on it.

Mia beams up at me before reaching for one of the sandwiches and taking a bite. I'm no expert when it comes to children, but if Mia is unhappy or afraid in her surroundings, she certainly isn't exhibiting any sign of it. In fact, she looks so happy and content that I'm starting to feel quite uncomfortable about the consequences her mother's reappearance in her life might have. I'm responsible for what is to be unleashed and I'd be lying if I said I'm not getting increasingly nervous about the outcome.

After our tea party, I hand Mia the stripy bag from The Bee's Knees and her eyes light up when she tears off the tissue paper and sees the unicorn jigsaw. We clear the magazines off the coffee table in the lounge and spend a very happy hour carefully selecting the pieces to create the frame, before filling in the middle of the puzzle. By the time we finish, Mia is yawning, so Polly takes her up to her bedroom for a nap, while I put the pieces back in the box ready for the next time she wants to do it. I'm just putting the lid on when Polly comes back into the lounge.

'Thanks, Liv,' she says. 'Mia is one happy, if sleepy, little girl right now. She asked when you're coming again because she and Mr Albert enjoyed your company so much.'

'That is such an adult thing to say. She's more like a miniature grown-up than a child.'

'I know what you mean; she's always coming out with stuff like that.'

'What do her friends make of it?' I ask.

'I don't know. She doesn't talk about school much.'

'I meant when they come here; they don't tease her, do they?'

A cloud passes across Polly's pretty features.

'She doesn't really have friends at the house. Tom's not keen on having kids running around shrieking and breaking things,' she says, shrugging her shoulders.

'That's a shame,' I say, 'particularly as she's an only child. It must be quite lonely for her, not having anyone to play with.'

'I think that's why she's so attached to Albert bear; he's like a playmate for her. You saw what she's like with him, chatting and then answering in his voice. It drives Tom crazy; he doesn't like her walking around with him because he says it's too babyish, so most days Mr Albert goes to bed before Tom gets home from work.'

A little shiver runs through me. Mia is five. I still used to talk to my teddy and cry into his fur if I was upset when I was eighteen. I even considered taking him on our gap year, until Sophie pointed out that he would get pretty grubby with some of the places we were going to be staying. It seems a bit harsh that a five-year-old isn't allowed to have her teddy bear for company, especially if she's not permitted to have real friends in the house either. I can't help wondering if maybe Polly came up with the compromise of Mr Albert 'going to bed' to prevent Tom from throwing him out altogether. Maybe Sophie isn't exaggerating my brother's controlling behaviour after all.

'And how about you, Polly?'

'Oh, I think it's quite sweet, particularly when she reads him a bedtime story,' Polly says, the corners of her eyes crinkling as she smiles at the thought.

'That's not actually what I meant,' I say. 'I was wondering if Tom allows you to have friends around?'

Polly's eyes take on a *deer in the headlights* look. She seems startled that I would have the front to ask such a question.

'Of course he does,' she begins defensively. 'At least, he would if I had any, but I've kind of lost touch with most of my friends since Tom and I got married.'

'Really? Even the girls from the practice who were bridesmaids at your wedding?'

'Tom said that me socialising with them could make things a bit awkward if he needed to reprimand them,' she says, her cheeks colouring slightly. 'I can see his point.'

I can feel my heart rate increasing. I feel indignant on Polly's behalf that my brother would think it's acceptable to expect his new wife to give up her friends, wherever they worked, just as he'd apparently forced Sophie to see less and less of Grace and me.

'Besides, I'm too busy looking after Mia most of the time. Not that I mind, of course,' Polly rushes on. 'She's an adorable little thing. And then there's the house to keep clean and tidy and Tom's dinner to make when he gets back from work, particularly if he's been on evening surgery. The last thing he'd want is to get home to a house full of chattering women.'

It's like I'm listening to a Stepford Wife. It's as though Polly has had her brain removed and replaced with a computer which has been programmed to serve Tom.

'Can you hear yourself?' I ask.

'Sorry?'

'You're talking as if your only function in life is to do whatever your husband bids. I wouldn't allow Jamie to treat me like that. Actually, no – no, I take that back. Jamie wouldn't want me to be subservient. Marriage is a partnership, not a dictatorship. Tom shouldn't expect you to give up everything outside of this house; it's not fair. Please don't try to tell me you're happy with the way things are, because I simply can't believe it.'

Polly's blinking furiously. I'm not sure if it's the shock of hearing a few home truths or if she's fighting back tears.

I take a step towards her, but she holds her hand up to keep me at a distance.

'I think you should leave now,' she manages to say in a strangled voice.

'Polly, please…' I start to say.

'No, really, I think you've said enough.'

I pick up my handbag and head towards the front door. I can't understand how the women in Tom's life seem to accept this kind of controlling behaviour as normal.

'Are you going to tell Tom what I said?' I ask.

'I don't know,' she replies, 'but please don't come here uninvited again.' She closes the door firmly behind me almost before I'm through it.

I can feel blood pulsing in my veins as I crunch across the gravel back to my car. My hands are shaking as I press the button on my key fob to unlock it. As I'm opening the driver's door, a movement in an upstairs window catches my eye. Perhaps our voices were louder than we thought, or maybe Mia wasn't as tired as she appeared. Either way, she is standing at her bedroom window holding Albert bear.

I raise my hand to wave goodbye and she reciprocates by moving her teddy-bear's paw up and down. The action brings a lump to my throat. Whatever doubts I may have had surrounding Sophie's version of her life with my brother have been swept away. Polly's reaction to my questions, defending and making excuses for Tom, has set alarm bells ringing. She's clearly very fond of my niece and feels protective towards her, but how much abuse would Polly be prepared to endure before she felt compelled to run, just as Sophie had done three and a half years previously?

I pull out of the driveway without a backward glance. I need to get home and talk things through with Sophie before Jamie gets back from work. Now that I've voiced my concerns, Polly might examine Tom's behaviour through new eyes. If she realises that it's not acceptable, she could pack her bags, and where would that leave Mia? My priority has to be the safety and happiness of my niece and, dreadful as it might sound, I'm not sure either of those would be best served if she was in the sole care of my brother.

CHAPTER 29

Sophie

Thursday afternoon

The bathwater is barely tepid, and the bubbles have long since dispersed, hardly surprising as I've been in the tub for the best part of an hour.

After clearing away the soup bowls, which in both Liv and my case meant pouring most of it down the sink as neither of us was hungry after our disagreement in the car, I rinsed them and left them to drain. I went upstairs to my room and sat on the bed for a while, trying to decide whether I should write to Luis. I've checked my phone regularly since arriving back in England, but he hasn't messaged me. It's hard to take since we've been virtually inseparable for three and a half years. In the end, I concluded that nothing has really changed in terms of the ultimatum he gave me and the choice I made, so there's very little to say that he hasn't already heard.

In an attempt to take my mind off the life I'm missing in Mexico, I opted for a relaxing bubble bath. I derived a few moments of pleasure from unscrewing the various colourful bottles of bathing gels that Liv has lined up on the shelf and sniffing the exotic-sounding aromas, trying to choose which I should soak in. Tempted as I was to go for something with lavender, as it's known for its calming properties, I selected one called ocean breeze. As the bathroom filled with the fresh ozone fragrance, I was transported back to Mexico and the life I thought was going to be mine forever. Then an altogether different memory forced its way into my head. The bath of our en-suite in Hailsham Crescent was full of water and I was kneeling in it. Tom had hold of my hair at the nape of my neck and I was choking. He appeared to be shaking as he glared at me with dark angry eyes, but nowhere near as much as I was at the memory. It took me several minutes before I felt calm enough to step into the bath without fear of my legs buckling beneath me. I inhaled deeply, closed my eyes and sank down into the hot water, allowing it to engulf me in a warm hug.

I must have fallen asleep because I've only just got out of the bath and am drying myself when I hear the front door slam and Liv calling out my name. I could be mistaken, but she sounds agitated.

'Up here, Liv,' I reply, wriggling into my jeans and throwing a jumper over my head.

I open the bathroom door and she launches herself at me, almost knocking me over with the force of the hug she wraps me in.

'I'm so sorry I doubted you. He's doing the same to Polly as he did to you. It's like history is repeating itself. The weird thing is, she either can't or won't see it,' Liv says, the words rushing out of her mouth at a hundred miles an hour. 'At least you recognised what he was doing was unacceptable and realised you had to get away, but Polly is either too scared of him to say anything or she genuinely doesn't see anything wrong with how he is treating her.'

'Slow down,' I say. I push her gently away from me and hold her at arm's length. 'Let's go downstairs and get a cup of tea and you can tell me exactly what happened.'

'Yes; yes, that's a good idea,' she replies, seeming slightly calmer now that she has unburdened herself.

'Did you see Mia?' I ask, leading the way down the stairs. While I want to know exactly what happened to change Liv's mind about

Tom, my priority is to make sure that Mia is all right. 'Did she seem okay?'

'Actually, she did. She loved the jigsaw I bought for her and she appeared to be completely relaxed in Polly's company.'

I'm not sure how that makes me feel. Obviously, it's a relief to know that my daughter is being looked after by someone who she clearly cares for, but I'm finding it difficult to suppress pangs of jealousy. It should be me looking after Mia, not a lookalike Tom married to replace me.

I immediately feel even worse for making that assumption. For all I know, he could have fallen head over heels in love with Polly, as he did with me in the beginning.

There's no doubt that Tom adored me for the first couple of years we were together, particularly when I got back after being away at uni. He was surprisingly demonstrative in public, so much so that our friends would often say, 'get a room, you two'. Once he'd put an engagement ring on my finger, he wanted to spend more and more time with me without our friends around, which, although I'd found endearing at the time, could have been the start of him trying to control my life.

I flick the switch on the kettle, having settled Liv in the lounge, and suddenly a vivid flashback of him shouting at me fills my mind. *You promised in front of our friends and family to obey me. Why can't you just do what you agreed? How many other promises are you going to break?* I don't remember what we were arguing about, but I do remember those blazing eyes as he pushed his face as close to mine as he could without actually touching me.

I'm trembling so much at the memory that I have to take some deep breaths and hold on to the work surface to steady myself. I drop my face onto the cool quartz to try to ease the blazing heat in my cheeks. How can someone who presents themself to the world as kind and amiable be so different behind closed doors? Tom's a real Dr Jekyll and Mr Hyde character and it seems Liv has now realised that too after spending a couple of hours with Polly. I ought to be feeling vindicated, but I'm too consumed with worry for Mia. What if Liv confronting Polly about Tom's behaviour forces her to reassess her situation? What if she decides to pack her bags and leave?

I make two mugs of tea and carry them through to the lounge, where I sit down on the sofa opposite Liv. She cups her hands around her mug and takes a sip even though the liquid is scalding hot.

'What happened, Liv?' I ask gently.

She raises her eyes and I can see she is struggling with her conscience. Liv has always adored and looked up to her big brother. In her eyes, he could do no wrong, so this must be torturous for her.

'Everything was fine while Mia was with us. We had a lovely tea party, with the teddy I bought her on her first birthday as the fourth guest at our table, before playing with her new jigsaw. When she started yawning, Polly took her up to bed for a nap. It was only when Polly came back down that some of the things she was saying began to ring alarm bells.'

'Such as what?' I ask, immediately feeling anxious.

'Tom doesn't let Mia have friends come to the house and he doesn't like her to talk to her teddy in his presence.'

The nails of my free hand are digging into my thigh. She's an only child, just as I was. My parents were always inviting my friends around to our house to play to prevent me from feeling lonely or isolated. And as for talking to my teddy, I'm pretty sure I was still doing that well into my teens, although I had no desire to take him on our gap-year travels and had a devil of a job to persuade Liv not to take hers. Although I think his attitude is selfish, not understanding that Mia would benefit from some company of her own age, it's not exactly a reason for alarm bells to be sounding.

'What else did Polly say to make you feel so concerned?' I demand. 'He doesn't smack her, does he, or lock her in her room if she's been misbehaving?'

'No, she didn't say anything like that. To be honest, I can't imagine Mia misbehaving. She's more like a miniature adult than a child.'

'Well, what then?'

Liv runs her finger around the rim of her mug. 'It's not only Mia who isn't allowed to have friends around to the house,' she says. 'Tom seems to want to prevent Polly from having contact with anyone but him. The exception is the school run, but Mia told me while we were doing her jigsaw that Polly always parks closest to the school gates and waits in the car for her. It could just be Polly being lazy or unsociable, but she didn't strike me as either. What if Tom has forbidden her from mixing with the other parents?'

A shiver runs down my spine. I'd started to question whether I'd deliberately mis-remembered him being so controlling towards me because I'd fallen out of love with him but was too weak to leave him. Hearing these things about his relationship with Polly has reaffirmed my initial belief: Tom needs to be in control of the people closest to him. It's as though he can't allow them any freedom, because he's afraid he might lose them. Trust is the foundation of any relationship and without it the cracks quickly start to appear.

I learned trust at a very early age. My dad used to take me to my swimming lessons on a Saturday morning because my mum couldn't swim and didn't like being in such close proximity to deep water. He would use my thirty-minute lesson time to have a swim, while I was being taught in the shallow end. Although I was comfortable in the water wearing armbands, I resolutely refused to put my head below the surface and the teacher said that was why I hadn't learned to swim yet.

After one lesson, shortly before my fourth birthday, I remember handing my armbands to the teacher, but instead of heading for the changing rooms as we usually did, Dad took my hand and walked me down the side of the pool. The deeper the water got, the darker the colour became and even holding his hand I'd felt increasingly nervous walking along at the side of it. Just before we got to the metal ladder leading down into the water, my dad stopped, dropped to his haunches so that he was at my eye level, and said, 'Do you trust me, Sophie?' It's funny how I can picture it so clearly when other parts of my memory are so patchy. I remember nodding. 'Good,' he said. 'I want you to stand here like a statue with your toes up to the edge while I get into the pool and then, when I tell you to, I want you to jump into the water. Can you do that?'

Although I was terrified and it took a few minutes of encouragement from him before I'd finally been persuaded to take that leap of faith, I felt a sense of freedom in those few seconds that I was airborne, totally trusting that my dad would never let anything bad happen to me. He allowed me to sink beneath the surface of the water momentarily, but I was able to feel his strong hands around my waist as he raised me back to the surface, saying, 'Brave girl.' I took a few strokes without armbands in my next lesson and was awarded my first certificate for swimming a width of the pool a few weeks later. I've been a confident swimmer ever since and used to really enjoy swimming in the sea next to Luis, with Vince keeping pace along the shoreline.

Of course, I wasn't aware at the time that my dad's actions were more about teaching me to have trust in others than learning how to swim. It saddens me to think that Mia may not be learning those important life lessons. Both my parents were responsible for the confident, independent person I became, which makes it even worse that Tom could undermine the values they instilled in me so completely. I'm also pretty sure neither of them would ever have tried to stop me from talking to my teddy bear. Come to think of it, my dad used to do Big Ted's growly voice when I was very young, and I actually believed it was Big Ted speaking. It breaks my heart that Mia may be missing out on those special moments that become cherished memories in adulthood. I can't let him deprive her of it; I won't.

'What are you thinking?' Liv asks, breaking into my thoughts.

What I'm really thinking is that I want to go straight around to my old house and remove my daughter from it, but common sense tells me this isn't an option. Not only am I pretty sure that Polly wouldn't just step aside and allow a woman she has never met before to barge her way in and leave with her stepdaughter, I'm also fearful of what Tom would do to Polly if he were to arrive home and find Mia gone.

'I think we need to share all this with Natasha Swann,' I say instead. 'She suspected that Tom might be treating Polly the same way that he treated me, and from what you've just told me, I'd say she's spot on. I wonder if it's too late to call her?'

'You should at least try,' Liv suggests. 'I don't think Mia is in any imminent danger, but there's simply no way of knowing how Tom will react when he finds out that you're not dead after all, and that you're back home.'

'You didn't tell Polly I'm alive, did you?' I ask, feeling panicky.

'Of course not, but he's going to receive the letter from Natasha's office in the next couple of days. If he were to suspect that you've come back to try to take Mia away from him, who knows what he might do.'

Liv's words scare me. Up until now, she has been prepared to defend her brother, trying to see things from both points of view, searching for reasonable explanations. If she's questioning Tom's behaviour, she must be really worried.

'You don't think he'd hurt Mia, do you?'

'I was actually thinking more of cases where fathers go on the run with their child rather than face the prospect of losing them. Tom will be afraid that a court might award custody to you as they always tend to favour the mother. He'll be scared about you explaining what drove you away in the first place. You could have stayed dead if you'd chosen to and he'll realise that, but you've come back to face the music. It won't take him long to work out that the only feasible reason is your desire to be reunited with Mia.'

As Liv is talking, I'm dialling Natasha Swann's number. The sooner she knows what is going on with Tom and Polly, the sooner she can decide on a course of action. It rings out four times and then goes to voicemail. I briefly explain what Liv discovered and ask her to call me back as soon as she gets the message.

'What do I do now?' I ask.

'We wait until she gets back to us.'

Liv using the word 'we' rather than 'you' means a lot to me. She has already gone out on a limb by inviting me to stay with her and Jamie, especially as Jamie is being forced to keep my existence from his best friend. But by using the word we, she has acknowledged that she believes Tom is responsible for the current situation and that she is going to help me fight to win any battle there may be for Mia, even though it will mean going against her own brother.

'I've missed you, Liv,' I say. 'Once I'd got back to Grace's apartment in Spain and the full implication of taking her identity dawned on me, I almost couldn't go ahead with my plan. The thought of never seeing you again or hearing your voice, and never sharing another secret with you or laughing at some stupid joke together, had me questioning whether I could go through with it. But my fear of Tom was greater. He stole everything from me: my child, my parents, my best friend, but most of all he stole the happy-go-lucky person I was. I was existing, nothing more, and I couldn't have gone on like that for much longer.' I can't stop my tears from leaking. 'I'll never be able to repay you for returning to Mexico and forcing me to face up to reality.'

She's by my side in an instant, her arms enveloping me, telling me that everything is going to be okay, just as she had when she was pressing her hands onto my arm to stem the flow of blood all those years ago. Liv is the closest thing to a sister I've ever known.

It's unimaginable to me now that we are reunited that I could have contemplated living the rest of my life without her in it.

We're still locked in a close embrace when we hear Jamie's key in the front door. Liv pulls away and raises her finger to her lips before heading out into the hall to greet her husband, who she expertly steers in the direction of the kitchen, giving me the opportunity to slip upstairs to my room until I feel able to face him. The phone call to my parents will have to wait until I'm feeling less drained. I want to be able to talk to them without dissolving into floods of tears and, tonight, I don't think I'm capable of that.

CHAPTER 30

Liv

Thursday evening

Jamie has shot me a few questioning looks throughout dinner. He's tried to engage Sophie in conversation, but she's been pretty monosyllabic. In the end, we all fall into an uneasy silence, broken only by the sound of cutlery against plates. When Jamie's mobile phone rings just as he is laying his knife and fork side by side on his plate, he uses it as an excuse to remove himself from the table, saying, 'What's up, mate?' as he heads towards the hall.

Sophie's eyes follow him. As he pulls the door to, she turns back to me. 'Do you think that's Tom?' she whispers.

'Maybe,' I reply. 'But Jamie has quite a few friends he calls "mate", so let's not go jumping to any conclusions.'

I don't know if Sophie was intending to finish her dinner, but that's clearly not going to happen now. I'm quite glad I resorted to defrosting something from the freezer rather than preparing something from scratch as the effort would have been wasted tonight.

I'm stacking the dishes to take through to the kitchen when Jamie comes back into the room.

'That was Tom,' he says.

It's a good job Sophie has her back to Jamie, so he doesn't see the panic register in her eyes.

'Everything all right?' I ask, keeping my tone light and conversational.

'I think so,' Jamie replies. 'He asked if you could give him a call back when I said that we were just finishing eating dinner. What's that about, Liv?'

For a moment I wonder if something has happened to Mum, but then Jamie continues.

'He said you called in to see Polly and Mia today. Were you going to mention it to me? I felt a bit of an idiot admitting I didn't know anything about it.'

'Sorry, Jamie. I'm just trying to be friendlier towards Polly, like you suggested. You don't normally want to know who I'm meeting up with for coffee.'

'No, of course not. It's just that this is an...' he pauses briefly, 'unusual situation. It's difficult for me seeing Tom at work and being unable to tell him that not only is his first wife back from the dead, but she's living under our roof. I hope the sudden interest in making friends with Polly is genuine, and not just you snooping around.'

Sophie pushes her chair back from the table.

'I'll take those,' she says, reaching for the stack of plates. 'And then I think I'll go up to bed, if you don't mind, I've got a bit of a headache.'

'Of course we don't mind. It's probably still jet lag,' I suggest, although I'm pretty sure it isn't. 'See you in the morning.'

'Night, Jamie,' she mutters as he holds the door open for her.

I take my time gathering up the place mats and drinks coasters and putting them in the drawer of the big old dresser that takes up most of the wall opposite our patio doors. It was my grandmother's, and nobody wanted it after she died, which I thought was quite sad. To be fair, it was an ugly piece of furniture in the original dark brown stain, but once I'd decided to claim it, I set about sanding it down and painting it duck-egg blue. It's now much-admired by people when they come to dinner at our house.

It's not long before I hear Sophie's footsteps going up the stairs, my cue to ring my brother back.

'Shall we go through to the lounge? My phone's in there. I'll put it on speaker if you like?'

Jamie shrugs, but follows me into the front room nevertheless. I was planning on telling him about my visit with Polly and Mia when we were in bed later as he's always more receptive to things when we're snuggled up close. Tom has put paid to that with his phone call, so having it on speaker is the next best course of action to reassure Jamie that I wasn't hiding anything.

I dial and it's picked up on the second ring.

'Hi Tom, it's me,' I say.

'Thanks for calling me back, Liv. Just a quickie really.' There's a pause, which I allow to hang in the air as I'm in no rush to offer any information. 'So, I was just wondering about the reason for your impromptu visit today, or had you already organised it with Polly?'

His voice sounds light and friendly, but I'm not fooled. He obviously wants to know if it was prearranged and, if so, why Polly hadn't told him about it in advance. I need to tread carefully because I don't know what she's said to him. When I called her yesterday, Polly had said not to mention it to Tom, so I'm in a tricky position. I decide it's safest to stick with what I've already said to Jamie and hope that Tom isn't too persistent.

'You and Jamie both seemed quite keen for Polly and me to get to know each other better. It was okay to pop in, wasn't it?'

'Yes, of course, although I'm not sure if she was up to it really. Mia's been off school for a couple of days with some bug or other, and Polly's gone up to bed early saying she doesn't feel too great. Whatever it is, I hope you won't come down with it.'

'It's nice of you to be concerned,' I say, 'but you know me, I've got the constitution of an ox. I'm sure I'll be fine.'

'Maybe it would be best to ring me first to ask about any future arrangements,' he says. 'Polly probably felt she couldn't refuse in case you thought she was snubbing you, even if she wasn't feeling a hundred per cent.'

'Okay, I'll bear that in mind,' I say.

After the way things were left with Polly earlier, with her virtually throwing me out of the house, I'm wondering if she's asked Tom to request that all future visits be arranged via him. I still can't comprehend how anyone can allow themselves to be under such close scrutiny from their partner.

'I hope they both feel better soon,' I add. 'Let us know if there's anything we can do to help.'

'That's kind of you to offer. You certainly made quite an impression on Mia today, bringing her the jigsaw. She really enjoyed the tea party too.'

He's clearly fishing for information. For the first time since he answered my call, I get the impression that he doesn't actually believe that I dropped in on the off-chance. Maybe it was something Polly said, or possibly Mia. Polly mentioned that the tea party was Mia's idea after she'd told her I was going to be calling in, so she might have let it slip to her dad. Whatever Tom thinks my motive was for today's visit, I'm pretty sure he has no idea about Sophie, or he wouldn't be this calm. It does raise the question of how he will react when he finds out though.

'Sandwiches and cakes, you can't beat them for a hastily put together tea party, although I must say it was delicious.' I resist the temptation to say that Mia's teddy, Mr Albert enjoyed it too.

'She is a bit of a whizz in the kitchen, as well you know.' He's definitely referring to the Baked Alaska incident, but I also get the feeling that he's having a bit of a go at me because I'm not.

'Well, I'll let you go. Remind Jamie that he's on his own in the morning, will you? I'm going to the dentist.'

I don't want Tom to know the call has been on speaker phone, so I raise my finger to my lips to prevent Jamie from replying. I'm a fraction of a second too late.

'No worries, I've got your appointments covered,' Jamie says.

There's a slight pause from the other end of the call.

'I didn't realise you had me on speaker phone, Liv,' Tom says.

'That's not a problem, is it? Jamie and I have no secrets,' I add, unable to keep the suggestion that he does out of my voice.

There's another short pause before he says, 'Of course not; see you tomorrow, Jamie,' before terminating the call.

'What?' Jamie asks, responding to my glare. 'I'm not a mind-reader; if you didn't want him to know I was on the call too, you should have said.'

He has a point, so I drop it, mostly because I want to ask him something and I want an honest answer rather than him being on the defensive.

'Question,' I say, turning to my husband. 'Would you expect me to check with you first if I wanted to have a friend around for coffee?'

'Don't be ridiculous,' Jamie replies in a voice much louder than it needed to be. 'I'm your husband, not your jailer.'

'So, do you agree that Tom ringing to quiz me about dropping in on my niece and sister-in-law is a little odd?'

I can see the nerve twitching in Jamie's cheek that only happens when he feels backed into a corner.

'Was your visit today Sophie's idea?' he counters without answering my question.

'What if it was?'

'Can't you see what she's trying to do? She's trying to make out that Tom's not a good father,' he says, the volume of his voice increasing further. 'She ran off, leaving her child behind without a second thought, because she hit a rocky patch in her marriage. Now that she's found out her lover boy can't give her children, she's come back to take the one that she previously abandoned. It's not right, and I don't like the way she's manipulating you into believing all the shit about Tom abusing her. I've worked alongside him for nearly ten years, and he wouldn't hurt a fly; I'd stake my life on it.'

'There's more than one way to abuse people, Jamie,' I say. 'It's not all about black eyes and broken cheekbones. But Sophie did tell me that her broken wrist just after she had Mia wasn't as a result of a fall.'

He looks momentarily taken aback.

'Then why didn't she accuse him back then?' he demands. 'Funny how this whole abuse story is only surfacing now that she wants something, namely Mia. You would never have put up with me raising a hand to you, and from what you've told me about how strong and independent Sophie was, I don't believe she would either, so why on earth would you believe all this crap? If Tom had really been abusing her like she's claiming, and she didn't feel like she could confide in you, her best friend, why on earth wouldn't she have gone to the police?'

'Because I was afraid,' Sophie says.

Jamie and I turn in unison to see her standing in the doorway.

'Sophie…' I start to say, but she interrupts me.

'I think maybe it's for the best if I move into a hotel. I don't want to cause any more friction between the two of you. Would you mind calling me a cab while I go and pack?'

'There's no need for that,' Jamie says. 'I'm just struggling to understand why you couldn't have been honest at the time if this stuff was going on. If it was really as bad as you say, you should have reported Tom to the police.'

'It would have been my word against his,' Sophie replies, resignation in her voice. 'He never said or did anything in front of other people. I remember him crying like a baby after the fridge incident, but a few minutes later he was screaming at me to stick to his story about falling.'

I wince and Jamie sinks down onto the sofa, a shocked expression on his face.

'I stuck with what he told me to say, because I was scared of what he might do if I didn't,' she continues, throwing me a meaningful look. 'And as for reporting him to the police, what could they have done without any witnesses? They'd have been inclined to believe Tom, an upstanding member of the community, and then what would have happened after they left? Do you see now, Jamie, why I didn't say anything? No one would have believed me if I had.'

I look from one to the other of them. I don't want this situation to drive a wedge between me and my husband, but I do think we owe it to Sophie to get to the truth, not to mention Mia and Polly. If my brother is capable of violence, it could end in disaster, so in a way we owe it to Tom too.

'Let's get through tomorrow, Sophie,' I say, hopeful that the psychoanalyst will be able to recognise if Tom's alleged abuse is real or imagined, 'then we can discuss whether or not it's the right thing for you to stay here. Okay?'

Sophie nods from her position by the door.

'I'm sorry if it feels as though I'm doubting you,' Jamie says, fiddling with his fingers and avoiding eye contact, 'but I've known Tom all of my adult life and it's really hard for me to accept that maybe I don't really know him at all.'

I know how my husband feels, except in my case, I've known Tom for the *whole* of my life. I don't want to believe he has issues either, so for now we have to give both of them the benefit of the doubt, although, since my visit with Polly, Sophie's version of events seems more and more plausible.

To prevent further discussion, I say, 'Are we agreed then? Nobody's going anywhere tonight.'

'Agreed,' Jamie says, finally raising his gaze to connect with Sophie's.

'Thank you,' she says simply, before turning on her heel and heading back upstairs.

CHAPTER 31

Sophie

Friday morning

I haven't slept well since I arrived back in England, but last night I barely slept at all after overhearing most of Liv and Jamie's heated conversation. His raised voice drew me out onto the landing at the top of the stairs from where I eavesdropped, my heart sinking with every accusation he levelled against me. Liv tried to defend me, but it was clear that even she isn't a hundred per cent sure that everything I've told her is true. I hate myself for dragging them into the mess that was my marriage, particularly as both of them have so much history with my husband.

It's weird to think of Tom in that way; he's moved on with his life and so had I until Liv spotted me on the beach in Tulum. I wonder what the odds were of Liv choosing to sit on that particular stretch of beach, only fifty metres or so away from where Luis and I regularly went swimming. A million to one? It really feels as though fate stepped in, and while I lay awake last night, staring at the weird alien face created by the shadow of Liv's ceiling lampshade, I came to the conclusion that it wasn't only for my benefit. I could have carried on living my life, blissfully unaware that I had ever given birth to my daughter. I wouldn't be harming anyone, because all the people I cared about back home thought I was dead. So, had fate intervened for some other reason? Was the whole purpose of me returning to England less about my life and more about doing the right thing for Mia and Polly? The longer I lay there staring up at the ceiling with eyes that refused to close, the more I convinced myself that must be the case.

I hear Liv and Jamie get up around 6.30 a.m. but decide to stay out of the way until after he's left for work. I've always liked Jamie; he's honest and loyal, and has eyes that reflect what he is feeling. Knowing that he's currently unable to trust me is upsetting but understandable. I'm feeling anxious enough with what lies ahead today, so making myself scarce seems like the best option.

Although I'm not hungry, I force myself to eat the scrambled egg on toast that Liv makes when I eventually show my face just after eight; at least it means I don't have to talk very much. Afterwards, I offer to do the dishes while Liv pops out for a few groceries. Apparently, their usual online weekly shop hasn't lasted so well with me around. I make a mental note to get some of my Mexican cash changed so that I can contribute towards my upkeep. Liv would never ask, but I'll feel better if I'm paying my way. I finish the dishes and head up to the bathroom to have a shower.

I'm just lathering up my hair for a second shampoo when I hear a car door slam. I assume it's Liv back from the supermarket until I hear the doorbell ring. Even if I wasn't in the middle of taking a shower, I can't answer the front door because nobody knows I'm here. It's only when the doorbell rings again in short persistent jabs that I wonder if maybe Liv has forgotten to take her front door key. I know she took it off her keyring to have a spare one cut for me in case I needed it, so maybe she didn't pick it up in her hurry to get back before we need to leave for my appointment.

I turn off the shower, wrap the bath sheet around me and start heading for the stairs. I'm about to call out that I'm coming when I hear a second car door slam. Perhaps it wasn't Liv after all. Maybe it was the postman trying to deliver a parcel. Before I can turn to head back to the bathroom to finish my shower, I hear Liv's voice. Her words turn the blood in my veins to ice.

'Tom,' she says in an unnaturally loud voice, 'what on earth are you doing here?'

I'm at the top of the stairs, and I'm literally frozen to the spot. A few metres away on the other side of Liv's front door is the man who made my life a living hell.

'It seems you're not so keen when the boot is on the other foot,' Tom says.

'I'm sorry, I don't follow,' Liv replies, still speaking loudly.

I realise she's trying to warn me. What if I'd called out, or worse still actually answered the door? It doesn't bear thinking about.

'Why are you shouting? I'm standing a couple of metres away from you,' Tom asks.

'Am I? Must be this damn ear infection. Everything sounds as though it's at the end of a tunnel. That's why I had you on speaker phone last night,' Liv replies.

Even in the state I'm in, I am in awe at the smoothness of the lie.

'Are you going to invite me in, or are we going to continue this conversation on your doorstep?'

I hear Liv's keys jangle and then the sound of them being dropped on the floor. She's clearly trying to give me as much time as possible to make sure I'm safely out of the way. The trouble is my legs have turned to jelly and I don't trust myself to move without falling. If Tom steps into the house and looks up to his left, he'll have the shock of his life. For a moment I entertain the idea that the shock might be enough to give him a heart attack and then all my problems would be solved. I dismiss the thought. Nothing fazes Tom and, besides, I don't wish him dead, I just want my daughter back.

'Here, let me do it,' Tom says with obvious irritation in his voice.

The sound of the key in the lock spurs me into action. I stumble into the bathroom to collect my clothes and just make it into the spare bedroom as the front door swings open. I hardly dare breathe for fear of being heard, but I will have to sooner or later because the thud of me passing out would certainly attract Tom's attention. I lean against the wall behind the bedroom door and inhale deeply through my nose, then release the air as gradually as I can.

'To what do I owe the pleasure?' I hear Liv ask. 'I thought you had a dentist appointment this morning.'

'I've been. It was just a check-up and the patient before me was a no-show. I was seen early and there's nothing wrong with my teeth, so I thought I'd call in on you on the way back as I was virtually passing your front door. It's not a problem, is it?'

'No, of course not, except I have an appointment to get to myself this morning. I don't even have time to offer you a coffee,' Liv says.

The appointment Liv is referring to is mine with the psychoanalyst. We're due there at half past eleven and I'm currently hiding in the bedroom with half a bottle of shampoo in my hair. Liv needs to get rid of Tom pronto if we're going to make it on time.

'I didn't come here for coffee,' Tom replies.

'So, why are you here? Mum's okay, isn't she?'

I can hear the concern in Liv's tone and it makes me feel guilty all over again for not being there to support her through her dad's cancer treatment.

'As far as I know, I haven't spoken to her today. No, I just wanted to ask you what you and Polly chatted about yesterday.'

'Nothing much,' Liv says. 'Mostly Mia, I think. I was surprised at how grown-up she is for a five-year-old. I really regret not seeing more of her. I'm going to make more of an effort from now on.'

'Like I said on the phone, she couldn't stop talking about Auntie Liv and she was the same over breakfast this morning. Polly hardly said a word. You didn't say anything that might have upset her, did you, Liv?'

'Not that I'm aware of. I like Polly; she seems a really sweet girl.'

'She is,' Tom replies. 'I'm glad you're going to give her a chance; I think you'll like her when you get to know her.'

'Maybe I struggled to get past the fact that she looked so much like Sophie.'

'Trust me, that's where the similarity ends. She's nothing like my former wife,' Tom says, adding, 'thank God.'

There is a saying that eavesdroppers never hear anything good about themselves and it's proving to be true.

'Tom!' Liv snaps, clearly outraged on my behalf. 'That's not a very nice thing to say about my best friend.'

'Maybe not, but you might not have known her as well as you thought you did.'

'I don't want to hear it, particularly when she's not here to defend herself.'

There is a certain irony in Liv's words, as she knows full well I can hear anything Tom has to say about me. Maybe she's afraid that I won't be able to stop myself from reacting and that is why she cut him off. Or she wants to protect me from whatever vitriol he is about to throw my way.

'Whatever. You always did view Sophie through rose-tinted glasses, even when she ran off to Spain to visit Grace without inviting you.'

'I was in no state to go anywhere after losing Alfie, as well you know.'

As she finishes speaking, my mobile starts to ring, making a heck of a racket as it vibrates against the wood of the bedside cabinet. For a moment, I can't imagine who would be ringing me. Definitely not anyone in Mexico as it's just after 5 a.m. there. Then I remember the message I left for Natasha Swann. It must be her returning my call, but I can't possibly answer it with Tom downstairs in the hall.

'Is that your mobile ringing?' I hear Tom ask. 'Did you forget to take it out with you?'

'Must have done,' Liv replies. 'I'll never get to it before it stops ringing, but I'd better check to see if there's a message. It might be them cancelling my appointment and I'd hate to have a wasted journey.'

'I'll come up and use the bathroom if that's okay and then I'd better be making tracks. Jamie will wonder where I've got to.'

My heart is thundering in my chest as I hear the two of them climbing the stairs. I'm trapped in a room a few feet away from a man who terrifies me praying that, having had no response, Natasha doesn't try Liv's phone, which is probably in the pocket of her coat.

'Come to think of it,' Liv is saying, 'I might have left it in the spare room when I was looking for my gloves this morning.'

More quick thinking from Liv as it would have looked suspicious if she'd come into the spare room instead of going to hers and Jamie's.

'Right, sis,' Tom says, a hint of sarcasm in his voice, 'and there was me thinking that you'd been sleeping in the spare room because you and Jamie haven't completely made up after your trial separation.'

'Sorry to disappoint,' Liv replies as she pushes the door open with me pressed flat against the wall behind it, 'but, actually, Jamie and I are closer than ever.'

'I'm pleased for you. If ever there was a perfect couple, it's you two.'

I hear the bolt on the bathroom door being shot.

Liv catches my eye and holds her finger up to her lips. As she hands me my phone, she retrieves her own from her pocket and flicks the little switch on the side to put it into silent mode. I nod and do the same with mine. I can feel beads of sweat forming on my forehead as she leaves the room, closing the door firmly behind her. I know I'm going to have to face Tom in the coming weeks, but I'm not ready for it yet, not until I have a few more memories of our life together to strengthen my resolve.

With the door closed, the voices are muffled so I can't really make out anything else that's said, but I do hear the front door slam a few minutes later, followed by footsteps running up the stairs.

'It's me,' Liv says, throwing open the door. 'Bloody hell! That was close. I couldn't believe it when your phone rang. Was it Natasha? Has she left a message?'

I glance down at the offending phone that had almost given the game away. It's a number I don't recognise, and the voicemail icon is flashing. I select the message and hit play.

'Hello, Sophie,' a female voice says. 'Just confirming your appointment this morning at 11.30 a.m. I've squeezed you in as a favour to Natasha Swann by cancelling my lunch date, so if you can't make it please let me know.'

I tap out a quick text response and press send.

'Right,' Liv says, 'you finish off in the shower and then we'll have to get going if we're going to make it on time. The traffic around Purley Cross is a nightmare, particularly on a Friday.'

It only takes me a few minutes to rinse the lather out of my hair and run some conditioner through it while I wash the rest of me.

I'm back in the bedroom sitting on the bed while I put my socks on, thinking what a narrow escape I've just had, when the image of me sitting on the bed I shared with Tom at Hailsham Crescent forces its way into my mind. It's the flashback I get most frequently and the one that frightens me the most. I can picture the knife as clear as day: it has a black handle with rivets through it and a long, wide blade which is glinting in the sunlight streaming through the window. It's the one I used to chop vegetables, so why have I got it in our bedroom?

I close my eyes trying to concentrate. What was I planning on doing with the knife? I see myself running my finger along the blade. My hands are trembling so much that a spot of bright red appears on my fingertip, but I don't appear to have noticed. Suddenly, my head shoots up as though I've heard something.

I can see fear in my eyes and I drop the knife as though it has scalded me before tucking it under my pillow and reaching for a tissue to mop the blood.

'Are you ready?' Liv calls up the stairs.

My eyes snap open and I'm surprised that the trembling was not only the Sophie in my memory; I'm shaking like a leaf. But the moment is gone. Whatever I might have been about to dredge up from the recesses of my mind is still locked there – for now at least.

'Yes, I'm ready,' I reply. I pull Liv's boots on and slip my phone into my bag as I close the bedroom door behind me. It's true in a practical sense, but am I actually ready to uncover the terrifying memories that my mind has been protecting me from? Scary as it is, I have no choice if I'm to move forward to the next phase of my life.

CHAPTER 32

Liv

Friday lunchtime

My stomach is starting to rumble. I've been back in my car, parked along the road from psychoanalyst Eleanor Rashford's home where she sees her clients, for the past twenty-five minutes, having initially walked down to Purley High Street to pass some time. While I was there, I popped into Brigham and Davis, the estate agents where I work, to confirm that I will definitely be returning to work on Monday, having taken last-minute holiday to return to Mexico and then ferry Sophie around.

Ray Brigham is a friend of Jamie's dad and so has been far more tolerant with my last-minute requests for leave than most employers would be.

I had a coffee with my colleague Jenny who has been picking up my workload while I've been off but declined a biscuit as I didn't want to spoil my lunch. I'm now regretting that decision. My stomach grumbles loudly, again reminding me that it's time to eat, as if I didn't already know.

I've clearly miscalculated how long Sophie would be on the analyst's couch. Eleanor Rashford made a point of saying that she'd squeezed Sophie in as a favour to her friend, so we both assumed the initial consultation would be no more than an hour. It seems we were wrong. It's also means we're running short of time to get back to Oxted to meet with Natasha Swann.

She called Sophie while we were on the drive over here this morning. Sophie put her call on speaker as it was me who had met with Polly the previous day and had concerns that all might not be right in her relationship with my brother. Natasha listened while I talked, without interrupting. When I got to the bit about Polly clamming up and asking for me not to visit again unless I was invited, she said, 'It sounds like she's definitely hiding something; the question is what?' That was when she suggested dropping into her office around three after she'd had a chance to go through Eleanor's initial assessment notes.

I glance at my watch. It's almost quarter to two. I'm going to have to interrupt their meeting if we're going to grab a quick bite and make it to Oxted on time.

I get out of my car, walk briskly down the road and climb the steps to the imposing front door, just as I watched Sophie do over two hours earlier. There are two bells at the side of the door, one of which says 'house' and the other 'clinic'. I press the latter and a few moments later a voice comes through the intercom which I recognise as Eleanor's from her voicemail this morning.

'Can I help you?' she asks.

'I'm really sorry to interrupt,' I say, 'but this is Liv, Sophie's friend, and I'm afraid we need to leave fairly shortly if we're going to make our meeting with Natasha Swann.'

There's a brief pause.

'Oh dear. You must have missed her. Sophie left over an hour ago.'

My initial reaction is confusion. If Sophie came out while I was in Purley chatting to my work colleagues, I'm pretty sure she would have messaged me and waited by my car until I returned. That's when I remember I put my phone on silent earlier, although I'm pretty sure I took it off again once Tom left. I reach into my coat pocket for it, and a quick glance shows me that there is no message from Sophie and that I did indeed turn the sound back on.

'Is there anything else I can help you with?' Eleanor asks. 'Only my next client is due at two and I'm just grabbing a quick bite to eat.'

'Um, did Sophie seem all right when she left?' I ask.

'I'm afraid I'm not at liberty to discuss my patients,' she replies.

The change of description from client to patient isn't lost on me.

'No, no, of course not. I'm just a bit worried that she might be feeling upset if you managed to help her unlock some of her memories. I've witnessed how she is when she has flashbacks of the way my brother treated her,' I say, to let Eleanor know that I'm fully aware of the situation.

There is another brief pause and then the lock on the pale blue door releases and she says, 'You'd better come in for a minute.'

The hallway is flooded with light as I push the heavy door open, and I haven't taken more than a couple of steps into it before a tall grey-haired woman wearing distinctive owl-rimmed glasses appears from a doorway to my left.

With no preamble, she says, 'I can't discuss the specifics of Sophie's case with you without her permission, but I can tell you that she learned a few things that she wasn't expecting. As a consequence, she was quite agitated when she left here. In fact, I was only happy to let her leave because she assured me you were waiting outside for her.' There's a hint of concern in her voice.

'In what way agitated?' I ask. Sophie is my responsibility. She came back to England because of me and is now wandering the streets in a bit of a state. 'Was she crying?' I continue, trying to imagine how emotional Sophie might be feeling if the full horror of her marriage to my brother flooded back to her all at once.

'No. She seemed more shocked than anything, but I would certainly feel more comfortable if she'd returned to your car as she said she was going to,' Eleanor says, rubbing her middle finger on her forehead as though trying to think what would be the best course of action.

My skin is starting to tingle. Something doesn't feel right. What on earth was uncovered in Eleanor's office that shocked rather than upset Sophie? Why has she gone off without contacting me?

'You don't think she's likely to do anything stupid, do you?'

'Such as?' she asks.

'I-I don't know. Did she seem as though she might harm herself?' I ask, remembering the incident with the knife Sophie had described to me and how she was unsure whether her intention had been to use it on herself or her husband. What have I done by encouraging her to come back and face up to her life with Tom?

'It's impossible for me to say. I've emailed my report to Natasha, so I would suggest giving her a call as a matter of urgency. I believe you were responsible for introducing the two of them, so Sophie may have given Natasha permission to discuss the case with you.'

The bell on the front door rings, catching us both by surprise.

'I'm sorry, that's probably my next appointment,' Eleanor says, 'and I really can't give you any more information.'

'Of course,' I say, reaching for the door handle and opening it, startling the young man on the other side. I rush past him down the steps, already dialling Natasha's number. Something about the way Eleanor Rashford was speaking is making me feel anxious; I need to find out what Sophie discovered about her past and then I need to find Sophie. I simply don't understand why she hasn't called me.

Natasha answers before I'm back at my car.

'Hello, Liv,' Natasha says. 'I'm just reading Eleanor's report now. Are you okay?'

Why would she be asking me that? I'm not the one on the receiving end of a shock, Sophie is. My heart starts pounding in my chest. I have to find out what is in the report and there's a chance that Natasha might not be willing to discuss it with me unless she believes I'm with Sophie.

'Well, obviously we're both a bit shocked,' I say, hoping my ambiguity suggests that I'm with her.

'Are you on speaker?' she asks.

'Not at the moment, but I can be if you want.'

'No, don't do that,' Natasha replies hurriedly. 'This is for your ears only.'

'Okay,' I reply cautiously.

'As you've probably realised,' she continues, 'Eleanor's report changes things somewhat. Tom must have had his reasons for keeping quiet, but there's little doubt that at least some of it will come out now, particularly if there's going to be a custody battle.'

I've reached my car, which is just as well because I'm leaning heavily on it for support. I'm trying to make sense of what Natasha has just said. What was Tom keeping quiet about? My mouth feels dry. Have I misjudged my brother? I've only heard Sophie's version of events, but she told them in such a compelling way, I genuinely think she believed it to be the truth. The alternative doesn't bear thinking about. She's my best friend; surely she wouldn't deliberately lie to me.

'Are you still there, Liv?'

'Yes,' is all I can manage.

'Has Sophie said much to you?' Natasha asks. 'It must be difficult with you being Tom's sister.'

I should probably tell Natasha that I haven't seen Sophie since her appointment and that I have no idea where she is. I have to find her and talk to her; give her a chance to explain. I initially struggled to believe some of the things Sophie accused my brother of doing, but after visiting Polly yesterday and hearing how possessive Tom is of both her and Mia, I interpreted it as him trying to exert control over them. Maybe I'm wrong and his motivation for being overly protective is a fear of losing them after the way he lost Sophie.

'We've been friends for a very long time,' I say, answering in a way that suggests Sophie is with me and I can't say too much.

'We need some time to talk things through. Can we cancel the meeting this afternoon and rearrange for Monday?'

'No worries, I'll free up ten o'clock,' Natasha replies before terminating the call.

I unlock the car and climb in, leaning my head against the steering wheel while I try to gather my thoughts. The text message alert sounds on my phone, which I'm still holding, and I lift my head to look at it, expecting it to be a message from Natasha confirming the appointment for Monday. I inhale sharply when I see it's from Sophie. With shaking hands, I open the message:

Liv, I don't know what to say except I'm so very sorry for all the upset I've caused. You were right about Tom all along, he's a kind and caring man and I'm the monster. I don't know how I would ever be able to face you, to look into your eyes and know that you'll never be able to truly trust me. So, I'm running away again and this time I really beg you not to come looking. I'm not worthy of a moment more of your time. Goodbye xx

I sit staring at the screen, reading the message over and over, searching for clues as to what she means and where she might run to. There's nothing. I can't deny it's an enormous relief to discover that Tom hadn't been abusing Sophie, but I'm horrified to hear her call herself a monster. The Sophie I've known for most of my life could never be described in that way. What on earth can she have done to make herself believe that she is?

I'm searching for an explanation for the meaning of the words in her text when a light bulb goes on in my head. I know where Sophie is headed and why she needed to slip away without me. If she's intending to disappear again, I'm certain she wouldn't go without seeing Mia. But what if seeing her little girl pushes her over the edge? What if she can't bear to leave Mia again and tries to take her with her?

I press Sophie's number on my phone. If I can just talk to her, I might be able to make her see that she doesn't need to run. The call hasn't connected. It's just ringing and ringing without defaulting to voicemail. I try again, but the same thing happens.

If I'm right, and Sophie is intending to try to see Mia, I need to warn Polly. I press her number and it rings four times before going to voicemail. There's no way I can explain what is going on in a message, so I hang up and try again several times. Polly still doesn't pick up. She probably doesn't want to talk to me after what I said to her yesterday and now I'm seeing things from a different perspective, I can't say I blame her.

What the hell do I do next? Jamie and Tom will be operating as they always do in the early afternoon. That leaves me. I have to get to Tom and Polly's house before Sophie does something she would regret, and I would never forgive myself for.

CHAPTER 33

Sophie

Friday afternoon

'Are you all right, miss?' the cab driver asks as we wait at a red traffic light.

I've been aware of him watching me in his rear-view mirror almost from the moment I got into the cab and asked him to take me to the top of Bug Hill in Warlingham. His question suggests that I must look a bit of a state.

'Yes, fine,' I say, shrinking further into the faux fur hood of Liv's coat. 'I've just had some bad news that I'd rather not talk about.'

He accepts my explanation and returns his attention to the road.

It's lucky that I'd already planned to change some of my Mexican pesos into pounds while we were out. Not only does it mean that I have money to pay for the cab, but I also have Grace's passport with me, which it looks like I'm going to need to use one last time, assuming that the paperwork Natasha Swann was so efficient in sending off hasn't yet been processed. I have no idea yet where I'm intending to run to. I haven't really thought about anything beyond seeing Mia. She's the reason I came back. Every fibre of my being knew it was a dangerous thing to undertake, I just didn't know why until I lay back on Eleanor Rashford's couch, after she'd asked me a few questions about my early life, and she began to regress me.

She started by asking about my life in Mexico. Her voice was warm and soothing and made me think of honey drizzling off one of those twisted spoons. I felt quite calm telling her about Luis and Vince and teaching Pilates classes. Working backwards, she asked how I came to be in Mexico in the first place, which took me back to the train crash in Spain. I began to feel uneasy, but she kept repeating in her low reassuring voice that we could stop at any point if it became too much for me. I didn't want to stop though; I wanted to find out what had forced me to flee.

When Eleanor moved on to questions about my life before the trip to Spain, I'd felt my pulse quicken and a panicky sensation in my chest. I took a few deep breaths and then the memories started to flow.

At first, my flashbacks are similar to the ones I've had before. I'm standing in the hallway of my former home with my case at my feet. Tom is holding Mia. As she reaches out to me, she drops her teddy. For the first time, I can picture my little girl's face and she's crying. Is it because she's dropped her teddy bear, or is it because she doesn't want me to leave her? I'm trying to remember, but Eleanor's voice is gently urging me to move on.

Now I'm in the kitchen and the fridge door is open. I'm reaching for a bottle of wine and Tom says, 'Should you be having that while you're still breastfeeding Mia?'

'I need a drink, Tom.'

'But it could harm our baby.'

'It's one drink. Why are you trying to remove every tiny pleasure from my life?'

'I'm not. And besides, you already had a glass of wine with dinner.'

The fridge door slams onto to my wrist. I can almost feel the agonising pain as I sink to the floor clutching my arm. Tom is towering over me.

'Now look what you've done. We need to get that checked out at the hospital, but you have to promise not to say how it happened,' Tom says. His face is inches away from mine, his pupils fully dilated, his eyes as black as coal. 'Do you hear me, Sophie? Not a word to anyone.'

I can see doctors and nurses at the hospital. They're asking me how it happened. I'm telling them I fell, just as Tom had instructed me to.

And then I'm in our bedroom. The knife I'd hidden under my pillow is lying on the floor at my feet. This time, Tom is there too. My hands are raised and I'm shocked that my wrists are covered in bruises. I watch as I attempt to hit my husband with clenched fists. He dodges the blows, his hands in front of his face protectively, before finally grabbing at my wrists to stop me. His lips are moving.

'It's okay, Sophie, I know you can't help it. You're not well.'

I'm screaming at him, over and over, my face ugly and contorted, 'It's all your fault, it's all your fault.'

'You don't mean that. I wish you'd let me get you the professional help you need.'

As though a veil is lifting, I realise that the look in his eyes which I'd previously believed was anger is actually fear and desperation. Maybe my bruises aren't a result of me protecting myself. Tom is holding my wrists to prevent me making contact with my blows. He's protecting himself from me. The memory of the fridge door closing onto my wrist floods my mind again. This time I can see that it is me who is slamming the door with all my might and deliberately trapping my own wrist.

I can hear shrieking and then Eleanor's voice as she brings me back to full consciousness which is when I realise that the noise is coming from me. My whole body is shaking, and I'm dripping with sweat.

'Try to breathe deeply,' Eleanor says in an effort to calm me. It's having no effect.

'I don't understand,' I say, still shaking violently. 'I was trying to hit Tom and I was shouting at him. He looked terrified of me. Oh my God, it wasn't Tom abusing me, it was the other way around.'

'Slow down,' Eleanor says in her soothing tones. 'The way you are now remembering events has obviously come as a dreadful shock, but let's just take a moment to examine what might have caused you to behave in this way. I think you may have been suffering from a severe case of post-partum depression, or PPD.'

'I don't understand,' I reply. 'I thought that was something new mothers had for a few days after the baby is born.'

'You're right to a degree. PPD is sometimes referred to as the baby blues and usually only lasts a few days or weeks, but for some mothers it can be much more severe. It can last for months or even years, which in my opinion seems likely in your case.'

I shake my head, unable to comprehend what I'm hearing.

'There are a few different scenarios,' Eleanor continues. 'After Mia's birth, you may have become obsessed and overprotective of her, not allowing anyone near her, even her father.'

The flashback of Tom holding Mia near our front door comes to my mind. If that had been the case, I'm pretty sure I wouldn't have left her to go and visit with Grace.

'On the other hand, you may have been struggling to connect with Mia. It's not that uncommon, particularly if you had a difficult birth.'

Did I struggle to connect with Mia? I don't think so, but I've been unable to remember any intimate moments with her, apart from her suckling at my breast when she was a new-born in hospital. I have no memory of her blowing out the candles on her birthday cake or a look of excitement on her face as she tore colourful wrapping paper off Christmas gifts. Why can't I remember these things? I don't even recall tucking her into bed at night and reading her favourite story? But when I was regressed, my little girl was reaching out to me, not wanting me to leave her. If she loved me, I must have loved her too.

'Or, you could have lost your sense of identity, seeing yourself only as Mia's mother rather than Sophie. When this happens, a wife can blame their husband for getting them pregnant and in extreme cases it can lead to violence towards them. I know that's a lot to take in, but any one of those scenarios might be what happened between you and Tom. Are you okay, Sophie?'

'I need to go now,' I say, swinging my legs down to the floor. I need to see Mia. I have to know what my feelings towards her are.

'Should I fetch your sister-in-law?' Eleanor asks.

Liv is the last person on the planet I want to see. She trusts me, believes in me, even argued with her own husband because of me, all based on what I thought was true. I simply can't face her. I need space to think.

'It's fine,' I reply. 'She's literally just outside.'

I make my next appointment, which I have no intention of keeping, and leave.

It's easier than I thought it would be getting away from the clinic without Liv seeing me. I wait until a couple pass the gate and then fall into step immediately behind them for a few seconds before ducking down between two parked cars. Within a couple of minutes, I get lucky. A double-decker bus approaches and I cross the road behind it, hidden from Liv's view, and hurry down a side street towards Purley town centre. I figure I have an hour or so before Liv goes looking for me. Hopefully by then I will already be with Mia.

I ask the taxi driver to drop me off at the end of Hailsham Crescent rather than pulling up outside my old house. It will add credibility to the plan I eventually managed to formulate in the back of the cab. What I say to Polly needs to be convincing enough for her to invite me into the house. You only get one chance to make a first impression and the first impression I make on Polly could mean the difference in me getting to see Mia or not.

Standing in the gateway of my former home for the first time in over three years gives me a strange feeling. All my memories prior to the session with Eleanor Rashford had painted Tom as the villain, but I now know that not to be the case. I close my eyes for a moment and there he is, a broad grin on his face, carrying me over the threshold of our new home even though we'd been married for a couple of years and I was heavily pregnant. How could my mind have got everything so wrong? I feel desperately sad for the loss of the life I once shared with Tom, but that is my past and heaven alone knows what my future will hold.

The urgency to lay eyes on my daughter takes over once again and I stride up the gravel driveway and knock on the door. I wait a few moments, my heart hammering in my chest so loudly that I'm worried Polly might hear it. I raise my hand to knock again but stop in mid action as the door is cautiously opened and a blonde woman peers around it. I'm fairly certain that her shoulders relax when she sees me, possibly because she was worried that Liv had ignored her instruction from the previous day.

'Sorry I kept you,' Polly says. 'I'm just in the middle of having lunch with my little girl. Can I help you?'

I should be grateful that she called Mia 'my little girl' rather than 'my daughter', but it still hurts to hear someone else describe her as that. She's not Polly's little girl, she's mine.

'It's my car,' I say, turning and waving my hand in the general direction of the road. 'I broke down at the top of Bug Hill, right on the bend, and I was just calling the police to report it being in a dangerous location when a car came speeding up the hill and only missed me by millimetres. I was so shocked, I dropped my phone and smashed it.' I hold out my mobile so that she can see the shattered screen. Replacing it is an expense I could do without, but I had to smash it after sending the text to Liv to add authenticity to my story. Judging by the compassionate look on Polly's face, it was worth it.

'Oh, you poor thing,' she says, 'you're shaking. You must have been terrified.'

She's right, I am shaking. I have been since I left Eleanor's after remembering the awful things I said and did.

'Didn't the other driver stop?' she adds.

'N-no, he just kept on driving.'

Polly has opened the door fully now and I can see past her into the hall that I chose the paint colour for, and beyond that to the kitchen. In my mind, I'm picturing a dark-haired child sitting at the big wooden table biting into a sandwich or dipping chips in tomato ketchup. I'm so desperate to see Mia that I want to push Polly aside, run through to the kitchen and scoop her up in my arms, but I know I can't. I have to wait to be invited in and then I'll get my chance.

'You saw the driver then,' Polly is saying. 'Did you manage to get his registration number?'

'Just a fleeting glimpse. It all happened so quickly.'

For a moment, Polly just stands there, unsure what to say or do next.

I won't get another chance; I have to make her invite me in. I relax my knees, as though my legs are about to buckle, and reach my hand out for the door frame.

'Do you think I might have a glass of water?' I ask.

As though a switch has flicked, she says, 'I can do better than that. Come in and I'll make you a cup of tea while you call the police.'

She stands to one side and I step into the hallway just as a child's voice says, 'Can you hurry up, please. Mr Albert and I are waiting for you and our soup is getting cold.'

I may have feigned my knees buckling a few moments earlier, but this time they go for real, and I stumble forward, landing in a heap on the circular rug with the abstract rose design, a wedding present from Grace.

'Oh, my goodness, are you okay?' Polly says, rushing forward to help me.

I hear chair legs scrape against tiles and the sound of footsteps. When I look up, I see a little girl standing in the kitchen doorway clutching a well-loved teddy bear. My heart feels as though it might explode.

'What's wrong with the lady? Did she trip on the rug?'

Exactly as Liv described, although Mia's voice is that of a child, her words are more adult.

'She's had a shock, Mia.'

Little does Polly know how accurate those words are. I've just laid eyes on my daughter for the first time in over three years. I immediately know that Eleanor's suggestion that I hadn't connected with her must be wrong. I've never before experienced such overwhelming love. Not with Tom, even in the early days, not with Luis. I'm struggling to breathe because my chest feels so tight.

'We need to help the lady into the lounge,' Polly continues. 'Then maybe you and Mr Albert can look after her while I make her a cup of tea.'

'Mia,' I whisper, allowing the word to linger on my lips. It's been so long since I've spoken her name in her presence.

Polly places her hand under my elbow to help me up, but Mia is still standing in the doorway.

'Daddy said we shouldn't have visitors without asking him first,' she says, her serious voice matching the concerned look on her face.

'It's all right, Mia, this is different. This lady needs our help, so I'm sure your daddy wouldn't mind.'

Slowly my daughter leaves her position next to the door and follows us into the lounge. Again, it's as I remember it, apart from the photographs on the bookcase. There is a new wedding photograph in pride of place and all the baby pictures are ones with

Tom and Mia, or ones of Mia on her own. There are also some family shots including Polly, which twists a knife in my heart. It should have been me in those photos. Why wasn't I happy with the life I had? I don't understand.

Polly moves the footstool so that I can put my feet up on it and then leaves the room to make me the promised cup of tea.

Mia has perched herself on one of the chairs and seems to be studying me intently. From beneath my lashes I am doing the same thing. She looks exactly as I imagine Liv looked at the same age. I'm longing to throw my arms around her and hug her and tell her how sorry I am for abandoning her, but of course I can't do any of those things.

'What colour is your hair?' she asks.

I reach my hand up to my head. I'm still wearing Liv's woollen hat into which I've bundled my mass of blonde hair.

'It's yellow, like your mummy's,' I reply. I'm fully aware that her response may break my heart into a million pieces. Liv told me that Mia referred to Polly by her name rather than mummy. Something deep inside me is desperate for that to be true. 'Would you like me to show you?'

'How do you know my mummy had yellow hair?' she asks, her voice filled with curiosity.

I catch my breath slightly before saying, 'I-I meant Polly.'

'Polly's not my mummy. She's married to my daddy, but my mummy died.'

My heart is pounding. I wonder how much Tom has told her about me. After all, she wasn't quite two when I went to visit Grace in Spain. Her voice was quite solemn, but she doesn't sound particularly upset, which maybe isn't surprising as she probably has very little memory of me, if she remembers me at all.

'Does that make you sad?' I ask.

'Sometimes, but Mr Albert always makes it better,' she says, hugging her bear into her chest.

'He must be very special; may I have a closer look?' I ask.

Mia hesitates before sliding off the chair and taking a couple of steps towards me.

'Would you like to hold him for a minute?' she asks. 'He might make you feel better too.'

'That's very kind of you, thank you,' I say, reaching out to take the teddy and in doing so touching the delicate skin of my daughter's hand. I have an overwhelming urge to wrap my arms around Mia and never let her go, but that would frighten her and that's the last thing I want. Instead, I pull Mr Albert into my chest and say, 'You know, that does make me feel better.'

I'm not lying. Breathing in the teddy's aroma, knowing that he is Mia's constant companion, is almost as good as burying my face in her dark curls.

'You can show me now,' Mia says.

For a moment, I'm not sure what she means.

'Your hair. I wanted yellow hair, like a fairy-tale princess, but mine's like Daddy's.'

I hand the teddy back to Mia with one hand and with the other I remove the woollen hat and allow my freshly washed hair to cascade over my shoulders.

'It's nearly as long as Rapunzel's hair,' she says, an element of wonder in her voice. She is staring at me without any attempt at disguising it, as only young children have the confidence to do. 'You actually look a lot like my mummy.'

My heart is battering my ribcage.

'You've seen a photograph of her?'

'Oh yes. Daddy made me a special picture book. He said if I sleep with it under my pillow every night, then she won't be alone in heaven.'

I raise my hand to my mouth to stifle my gasp. How could Tom say such a kind and thoughtful thing after the awful way I treated him?

'Are you all right? Should I fetch Polly?'

'What if your mummy's not in heaven?' I ask, ignoring her questions.

'She will be,' Mia says, nodding her head. 'Daddy said she was a good person and everybody knows good people go to heaven.'

I'm close to tears.

'I meant, what if your mummy didn't die. What if she lost her memory for a long time, but then things started coming back to her? Once she remembered she had a daughter, the first thing she wanted to do was return to her home to see her.'

A crash of crockery from behind me causes me to turn. Polly is standing in the doorway with a look of horror on her face, a smashed cup and saucer at her feet, the contents splattered across the cream carpet.

I turn back to face Mia. I want to tell her that I'm the person I was describing. I'm her mummy and I want her to know that, but she looks frightened.

'Are you my mummy?' she asks, her eyes as wide as saucers and a slight tremor to her voice.

What should I say? My reason for coming here was to see Mia and make sure she was happy and well-cared for. I don't think there can be any question about that. Polly has shown how kind-hearted she is, and Mia clearly adores her. I should leave, letting her believe the things Tom has told her about me. Better for her to think of her mummy in heaven than for me to admit to being her mum and then running off again. It wouldn't be fair on Mia. But now that I've felt that all-consuming surge of mother-love, I don't know if I can bear the thought of never seeing my little girl again. I was sick before, Eleanor explained that to me, and I've had the chance to think about the dreadful state I must have been in on the journey over here. I don't have that excuse this time. And anyway, I'm not sure I want to run and leave my daughter behind. I want to be a part of her life.

It may not be under the best circumstances, but Mia is still staring at me waiting for an answer to her question and I may never get another chance.

'Yes, Mia, I am your mummy.'

CHAPTER 34

Liv

Friday afternoon

I've never been one for road rage, but on the drive from Purley to Warlingham, which takes me along the busy Kenley Road, I've honked my horn three times and even lowered my window to shout abuse at an elderly man who wasn't completely over his side of the road while he was waiting to turn right. In the end, I mounted the kerb to get past him, narrowly avoiding a bollard which I hadn't noticed because I'd been too busy getting irate. It's just as well it was so busy as there are speed cameras along that stretch of road and I would definitely have been fined if traffic had allowed me to go faster.

I've been in two minds whether or not to leave a message for Jamie asking him to ring me as soon as he's out of surgery. The main thing stopping me is that I don't know for sure what Sophie discovered and I don't want to make things worse than they already are by making assumptions.

All I keep thinking, as I take chance after chance that I never normally would, is that this is my fault. If I'd left things alone, as Sophie begged me to in her letter, none of this would be happening. I wouldn't be driving like a maniac, worried sick about what Sophie might do. I'm certain she's headed for my brother's house to see Mia. That was the thing that changed her mind and brought her back to England and I just know she won't leave without seeing her. But it's what she will do next that worries me. Will she be able to settle for having seen her daughter and then just disappear as she did before? It's possible. She still has Grace's passport, which she could use to flee the UK.

But what if just seeing her daughter isn't enough for Sophie. It could reignite a fierce maternal bond and she may decide to run away, taking Mia with her.

Don't be ridiculous, I tell myself as I take a left at the roundabout at the bottom of Hillside Road and then drive over the mini roundabout near the station without giving way. This time the road rage is hurled in my direction and not without some justification, but I'm too stressed out to care.

I press my foot down harder on the pedal and accelerate up the hill. Even if Sophie does try to take Mia, Polly won't just stand by and let her do it, I rationalise. She'd ring Tom; in fact, he might be on his way home right now. If only Polly had picked up the phone when I tried to call her, I could have warned her that Sophie was on her way.

Calm down, I try to tell myself. Why on earth would Polly let Sophie into the house in the first place? And, in any case, Mia's not a baby, she'll have learned all about 'stranger danger' at school and wouldn't willingly go off with someone she doesn't know. I'm telling myself all these things, but I'm still terrified of what I'm going to find.

I turn left at the T-junction, then pull into the right-hand lane, waiting to turn by the green where we used to walk when Mia was a new-born. Memories of happy baby talk fill my mind. 'It'll be your turn next,' Sophie used to say. 'Becoming a mother is just the most fulfilling thing you could ever imagine.' But within weeks, she'd stopped calling me to go for walks with her and Mia. I didn't question it at the time, thinking she must be so busy getting used to all the differences in her life, but I should have made more of an effort to make sure she was okay.

The stream of traffic is constant.

'Come on,' I mutter under my breath, tapping my fingers agitatedly on the steering wheel.

Finally, I manage to pull across the flow of traffic in a gap that wasn't really big enough, resulting in yet another irate motorist flicking a 'V' sign at me. I don't care.

My head is full of 'what ifs' and 'why didn'ts' as I pull out onto the road that leads to the top of Bug Hill. The next thing I know, someone has smashed into the back of my car. The impact throws me forward and even with my seat belt on I bang my head on the windscreen. I want to drive on. I need to get to my brother's house. But I can feel myself getting hot and I know I'm about to pass out. I reach into my coat pocket as the driver's door is wrenched open.

'What the hell were you doing?' an angry voice demands. 'You could have killed someone, pulling out in front of me like that.'

I can feel warm liquid trickling down my forehead, which I presume is blood. With an almighty effort, I hand my phone to the stranger.

'Call Tom and tell him to go home immediately. Mia's in danger,' I manage to say before darkness engulfs me.

CHAPTER 35

Sophie

Friday afternoon

I'm not sure what I expected Mia to do once I revealed my true identity to her. Polly's reaction though was very predictable. She recovered almost immediately from the shock and was across the room in a matter of seconds, grabbing Mia's hand and pulling her away from me.

'Who the hell are you?' she demands, positioning herself protectively between me and my daughter.

'Like I said, I'm Sophie. Mia's mum and Tom's wife,' I say, sounding far calmer than I'm actually feeling.

'You can't be. She's dead,' Polly says. 'I've seen the newspaper cuttings of the crash. Nobody could have survived that.'

Now is not the time to get into an explanation of how I survived the train crash. Liv is probably on her way over here as we speak. She'll have worked out that I wouldn't just disappear without trying to see Mia and she could well have contacted Jamie, or even Tom, in her panic. Before I gained entry to the house, I didn't really have a plan of what I was going to do beyond seeing Mia. Now that I've seen her and she knows who I am, I can't just walk away and leave her. I've already been deprived of my daughter for three and a half years and I want her back.

The two-year period of my life which my mind had locked away is all coming back to me now in awful technicolour. I'm absolutely certain that I loved Mia unconditionally, taking out my frustration with the way I was feeling on Tom instead. I would try to goad him into hitting me. I can even hear my words, 'Go on, Tom, you know you want to,' but he never succumbed, no matter how hard I pressed his buttons. He must have had the patience of a saint not to react.

I was ill, I realise that now, but at the time I refused to accept it and became agitated every time he suggested seeking medical help. It's weird the tricks our minds can play on us, making us see things in a certain way when the opposite is true. Tom was trying everything he could to keep our little family together and I repaid his kindness with abuse. I have no idea how he will react once he finds out I'm alive. He's settled and happy with Polly and Mia, have I really got the right to tear all that apart?

'I want you to leave now,' Polly says when I don't respond, 'or I'll call the police.'

Mia is peering out from behind the folds in Polly's skirt. She doesn't look afraid, just curious.

'Is that what you want, Mia?' I ask. 'Do you want mummy to go away again?'

'That's an unfair question to ask a five-year-old,' Polly responds.

She's right. My words came out all wrong. I just need to know if Mia wants me to be in her life as desperately as I want her to be in mine.

'You shouldn't have come here, gaining entry in such a deceitful way,' she continues. 'And to think I actually felt sorry for you.'

'I've come a long way to see Mia. If I'd turned up on the doorstep and told you who I was you either wouldn't have believed me or you'd have closed the door in my face. I couldn't let that happen. I had to see my little girl.'

'Well, you've seen her, so now I think you should leave,' she says, raising her voice slightly to exert her authority.

'Please don't shout, Polly, you'll scare Mia.'

Polly drops to her knees and pushes Mia's dark curls back off her face.

'Don't be scared, darling,' she says. 'I'll call your daddy to come home, and he'll sort all this out.'

'Will you also tell him how you left his daughter alone with a stranger, without recognising the danger you placed her in. Mia might not be so lucky next time.'

I know how hurtful and wounding my words are, but I'm unable to stop myself.

Polly's shoulders slump forward momentarily, but she forces them back and gets to her feet.

'What is it you want, Sophie?' she asks, her voice back to a normal volume. 'Is it only Mia, or do you want steal everything I've loved over the past three and a half years, Tom included?'

Her question is like the slap across the face you give to someone when they've become hysterical. I've given no proper thought to my future, I just know I want Mia to be part of it. But am I really prepared to destroy other people's lives to achieve it?

The sound of tyres screeching to a halt on the gravel driveway is followed by a car door slamming. Liv has got here sooner than I thought.

I don't know who is more shocked, me or Tom, when he appears in the doorway moments later.

'What the hell's going on?' he manages to say.

'Daddy,' Mia says, running towards Tom and clinging on to his legs as though her life depends on it.

'You're safe now, baby,' he says, sweeping her up in his arms and burying his face in Mia's hair for a moment.

His voice is gentle and the image of the two of them in a tight embrace is at once heart-warming and heartbreaking. Part of my reason for coming back to England was because I was afraid for Mia and the life she would lead with a controlling, abusive father. I now know that Tom is neither. Mia loves her daddy and it's plain to see the feeling is reciprocated.

He looks from one to the other of his two wives, confusion having replaced shock. Eventually his gaze rests on me.

'Sophie, is it really you?' he asks, walking over to the armchair to sit down, still firmly holding Mia against his chest.

There's a quiver in his voice. I'm not sure if it's from emotion or disbelief.

'Yes, Tom, it's me. I survived the accident, but for a while I… I didn't know who I was.'

How true those words are on so many levels. There was a short period of time when I genuinely didn't know if I was Grace or Sophie, and for a long time in Mexico I didn't know what my mind was preventing me from remembering. But, mostly, I've realised that giving birth to Mia, no matter how much I loved her, stole my identity just as Eleanor had described. I ceased being Sophie and became Mia's mum and it was something I was incapable of dealing with.

'Where have you been all this time?' Tom asks. He's rocking gently back and forth and I'm not sure if it's for his benefit or Mia's.

'Mexico.'

He stops rocking.

'Is you turning up here something to do with Liv's holiday there?'

'Yes. She thought she recognised me on the beach.'

'Really? Why would she think it was you when we all believed you were dead?'

'It was my tattoo,' I say, subconsciously fingering my forearm through Liv's quilted coat. 'You didn't want me to have it in the first place and now it looks like it's ruined everything.'

For the first time in several minutes, Tom transfers his gaze to Polly.

'What is she doing here? Am I the only one who didn't know she was back from the dead?'

'I didn't know it was her,' Polly replies. 'She came to the door asking for help saying her car had broken down. I'm so sorry, Tom. I would never have let her in if I'd known.'

'Don't blame Polly,' I say. 'She was just being a good Samaritan.'

'Why are you here? The guy ringing on Liv's phone just told me to get here as soon as possible because Mia was in danger. What did he mean?'

My grip tightens on the arm of the sofa.

'What guy? Why didn't Liv call you herself?' I ask.

'She was in a car accident. In her rush to get here because she was worried for Mia's safety, Liv pulled out in front of the guy and he ran into the back of her.'

Polly and I gasp at the same time.

'Oh God,' I say. 'Please tell me she's all right. I'll never forgive myself if anything happens to her.'

'She banged her head and passed out. They've taken her to East Surrey Hospital to check her over. Jamie is on his way there now.'

'I'm so sorry, Tom. I wish I'd just stayed away.'

'So why didn't you?' he asks. There is no anger in his voice, just sadness. 'We all shed a lot of tears when we said goodbye to you.'

'Even you?'

'Especially me.'

'After the way I treated you?'

'You couldn't help it; you were sick,' he says, his voice full of compassion. 'I tried to protect you by keeping things secret like you asked me to, but in the end, I did more harm than good. I wish I'd sought the professional help you needed even though you said you didn't want it. Things would have been so different for all of us.'

All the dreadful thoughts that I've allowed to fill my head about my husband dissolve in the tears that are streaming down my face.

'Mummy's crying, Daddy. Shall I fetch her one of my special hankies?' Mia asks.

'I'll go,' Polly says, rushing out of the room.

I can't be sure, but I think she may be crying too.

'What a mess,' I say, sniffing.

'Yes,' Tom says. 'What an almighty mess and I've no idea how we go about fixing it.'

'Do you think Mr Albert might help?' Mia asks.

'I'm not sure your toy can help this time,' Tom replies, ruffling Mia's hair.

'Mr Albert's not a toy, he's my friend.'

She slips off Tom's knee and walks over towards me. Without coming too close, she holds the teddy bear out at arm's length just as Polly comes back in the room with a handkerchief. She hands it to me with a faint smile before going over to perch on the arm of the chair where Tom is sitting. She rests her hand on his shoulder in a gesture clearly intended to comfort him after the shock of walking into his home and discovering I'm back from the dead.

Clutching Mr Albert in my left hand, I wipe my tears with the hankie in my right. It's gently fragranced and I immediately recognise the scent. Tom must spray my perfume onto Mia's hankies. I'm guessing he told her it was my favourite and does it to comfort her. I make eye contact with him for a second before he drops his gaze. I wonder if either Mia or Polly know that it's called True Love, the fragrance Tom bought for me on our first Christmas together.

CHAPTER 36

Liv

Friday late afternoon

'What on earth were you thinking?' Jamie says the moment my hospital bed is locked in place and the nurse has pulled the curtains around it to give us some privacy. 'You could have been seriously injured if that car had been travelling any faster, and the other driver too.'

I've just been wheeled back onto the ward after the final test to make sure I don't have any undetected injuries. Jamie has been waiting in the general area and has clearly got himself more and more worked up as time ticked on, judging by the pallor of his skin and the worried look in his eyes.

At the scene earlier, the paramedics put a brace around my neck and then gently eased me onto a board before lifting me onto the stretcher. Their concern was that I'd blacked out after a fairly minor impact, so they wanted to be sure that I hadn't suffered an injury to my spinal cord. I wasn't passed out for long, but the moment I came around, I asked the driver I'd had the collision with, who was now looking concerned rather than angry, whether he had managed to reach Tom. He replied that he had, and that Tom was on his way home. He also volunteered to stay with me until the paramedics arrived. Apparently, he'd been told to try to keep me awake if I regained consciousness, so he took the opportunity to take my insurance company details and my name and address, none of which I objected to because I was clearly to blame. By the time he'd finished tapping everything into his mobile phone, I could already hear the wail of the ambulance in the distance.

'I'm sorry, Jamie,' I say, touching his fingertips. 'I was too preoccupied worrying about Mia and wasn't paying attention to the road. It was entirely my fault.'

'Why were you worried about Mia? Is she sick or something? Tom didn't say much when he stuck his head around my door to tell me he had to go home because there was an emergency.'

'Haven't you heard from him?' I ask, feeling the panic rising in my chest.

'No, I didn't want to bother him,' Jamie says. 'Whatever the emergency was, I figured he was dealing with it. What I don't understand is why Polly rang you for help rather than Tom – and where the hell is Sophie?'

'What makes you think Polly rang me?'

'Why else would you be on your way to Tom's house?'

I spend the next few minutes explaining to him what happened with Sophie at Eleanor Rashford's and my subsequent phone conversation with Natasha Swann.

He shakes his head. 'I knew Tom wasn't a wife-beater. Hold on a minute; what was the emergency at home?'

'I was worried that Sophie might decide the only way she could be with Mia is if she ran off with her.'

'Kidnap her own daughter? Why on earth would Sophie do that?'

'Because she loves Mia and was probably scared to death that Tom wouldn't allow her access.'

'You both need to stop seeing Tom as the bad guy here, Liv. Has it occurred to you that he might have been covering things up in his marriage because he was trying to hold his family together? He absolutely adored Sophie and would have done anything for her. I know he's married to Polly now, but you don't stop loving someone just because they've died. Your mum still loves your dad, doesn't she?'

'Of course, and we both still love Alfie,' I say, reaching for Jamie's hand.

He lifts my hand to his lips and kisses it, causing butterflies in my stomach. I love my husband as much as I did on our wedding day, in fact more if that's possible.

'Tom could have a problem balancing his new life with his old if Sophie doesn't go running back to Mexico. He and Polly are good together and she's brilliant with Mia,' Jamie says, reminding me that we don't know what happened at the house.

'Can you ring Tom and find out if everything's okay?'

Jamie reaches into his pocket for his phone.

'There's no signal in here,' he says. 'I'll call from the reception area. There's a coffee shop there, do you want anything?'

I shake my head. I'm far too anxious about Mia to even contemplate eating until I know she's all right.

'Okay, I won't be long. Try not to worry,' he says, leaning over the bed to kiss my forehead.

I smile up at my husband. I'm so thankful that we were able to sort out our differences. I don't want to live my life without him by my side.

'Ask him if Sophie's been in touch with him, will you?' I say as Jamie is leaving the room.

He turns back to look at me.

'Are you sure I should? If you were wrong, and Sophie has been nowhere near the house, is there any point in Tom knowing that she is still alive?'

'He'll know soon enough and I'd rather he hears it from us. It's going to be awkward explaining to him why I didn't tell him about Sophie being back in England. I hope it doesn't drive a wedge between us again.'

'*We*, Liv,' Jamie says. 'Why *we* didn't tell him Sophie was back and living at *our* house. We're in this together, okay?'

I nod and rest my head back on the pillows as he goes off to make the phone call. I have no idea how the whole Sophie situation is going to pan out. I hope she doesn't just disappear again, because I've missed having her in my life, but I'd understand if she felt she couldn't face up to what happened in the past.

I must have dozed off because I'm woken by a knock at the door.

'Come in,' I say.

A young nurse comes into the room wheeling a trolley.

'I'm just going to do your blood pressure,' she explains.

I wiggle my way into a more upright position, and she wraps the cuff around my upper arm and starts inflating it with her eyes firmly fixed on the digital read-out.

'It's good news about the baby,' she says.

'Are you sure you're in the right room? I'm here because I had a car accident.'

She turns to look at me, a flicker of concern in her eyes.

'You are Olivia Nelson?' she asks.

'Yes.'

'Phew, that's a relief,' she says. 'I wouldn't want to get sacked on my second week on the wards.'

I don't want her to get sacked on my account, so I let her concentrate on what she's doing. The cuff around my upper arm gradually deflates and the machine beeps. I wait until she has finished recording the read-out.

'So, what did you mean about the baby?' I ask as she's removing the cuff.

'The urine sample came back, and it shows you are still pregnant,' she says smiling as she loads everything back onto her trolley. 'That's good news to end your less than brilliant day.'

Her words are only truly sinking in when Jamie comes rushing into the room looking slightly flustered.

'Flipping heck, it's all been going on at Tom's…' he starts to say, but the tears streaming down my cheeks stop him in mid flow. 'What is it? Are you in pain?'

He's by my side in an instant, reaching for a tissue from the box on the cabinet and handing it to me, anxiety etched onto his face.

'I'm pregnant,' I manage between my sobs. 'We're going to have a baby.'

CHAPTER 37

Sophie

Friday evening

It's indescribably weird watching my daughter climb the stairs of my former home on her way to bed, holding the hand of a woman I met for the first time less than five hours ago. When they reach the landing, Mia turns and waves Mr Albert's paw at me just as Liv described her doing through the window the previous afternoon. I wave back and blow her a kiss. She lets go of Polly's hand for a moment to catch the kiss, which she puts in the pocket of her unicorn nightdress before padding across the carpet to her bedroom. That small gesture brings me immeasurable joy. There have been times over the past few days when I've doubted the wisdom of my decision to leave my life in Mexico, but my daughter catching my kiss and holding it close to her heart reaffirms that I made the right choice.

'You'll have to excuse her with that damn teddy,' Tom says. 'I've been trying to wean her off it, but she's not having any of it.'

'She's needed Mr Albert,' I reply. 'Mia's had to be a pretty brave little girl thanks to me. He's been a constant companion for her; someone to share her worries with.'

'That's exactly what Polly said. If it had been left to me, he would have been tied to the front of the bin men's lorry a couple of years ago.'

'Please tell me you don't mean that?' I say.

'Of course not. He'd have been front and centre in the charity shop window. I'm joking, Sophie,' he says in response to my shocked expression. 'I thought you knew me better than that.'

With those few words, Tom has hit the nail on the head. I used to know my husband so well, but there has been a lot of water under the bridge since our carefree days before Mia was born. For the first time since he appeared in the doorway of his lounge looking concerned, I take a proper look at the man I envisaged spending the rest of my life with. Outwardly, he hasn't changed much in the three and a half years since I last saw him apart from a few silvery grey strands of hair around the temples and maybe one or two more lines around his eyes. But I can't help wondering what the stress of trying to care for me for almost two years, followed by the trauma of losing me, has done to him on the inside. It's little wonder he needed someone to help him cope, and from what I've seen of Polly he couldn't have chosen a kinder person.

'What are you thinking?' he asks.

'I was just thinking how lucky you are to have Polly. She clearly adores you and she's so good with Mia. You know, when I came here today, I wasn't sure whether you would have told Mia anything about me. It took me by surprise when she said I looked like her mummy; I thought she meant Polly.'

'She's always known that Polly wasn't her real mummy, even though she couldn't really remember much about you. I wanted her to have pictures of you, so I made a little album for her,' Tom says, looking slightly self-conscious.

'Mia told me. She also said she sleeps with it under her pillow so that I wouldn't be alone in heaven. I can't believe you were so kind about me after I'd treated you so badly,' I say, struggling to keep the wobble out of my voice.

'It wasn't your fault, Sophie. I kept telling you at the time that you were sick and needed professional help, but you saw it as a sign of failure. You were an amazing mum, you know.'

His words almost floor me.

'Was I? You're not just saying that?'

'No. However upset or angry you were with me, you were always so loving with Mia. That's what I couldn't understand. I read up so much on postpartum depression and more often than not it's the mother failing to bond with their baby that causes problems. You couldn't have loved Mia more if you tried,' he affirms, a wistful expression on his face.

'You've no idea how much it means to me to know that I was a good mum,' I say, relief flooding through me. 'What's really sad though is that despite being able to recall some of the awful times, I can't reach any of the time I spent with Mia. I was so afraid I might have been horrible to her too.'

'Trust me, you weren't. We had some happy family time together. Memories of pushing the pram along the seafront in Worthing with people stopping us to tell us what a beautiful baby Mia was kept me going in the darkest moments.'

Hearing Tom say that underlines that it wasn't only me who lost so much.

'I wish I could remember that,' I say.

'Give it time, Sophie. You had two massive traumas to deal with. There's little wonder that your memory shut down to protect you.'

I can't believe Tom is still so considerate towards me after all I've put him through.

'Does Polly always read Mia her bedtime story?' I ask, feeling the need to change the subject before I get too emotional.

'Usually. Mia prefers it because Polly puts on all the characters' voices. She says I'm boring,' he comments good-naturedly.

'I couldn't possibly comment,' I reply, unable to resist a little chuckle. 'Seriously though, Polly really does seem to love Mia. It makes me feel better knowing that she'll be growing up with someone so caring.'

Tom is giving me a strange look.

'What?' I ask.

'Am I missing something? I thought you'd come back because you wanted to be a part of Mia's life. Don't tell me you've put her through all the drama this afternoon just to disappear again?' he demands, the lightness of tone gone from his voice. 'That's not very fair.'

'But… I didn't think you'd want me around. You and Polly are obviously so happy together and Mia adores you both. I'd just be in the way, wouldn't I?'

Much as it breaks my heart to admit it, they make a perfect little family and it would be wrong of me to disrupt the safe haven they have created for Mia.

Neither of us notice Polly come back downstairs after settling Mia to sleep, so when she speaks it takes us both by surprise.

'No, you wouldn't, Sophie. Mia didn't want a story tonight, she wanted to talk about how her prayers had been answered and heaven had let you come back to earth. You can't walk away and destroy your little girl's faith.'

'I-I don't know what to say…'

'Then don't say anything until you've had time to think things through,' Tom says. 'But Polly's right, we all want the best for Mia and the best is for to have her mummy and daddy and Polly – it will make her feel very special.'

My heart feels as though it might explode. After discovering that my mind had played a terrible trick on me in making me think I was running away from an abusive husband, he turns out to be exactly what I always thought he was before I became ill. I know it's too late for us as husband and wife, but I will always love Tom and there will always be a special place in my heart for him.

He and Polly are standing in front of me holding hands and each extending an arm to include me in a group hug. It takes me back to my schooldays with Liv and Grace. We were there for each other then, and now Tom and Polly are inviting me into their lives to involve me in Mia's upbringing.

'Thank you,' I say, stepping into the embrace.

My day really couldn't have ended any better.

CHAPTER 38

Liv and Sophie

Saturday afternoon

It was quite difficult to persuade Jamie to go and play football this afternoon, but between us, Sophie and I managed it.

The two of them turned up at East Surrey hospital at half past nine this morning and then the three of us sat around twiddling our thumbs and making small talk until the doctor said I was fine to go home. To be honest, I was happy to have spent the night in hospital, because after I told Jamie about the baby, he was so excited, he wouldn't stop talking, so I don't imagine I would have had very much sleep at home.

Obviously, I'm as excited as he is, but mine is tempered with a degree of trepidation. I managed to get to eighteen weeks with Alfie and he still wasn't viable. There's a long way to go before I hit the magic twenty weeks and until then, Jamie and I have agreed that the only person who needs to know about my pregnancy, is Sophie. She is living with us and even if she didn't notice my thickening waistline, it would be virtually impossible not to let something slip.

Jamie was all for me going for a rest when we got back from the hospital, but I wasn't having it. 'I'm pregnant, Jamie, not ill. I'm twenty-four hours more pregnant now than I was this time yesterday and you weren't suggesting I go for a lie-down then.' He stopped fussing for about ten minutes before questioning whether I should be carrying the linen basket downstairs to put a wash on. That's when I suggested that his football team needed him, and after catching my pleading look over his shoulder, Sophie promised to look after me until he got back.

She's been true to her word. After Jamie left, she filled me in on everything that had happened at Tom and Polly's yesterday and I'm over the moon that they want her to be a part of Mia's life without a fight for access. I'd wrestled with my conscience when I'd thought I was going to have to back Sophie over Tom in the interest of what was best for Mia. He can be a bit of a know-it-all at times, but he's my big brother and I love him. I'm hopeful that things will get back to how they always used to be between us, especially when he finds out he's going to be an uncle, I think, resting my hands lightly on my tummy.

Sophie's gone through to the kitchen to make me a cup of tea and then she's suggested an afternoon of watching a film with our feet up. While I quite fancy the idea, there is something she needs to do first.

I get the distinct impression she has been putting off calling her parents, which is understandable. What on earth do you say to two people so devastated by your death that they moved as far away from Surrey as they could to avoid the sympathetic look in people's eyes? But Sophie's been back in the UK for almost a week, and I can't let her put it off any longer.

'Here we go,' she says, walking into the room carrying a tray with two mugs and a plate full of Jaffa Cakes on it.

As she places it on the table, I'm immediately transported back to the night that I read her letter. It feels a lot longer than two months ago and although it's been a bit of a bumpy ride, I'm so glad she's back home. Despite missing her, I hadn't realised just how much her 'death' had affected me, although now of course I'm grieving for Grace. We were all such close friends for so many years until life pulled us in different directions. It's terribly sad that Grace was denied a happy settled family life, particularly as she didn't have the most loving home life when she was growing up. A tear squeezes out of the corner of my eye.

'Are you okay?' Sophie asks, sitting down next to me on the sofa and gently touching my forearm.

'I was just thinking about Grace and how unfair so many things in her life were.' I feel Sophie tense up. 'I'm not only talking about the accident. I keep telling you it wasn't your fault.'

'I'll always blame myself for it though, whatever you say.'

'Well, you shouldn't. None of us can control fate, not even you, Sophie,' I say, brushing the tear from my eye with the back of my hand. 'We both have guilty feelings about Grace, but I'm not sure she'd want us to. Although her life was short, she really did live it in her own way.'

'You're right. One of the few things I remember her saying when I went to see her in Spain, was, "If I died tomorrow, I can honestly say I've lived." How prophetic that turned out to be, but it did bring me some comfort on the days my grief for her loss overcame me.'

A shiver runs through me.

'Once she has a resting place, we should make a promise to visit it on her birthday each year,' I say.

Sophie smiles wistfully.

'I always lit a candle for her and said a small prayer, even though she wasn't religious.'

'Then we'll both do that from now on,' I say.

We sit in silence for a few moments before Sophie hands me my mug saying, 'Here, you'd better drink your tea before it gets cold or you'll be telling Jamie I didn't look after you properly. Do you want one of these?' she asks, offering me the plate of Jaffa Cakes. 'I thought you didn't like them.'

'I don't; they're gross,' I reply, feeling my stomach lurch at the mere thought of biting into one. 'I buy them so that Jamie has something sweet to eat and I won't be tempted. You know, I was starting to feel really pissed off that all my waistbands were feeling tighter than usual, but now I know why, I don't care.'

'Oh Liv,' she says, settling next to me on the sofa, 'I can't begin to tell you how happy I am for you.'

'Our secret, remember,' I say. 'We're not even telling our parents until I'm at twenty weeks.'

'Mum's the word,' Sophie replies, mischievously raising a Jaffa Cake to her lips and pretending to lock her mouth with it. She always did have such a sense of fun. 'What film do you fancy?'

'Actually, Sophie, talking of parents, isn't there something you need to do first?'

She sighs. 'I want to call them, Liv, really I do, but I don't know what to say. I'm actually terrified that one of them might have a heart attack or something with the shock of it.'

'It's never going to get any easier,' I say. 'But the sooner you get it over with, the sooner you can start to rebuild things.'

'What if they can't forgive me, Liv? It was an unspeakably cruel thing to do.'

'You were sick, Sophie. You couldn't help the desperation you felt, and I'm sure they'll understand that when you explain things to them.'

Now that I understand how acute Sophie's PPD was, I've been able to accept that she did what she thought was best for everyone at the time. I'm not sure if any of us would have been able to recover if she'd taken her own life as a way to escape the abyss she had sunk into. I know now that Tom was only doing what Sophie asked him to in not seeking professional help for her. I can only imagine the regret he must feel for going along with her wishes, but I don't need to imagine my own guilt for not recognising something was seriously wrong. Sophie had so many of us who would have done anything to help her if we'd known she was struggling, but her illness wouldn't let her reach out to anyone for help.

Wrapping her fingers around her mug, Sophie takes another sip of tea. She's nervous, of course she is, but this is the last major obstacle standing in the way of the rest of her life.

*

Liv's sitting next to me while I nervously touch my parents' number on the screen and wait for what feels like an eternity for them to pick up. It's a good job Liv is squeezing my hand for reassurance, because I'm not sure I can go through with it.

When my dad eventually answers, the line is a bit crackly, but I can hear the question in his voice.

'Liv?'

It catches me by surprise for a moment, but I quickly remember that I'm using Liv's mobile phone and he must have the number stored. Just hearing his voice starts me trembling. How could I have conceived a plan that would completely cut my parents out of my life, and how will I ever be able to explain it to them?

Liv said to keep things as simple as possible on this initial call and she squeezes my hand now as a reminder.

'It-it's not Liv; it's me, Dad,' I say, my voice shaking as much as my hands.

'Who the hell is this?' my dad snaps, his voice a mix of shock and anger.

'It's Sophie.'

A few seconds tick past and there is nothing from the other end of the line. I glance at Liv whose eyebrows are raised questioningly. I shake my head. She mouths the words *try again* at me.

'Dad? Are you still there?'

'I don't know who you are or what kind of sick joke this is, but if you ever dial this number again, I'll call the police.'

The line goes dead. I move the phone away from my ear and stare at it for a moment. I don't know what I expected really, and I can't blame him for reacting in that way. It was never going to be an easy call.

'He hung up,' I say, replying to Liv's unspoken question.

Before she can respond, the house phone starts to ring.

'Let me,' Liv says, reaching for the phone and lifting it from its cradle. 'Hello,' she says, flicking it onto speaker.

'Have you had your mobile stolen?'

It's my dad speaking. The line is much clearer and I can hear he sounds shaken.

'Hello, Mr Baxter, it's Liv. I know why you're ringing and, in answer to your question, no, I haven't.'

'Did you just ring me then?' he asks, sounding totally confused. 'I had a call from your phone from a woman claiming to be Sophie, but we all know that's not possible.'

'Obviously, this will come as a complete shock,' Liv says gently, 'but... it was Sophie. She's here with me and I've got you on speaker phone so she can hear you too.'

In the background, I hear my mum say, 'Are you speaking to Liv? What's she saying, Peter? Who was that on the phone just now?'

The tightness in my chest on hearing Mum's voice feels like my heart is being gripped in a vice.

'That's what I'm trying to find out, Laura,' my dad replies. 'Liv says it was Sophie; she says she's there with her now.'

'Mr Baxter, can you still hear me?' Liv asks. 'I'm putting Sophie on the line.' Handing the handset to me, she says, 'I'm going to give you some space. Call me if you need me.'

The door closes behind her and I take a deep breath.

'Mum, Dad, it really is me,' I say, fighting to keep my emotions under control but already feeling tears pricking the back of my eyes.

I hear Mum say, 'Give me the phone, Peter.'

There's a rustling sound and then her voice, as clear as a bell.

'Sophie?'

'Mum.'

'How is this possible?' she gasps. 'We thought you were dead.'

'I know. I'm so sorry for everything you've been through. I should have found another way.'

'I don't understand. Where have you been all these years, darling?'

Her use of the word *darling* breaks me. Tears are streaming down my cheeks as I lose the battle with my emotions.

'In Mexico,' I manage through my sobs. 'Liv found me and brought me home.'

CHAPTER 39

Liv

Saturday afternoon

I stand outside the lounge door for a few minutes to make sure Sophie is coping with the enormity of trying to explain things to her parents. I'm trying to decide whether to head upstairs for a bath when I notice through the glass panel of our front door that someone is on the other side of it. I'm assuming it's someone delivering flyers as it's far too late for our postman. I wait for a few seconds, but when nothing appears through the letterbox my curiosity gets the better of me and I open the door.

'Tom!' I exclaim. 'What are you doing lurking around on my doorstep?'

'I was just about to knock,' he says, looking mildly embarrassed.

'If you've come to see Sophie, she's on the phone to her parents, but you can wait in the dining room for her, if you like?'

'Actually, sis, we did all our talking yesterday evening; it's you I've come to see.'

'Oh, right. Well, you'd better come through and I'll make us a cup of tea,' I say, realising I've left my half-finished one in the lounge.

Tom follows me through to the kitchen and while I'm making the tea asks me how I'm feeling after the accident. He doesn't make any wisecracks about women drivers, for which I'm grateful. I remember that he's stopped taking sugar and apologise for the lack of biscuits to offer him as I lead the way into the dining room, explaining that the Jaffa Cakes are in the lounge with Sophie.

'No need to apologise. I haven't had a Jaffa Cake since I lived with Mum and Dad. I think I must have overdosed on them as a child, I can't stand them now.'

I smile.

'Me neither. At least that's something we agree on,' I say, making eye contact as we sit down on opposite sides of the dining table.

'We always agreed on most things before Sophie got sick,' he says.

'True, but only because you're my big brother and I thought you could do no wrong.'

'But I did do wrong,' he says, blowing on his tea. He's either doing it to cool it down or to buy himself some time. When he starts to speak again, I know it was the latter. 'I should have got professional help for Sophie when she was so sick, or at the very least talked to you about what was going on, even though she didn't want me to. I let her down, and it nearly cost her her life; in fact, it did cost her the life she had always known at the heart of a loving family, surrounded by friends. What a conceited idiot I was to think I knew what was best for her.'

It's strange to hear my brother talking like this. Throughout my life, he's always been confident and self-assured, but those few words, admitting that he made some bad decisions when Sophie was so ill, have taken more strength and courage than he probably realises himself. He was a husband and father trying to hold his family together in the way he thought was best at the time.

'You shouldn't be so hard on yourself,' I say, once again feeling a huge amount of guilt that I'd been so absorbed in my own life that I hadn't noticed the strain that Tom was under. I should have made more of an effort to maintain my close friendship with Sophie instead of playing happy families with Jamie and, if I had,

I would surely have spotted that something was seriously wrong. 'According to Sophie, in her darkest moments, she'd threatened to leave you, taking Mia with her if you breathed a word to anyone about her violent episodes. It was a pretty impossible situation, and you were clearly motivated by love and the desire to protect the people closest to you.'

'I can't begin to tell you what a relief it is to hear you say that, sis,' Tom says, the tension in his shoulders visibly melting. 'I've hated the friction between us.'

'Me too,' I say.

'I don't blame you for being angry with me when I started seeing Polly. You saw it as a betrayal, but the truth is, I wouldn't have survived without her after Sophie... went. I felt like it was my fault for suggesting the trip to see Grace. I've never told anyone other than Polly, but I was close to taking my own life. Only having Mia to look after stopped me, and I knew I wasn't doing a great job of that on my own."

'Oh my God, Tom, I had no idea you were in such a terrible state,' I say, shocked to hear my brother confessing this. 'Why didn't you talk to me at the time? Or Jamie; he's your best friend. He would have done anything to help you through your grief, but you pushed him away,' I add, remembering the times Jamie had voiced his concerns about Tom bottling his emotions up.

'How could I? I'd spent the previous two years keeping you both at arm's length, insisting everything was fine when in reality it was all falling apart at the seams. And besides, you were both still trying to come to terms with your own grief after losing Alfie. It didn't feel right to burden you with anything else. I honestly don't know what would have happened to me and Mia if it hadn't been for Polly. I'm not exaggerating when I say, she saved me.'

His words really hit home. If only I'd known then what I know now.

'I'm so sorry for the way I've been with you and Polly. I should have tried to see things from your point of view and understand what you needed instead of being so accusatory.'

'With the benefit of hindsight, we could all have done things differently,' he says.

For a moment our eyes lock. I don't know what Tom is thinking, but I'm filled with regret for all that I've missed out on in the past three and a half years.

'I love Polly very deeply, you know. She's an incredible woman because she knows I never stopped loving Sophie and she was able to accept that. I'm extremely lucky to have her.'

'But what will happen now? Do you think Polly will be able to accept you loving Sophie knowing that she's still alive?'

'My love for Polly is total. I will always have a special place in my heart for Sophie and what we had together, and I've told Polly that. But I've also told her that she is the one I want to spend the rest of my life with. Sophie is going to be in our lives because of Mia and what's best for her, but things can never go back to how they were.'

It feels good to be having this conversation with my brother, but it's also making me question what kind of a person I am to ever have doubted him.

'I can only apologise for the way I've been with you lately. I should have trusted that you were the person I always believed you to be. Jamie never lost faith in you, even when Sophie thought she was remembering dreadful things. He had your back in a way that I didn't, and I feel really bad about it.'

'Jamie's a good egg. It might not have come out the way I intended it to that day at Mum's, but you are lucky that he is completely loyal to you. I'm not sure too many blokes would have agreed to have their best mate's ex-wife living under their roof and making pretty damning accusations while being expected to keep it secret.'

'You know, I've always had my suspicions that you like him better than me.'

For a moment he's not sure whether I'm joking, but when he realises I am, he gets up from his chair to come and give me a hug.

'I'm not gonna lie, I'm pretty hurt that you thought I could ever lay a finger on Sophie.'

I start to pull away to protest, but he stops me.

'But she was very honest about the stuff she told you and I can see how damning it must have looked. Even what you saw at our house, with me not letting Mia or Polly have friends around, must have added fuel to the fire.'

'It did. Tell me to mind my own business, but why did you decide that? When you rang me after I'd dropped in to see them, you seemed so mistrustful.'

'Polly was unnaturally quiet. I thought maybe you'd said something to upset her. Everything I did was to keep my girls safe, you know. I couldn't bear the thought of anything happening to them after what happened to Sophie,' he says, shaking his head. 'I can see now that it wasn't very fair to either of them.'

'No, but understandable now that I know the whole story.'

As though a thought has just occurred to him, Tom says, 'Talking of the whole story, has anyone been in touch with Grace's parents yet?'

'Sophie's written to them. How sad that their relationship with their daughter was so broken that they didn't seem to question her disappearing without trace from Spain. Maybe now they know the truth they'll be able to show Grace the love in death that they seemed unable to when she was alive.'

In my head, I picture her happy smiling eleven-year-old face on the first day we met at Birchdale School. We had so many good times together, but her life was tinged with unhappiness from the moment her brother was born. I lay my hand on my stomach and promise my unborn child that I will always love them no matter what life brings. I'm tempted to tell Tom that I'm pregnant, but stop myself. There will be plenty of time for that when emotions are not running so high.

'It's tragic really,' Tom says. 'I can't imagine anything ever lessening the love I feel for Mia.'

'But you will loosen your grip a bit now, won't you, and give Mia and Polly a bit more freedom?'

'For sure. Polly and I had a long heart-to-heart after Sophie left last night and the first change is for Polly to come back to work at the surgery part-time. Trust me, things are going to be different from now on.'

'That's good to hear. Thanks for coming to clear the air. I'm so happy to have my big brother back.'

'Me too. Listen, I'm going to have to go,' he says, glancing at his watch. 'I was so long standing on your doorstep plucking up the courage to come in that I didn't leave myself much time and I don't want to be late picking the girls up.'

'Has Mia had dancing class?'

'That was this morning. This afternoon she persuaded Polly to take her to the shop where Auntie Liv got her jigsaw from because she loves it so much.'

'There'll be plenty more gifts for Mia from The Bee's Knees, I promise,' I say as I show him out. 'I've got a lot of catching up to do on Auntie duties.'

CHAPTER 40

Sophie

Monday morning

It was strange sitting in the passenger seat of a car being driven by my ex-husband on the journey over to see Natasha Swann earlier this morning. Legally, he is still my husband, but, as we discussed on Friday, both Tom and I know that however much we once loved each other, that time in our lives has passed. Neither of us feels bitter about the way things turned out for us. We're both grateful for the time we had together and, of course, for our beautiful little Mia.

Tom came into the meeting at Natasha's for a few minutes before he needed to get back to work, having left Jamie holding the fort for him. He made it clear that as far as he was concerned what had happened when I was struggling with PPD was history and that he and Polly want me to be involved in Mia's upbringing. I'm incredibly grateful to Polly for her understanding of what will be best for Mia, and reminded of what a kind and caring husband Tom was before my illness ruined our lives together. Not all men would have endured what he did in an attempt to keep our little family together. It will be a different family dynamic now for Mia, but one in which I hope she will thrive.

Natasha is going to handle the legalities of Tom and my divorce so that he will be free to remarry Polly. They're not planning a big family celebration, just a quiet registry office affair with Jamie and Liv as witnesses. As Polly pointed out, she's already had her day in the spotlight so is keen to get on with their lives with the minimum amount of fuss. I'm really warming to her. Even though in some respects she has taken the life I would have been living if things had been different, I don't feel any animosity towards her at all. In fact, I'm glad that Tom found someone to build new memories with to replace the unhappy ones of our time after Mia was born. Maybe one day they'll have a little brother or sister for Mia, a bittersweet thought for me.

My future plans are less certain than Polly and Tom's. I can't leave the country until my identity is established beyond doubt, not that I was planning to once Tom made it clear that he wants me in Mia's life. I'm looking forward to making her tea when she gets home from school and reading her an occasional bedtime story; all the things that I was unaware I was missing for so long. I will need to be cleared of any wrongdoing with regard to living for three and a half years as Grace. Natasha seems to think it will be a fairly straightforward process once Eleanor Rashford has submitted her report citing amnesia due to the trauma of the train crash in Spain. The fact that I returned to England so promptly after the encounter with Liv when my memories started to return should also work in my favour, she said.

Jamie and Liv have been incredibly kind. They've agreed that I can continue living at their house for as long as I need to. Eventually, I want to get a place of my own, but that will have to wait until all the legal paperwork is completed and I'm able to get myself a job. I'm hoping it won't be too long or they might find themselves with a live-in nanny.

The thought of Liv being pregnant brings a smile to my lips. Obviously, she's not showing yet as she's only ten weeks pregnant, but there is already a serene aura about her. In some ways, having me there to keep an eye on Liv and make sure she doesn't overdo things is a blessing in disguise after what happened with Alfie, which might not have been the case if my parents still lived in the area.

I close my eyes trying to picture my parents' faces. It feels like such a long time since I've seen them, because so much has happened in the interim. Once they were able to get past the initial shock of me being alive, Mum and Dad wanted to know everything, but I kept the story about my memory loss and running away to Mexico as sketchy as possible. I'm not sure they need to know why I fled Spain; what they don't know won't hurt them, and goodness knows, I've already hurt them enough for one lifetime. They're planning on getting a flight from Shetland as soon as they can, and I can barely contain my excitement at the prospect of seeing them again.

I've been so lost in my thoughts that I'm surprised when the taxi comes to a standstill and I open my eyes to see we've already arrived at Jamie and Liv's. I hand over ten pounds and head down the path.

The moment my key is in the front door, Liv calls out from the front room, 'There's someone here to see you.'

My heart leaps. Mum and Dad must have been able to get a flight sooner than they expected. I push open the door, a broad smile lighting up my face, which is where it freezes.

'W-what…. I don't understand,' I say, my throat feeling tight.

'I'll leave you two to talk,' Liv says, brushing past me standing in the doorway and giving my arm a light squeeze.

'I tried to call you, Sophie.'

My mind flicks back to Friday afternoon and me crushing my mobile phone underfoot so that I could show the shattered screen to Polly.

'H-how did you find me?' I ask, edging forward to lean on the back of the sofa. I feel light-headed; I can hardly believe my eyes.

'I remembered some of the address from the letter you wrote to Liv and did a bit of investigating. As soon as I knew where you were, I booked my flight and tried to call you, but I couldn't get through. I thought maybe you didn't want to speak to me,' he says, 'and I wouldn't blame you, Sophie.'

There; he did it again. Luis called me Sophie instead of Grace for a second time.

'What are you doing here?' I whisper. I'm still struggling to believe that Luis has flown halfway around the world and is standing in the front room of my best friend's house when I thought I would never see him again.

'I eventually came to my senses and realised that I almost made the biggest mistake of my life,' he says, getting to his feet and moving towards me. 'Whatever it takes, whatever problems we have to overcome, I want to be with you, if you'll still have me.'

Falling into his arms feels like the most natural thing in the world. What Tom and I had was so special at the time, but events conspired to destroy that. I've already accepted that was my past and my future will be different, but never in my wildest dreams did I imagine I would be spending it with Luis.

Then reality kicks in and I realise the hopelessness of our situation. Luis lives in Mexico; he loves Mexico and his life there. I can't leave England because I have a responsibility to my daughter.

'I love you, Luis,' I say when he finally releases me from his tight embrace. 'If I could spend the rest of my life with you, I would, but I can't come back to live in Mexico.'

'I know...' he tries to interrupt, but I continue speaking.

'For now, I have to be here so that I can be a part of Mia's life while she's growing up. Back in Tulum, you asked me to make an impossible choice and I chose her,' I say struggling to hold back my tears. 'There was only one decision I could make. She's my little girl and I love her.'

He gently strokes the hair back off my face and tilts my chin up so that I am looking into his velvet brown eyes.

'Can I speak now?' he asks.

I almost don't want him to. I've told him why I can't go back to Mexico with him. Nothing he says will change my mind and my heart will be broken all over again.

'Liv explained that you and your husband have agreed to raise Mia together, and I think that's the best thing for her.'

The tiny bubble of hope that had been forcing its way to the surface has just burst. Luis sought me out and travelled halfway around the world to try to persuade me to go back to Tulum with him. Now he knows I can't this is turning into the tearful goodbye I tried to protect myself from when I left Mexico. It's devastating, but unavoidable.

'She needs the love of both her mother and father, but if you and Tom will let me, I will love her too.'

My heart feels fit to burst. With those five words, Luis gives me hope that we can have a future together.

CHAPTER 41

Sophie

Four months later

The sound of children's laughter fills the air. Mia has invited some of her friends around after school for a teddy bears' picnic on the lawn, while Liv and I keep an eye on them from our comfy chairs on the decking. Every now and then, I adjust the parasol to keep Liv in the shade and me in full sunshine. June, which can be a mixed month weather-wise, was gloriously sunny and the first few days of July have followed suit. I hope it stays that way when the schools break up for the summer holidays next week, not that it will affect us for the first three weeks. I'm looking forward to showing Tom, Polly and Mia the sights of Tulum and, of course, introducing them to Vince. I'm pretty sure Mia will fall in love with him and then drive Tom crazy begging for a puppy. At least he's in the right profession to choose the most child-friendly breed.

I was taken aback when Tom suggested flying out to Mexico for a family holiday, particularly when he said it would be good for Mia to get to know Luis better as he is going to be a constant in her life. No one was more surprised than me when on his visit at the end of May Luis went down on one knee, presented me with a diamond solitaire ring and asked me to marry him. It's much more modest than the two-carat ring Tom gave me, but I'm not bothered at all, I absolutely love it. I'd never been able to bring myself to sell my first engagement ring, but when I offered to return it to Tom, he wouldn't hear of it, suggesting instead that I should sell it to add to the money he has already given me for my new home.

I've had an offer accepted on a small cottage in Woldingham, halfway between Liv's and Tom's, so the perfect location, and Mum and Dad are selling up and returning to Surrey to be close to me and their granddaughter. They were both totally besotted with Mia after making her reacquaintance in March. I'll have to be pretty strict with them as they are desperate to make up for lost time and have a tendency to spoil her.

All being well, I should have completed on the house by the time Luis moves over in September. We've had lots of discussions about Vince and what would be best for him. Josefina offered to have him, but in the end we decided he should swap the beach walks for the stunning countryside walks around Woldingham after his quarantine period. Eventually, we're planning on moving back to Mexico to live, but not until Mia is in her late teens, although there will doubtless be plenty of trips home in the interim to visit Luis's family.

Both Jamie and Tom really like Luis and using their contacts have managed to get him a job in an animal shelter. I'm so pleased as it will give him a sense of familiarity which he'll need if he's going to adapt to his new way of life. Sometimes I have to pinch myself when I think of all he is giving up just to be with me. If I mention it, he laughs it off and says he always wanted to visit England and I've just given him an excuse. Mia has been a bit shy around Luis, but I think the visit to Mexico will change that. Luis, on the other hand, took to Mia straightaway and talks about her constantly during our nightly WhatsApp calls.

Funnily enough, I'm also now doing the same job I was when I lived in Tulum. I'm teaching Pilates classes at lunchtimes and in the evening, which leaves me free to pick up Mia from school every day and bring her home to Tom's for her tea before he and Polly get back from work. It's hard to imagine that if Liv hadn't visited Mexico in January, I wouldn't have got to experience the exquisite joy of spending time with my little girl.

'Mummy,' Mia's voice calls out, 'we've run out of tea.' She waggles her plastic teapot in my direction.

Although I'm getting used to hearing Mia call me Mummy, I still grin like a Cheshire cat every time she does.

'It has a nice ring to it, doesn't it?' Liv says, watching me scramble to my feet.

'It won't be too long before your little girl is calling you that,' I say, glancing down at the rounded bump beneath Liv's cotton sundress.

She and Jamie opted to know the sex of their baby at the twenty-week scan, so when they finally told everyone their news, they were able to announce that they were having a daughter. I'm glad. No child could ever replace Alfie, but I think it will be easier to have a girl first and Mia is utterly thrilled at the idea of having a baby cousin. When Liv told her, she immediately asked both Polly and me if we have babies in our tummy too; she isn't quite old enough to be fully au fait with the birds and the bees. I had a moment of sadness at the thought of never again experiencing the unconditional love I felt when I first held Mia in my arms as a new-born, but motherhood wasn't plain sailing for me. Luis has said he will look in to getting a reversal if that's what I want, but I'm not sure it is. Having Mia back in my life is incredibly fulfilling, it might tempt fate if I ask for too much.

'Can I get you anything while I'm up?' I ask, slipping my feet into my sandals.

'A mint tea would be lovely; it's supposed to help with heartburn,' Liv says, pulling a face.

'Mummeeee, can you hurry up please. Mr Albert is positively dying of thirst.'

I exchange a look with Liv. Mia is mixing more and more with her own age group, but she still comes out with some very adult stuff for a five-year-old.

'Tell Mr Albert that patience is a virtue,' I say, heading down the stone steps and over to where they have the picnic blanket laid out, strewn with sandwiches, biscuits, cakes and fruit sticks.

'Patent is a fur shoe,' Mia is saying to Mr Albert as I approach. 'What does that mean, Mummy?'

Stifling a laugh, I reply, 'Patience is waiting quietly for something.'

'What does that have to do with fur shoes?' she asks, a puzzled look in her eyes. She may have Tom's unruly mop of dark curls but her eyes are exactly the same shade of blue as mine.

'Nothing as far as I know. I said *virtue*, as in being good.'

All four girls roll around giggling on the rug, while I reach for the two plastic teapots to take them for a refill of orange squash. I deliver it to them and then head back to the kitchen, where the kettle is coming to the boil for Liv's mint tea. I'm about to pour the water into the cup when Liv calls to me.

'Sophie! Come quick.'

I rush outside imagining all sorts of disasters and stop in my tracks when everything looks just as I left it moments before.

'What is it, Liv? You scared me.'

'Give me your hand,' she says.

I move towards her and drop down to my knees at her side. She takes my hand and places it on the top of her swollen belly. A second later, I feel a firm kick beneath my palm, followed by another and another.

I gasp at the intimacy of the moment, feeling the movements of Liv's child before she takes her first breath.

'She doesn't kick that often and it's usually in bed at night, so only Jamie gets to feel it,' Liv says, unable to suppress her delight at being able to share it with me.

'I think you might have a dancer in there,' I say.

'A dancer who we've decided to call Grace,' Liv says. 'I hope you approve of our choice?'

'It's perfect,' I say with a smile, removing my hand from Liv's tummy to cross my chest the way all three of us did on the first day of senior school.

Liv follows my lead and we lock eyes as we say in unison, 'Friends forever.'

A LETTER FROM JULIA

Thank you so much for choosing to read *The Woman on the Beach*. If you enjoyed it and want to keep up to date with all my latest releases, please sign up at the following link. Your email address will never be shared and you can unsubscribe at any time.

www.bookouture.com/julia-roberts

Very often, the ideas for my books are triggered by people-watching, but in the case of *The Woman on the Beach* it was dog-watching. My husband and I were on a last-minute holiday in Mexico in advance of me undergoing quite major ankle surgery. Towards the end of our stay, I watched in fascination from the shade of my sun-lounger as a dog behaved in exactly the same way that Vince does in my book. He was so well-behaved waiting for his owners while they swam, and then clearly delighted when they eventually emerged from the ocean, which he showed by covering them in doggy kisses. That's when my imagination took over.

I created a story around the couple and their dog and how their seemingly idyllic lifestyle could be shattered by a ghost from the past. I also had to create a reason for Liv to be holidaying on her own… I did put Liv through the wringer a bit, didn't I? She truly deserved her happy ending.

I really enjoyed writing the chapters set in the past with the three friends, Sophie, Liv and Grace. They are a similar age to my own daughter, Sophie, so giving the other two names was as easy as remembering some of her contemporaries at school, and their behaviour was also more about memory than research, if you know what I mean!

In fact, the incident in the bar in Tulum, which triggers the whole chain of events leading to Tom and Sophie getting together, was an exaggeration of something that happened to my daughter when she was on holiday in Zante with a group of friends. The phone call no mother wants to receive when their child is a couple of thousand miles away starts with, 'Don't worry but…' My daughter's friend was ringing from the hospital where my Sophie was having stitches in her arm after being cut with a bottle during a brawl in a bar that she had tried to break up! Fortunately, my daughter's injury was nowhere near as severe as Sophie's in the book, although she did later have a tattoo… or several!

So not much research required there, nor for the location of the train crash as I know the area of Spain around Denia and Javea really well having holidayed there for years. And I've been doing Pilates as my main method of exercise for over twenty years so that was easy to draw on too, although my editor and I did have different opinions on whether the exercise should be called 'the hundred' or 'the one hundred' – I can't remember what we settled on in the end, but it was only a minor detail and probably down to individual teachers.

However, I did have to look into partial amnesia and how a trauma can completely lock the memory surrounding events or periods in a sufferer's life. It truly can take years of therapy to recover certain things from the recesses of our mind and sometimes the loss of an event or period of time is permanent. Thankfully, in Sophie's case it wasn't, and she was able to realise that Tom's actions, which she had remembered as being sinister and threatening, were his attempts to hold his family together as her post-partum depression deepened.

I've left some things open ended for you to reach your own conclusions on, such as whether or not Luis will have a reversal of his vasectomy and whether Polly and Tom will start a family together and give Mia a brother or sister.

I hope *The Woman on the Beach* has given you food for thought. If you'd been Liv, would you have gone back to Mexico looking for Sophie after she specifically asked you not to? Was her letter the cry for help that Liv perceived it to be?

And what about Sophie's impossible choice? Could you have left an idyllic life in Mexico with a man you love or would you have taken Liv's word that your daughter was happy and settled and left things as they were in the belief that it was the best thing for Mia?

I hope you loved *The Woman on the Beach*. If you did, I'd be most grateful if you would take a few minutes to write a review. Not only is your feedback important to me, it can make a real difference in helping new readers discover my books for the first time.

I love hearing from my readers – you can get in touch on my Facebook page, through Twitter, Instagram, Goodreads or my website.

Thanks,
Julia Roberts

JuliaRobertsTV

@JuliaRobertsTV

@juliagroberts

www.juliarobertsauthor.com

ACKNOWLEDGEMENTS

This is where I say a huge thank you to all the members of 'Team Julia' for their work on *The Woman on the Beach*.

As with my previous Bookouture books, my editor is Ruth Tross and I have to thank her for her belief in this book. When I first came up with the plot, I absolutely loved it, particularly telling the story from both Sophie and Liv's perspective but also with the 'historic' chapters. It seemed like a great idea at the time but the actuality of writing it was a lot more difficult than I'd anticipated, so much so that at one point I asked if I could write something completely different. Ruth was having none of it! She believed in this book and made suggestions of how to achieve the story I wanted to tell. She has the patience of a saint; it can't be easy trying to work out a publication schedule when your author has a cataract operation looming. Thanks to her professionalism, we got there in the end. She's a pleasure to work with, tremendously supportive, enthusiastic and honest, and I feel very fortunate to have her as my editor.

Once again, I've worked with a new copy editor, Jade Craddock on *The Woman on the Beach*. I'm going to be honest and say that, at times, I was shouting at all her comments in the margin – why did she need all these questions answered? The point is that a copy editor is seeing your book for the first time so sees it with fresh eyes. What seems obvious to me because I know the story so intimately would not necessarily be that obvious to a reader, hence all the questions! There was one particular chapter that had me struggling until the 'eleventh hour'. All I kept thinking was that Jade must think I'm a rubbish author – that's what made me persevere until the light-bulb moment came. So, a massive thank you to Jade for all the 'cattle-prodding', as a result of which she got the responses she wanted from me to make this a better book.

When I asked Ruth what the title was going to be, she said, 'It's actually a line from the book – I hope you'll approve.' I definitely do. Liv seeing 'the woman on the beach' was the catalyst for the story, so is the perfect title. I also love the cover, although here's a little insider information. Sophie was originally wearing a yellow dress when Liv spotted her on the beach in Mexico. Because the colours of the cover looked so good (they are the team colours of Crystal Palace F.C., who I support) I changed Sophie's dress from yellow to red because it always irritates me if the cover depicts something different from the words. I had lots of positive feedback when the cover was revealed by the Bookouture publicity team, headed up by Kim Nash, and my thanks go especially to Sarah Hardy for the work she has put in to help spread the word.

I always thank my family for the part they play in each new book. They are the ones who see the hours spent at the computer throughout each stage of the process and have to put up with me vaguely nodding my head during conversations at the dinner table when my mind is clearly elsewhere. During the writing of this book, my son and his girlfriend, who lived with us throughout lockdown, were in the process of buying their first house together, so there were a few stressful moments to deal with as I'm sure you can imagine. Now it will just be me and my husband, Chris, in the house, I'm hoping for less drama and fewer distractions although I'm currently experiencing 'empty nest syndrome' – no pets or children in the house for the first time in forty-two years! Maybe that could be the theme of my next novel? It's no lie when I said that Chris has complete faith in my ability as a writer. I've said it before, and I'll say it again: he truly is 'the wind beneath my wings' and I know I'm very lucky to have him even though I don't always show it.

Finally, I want to thank you for choosing to read *The Woman on the Beach*. It hasn't been the easiest book to write, but I hope you agree it was worth it in the end.